Luz rose and went on powdering her face. "I don't like it any more than you do. But don't forget, darling, we're working a con here. There's no other way."

For a moment, he didn't know what to say. "Okay," he finally admitted. "I guess you're right. I guess we can't avoid it."

He studied her as she shook her head and stood back from the mirror to appraise herself.

"You know," he said, "it absolutely amazes me—it's like you're a totally different person."

"No," she replied with a smile, "just a whole lot more of the same one. For the first time in my life, I know what I want. I'd kill for you. Compared to that, this'll be easy."

"Listen," he said, "you still have Marty's number?"

She nodded.

The
LONGEST
ODDS

BARRY
SHEINKOPF

LYNX BOOKS
New York

THE LONGEST ODDS

ISBN: 1-55802-213-9

First Printing/February 1989

This is a work of fiction. Names, characters, places, and incidents are either the product of the author's imagination or are used fictitiously. Any resemblance to actual events, locales, or persons, living or dead, is entirely coincidental.

This book is published by Lynx Books, a division of Lynx Communications, Inc., 41 Madison Avenue, New York, New York, 10010. The name ''Lynx'' together with the logotype consisting of a stylized head of a lynx is a trademark of Lynx Communications, Inc.

Printed in the United States of America

0 9 8 7 6 5 4 3 2 1

For Patrick John Kelley,
Who knew how to travel

The longest odds are those on getting even.

—Gambler's adage

The
LONGEST
ODDS

Chapter

1

A black Mercedes 240SL screeched to a stop in front of an office tower in downtown Rio. Four men jumped out into the moonless night. "Hurry!" growled one, an American executive with flashes of gray in his hair and a slight paunch.

The driver, a Venezuelan, moved quickly to the back of the car and lifted a large suitcase from the trunk. He followed the others up the expanse of steps and into the lobby.

The man who had given the orders nodded to the uniformed guards, who were wide awake and alert. The shorter one looked up politely and returned to his security console; the shift boss came around front and exchanged a murmured pleasantry with the American.

"I'm not expecting visitors," the gray-haired man said to him as they passed.

"Very good, Senhor Preston. We'll call first."

"*Obrigado.*"

"Senhor Rigg," the shift boss added respectfully to

the other American, a man with auburn hair and sharp eyes who worked for Preston in what the guard understood to be an important capacity.

"*Boa noite,*" Rigg replied, slowing for a moment. "Anyone come down yet?"

The shift boss shook his head and, when Preston and the three others moved off, issued a few orders over the intercom. He had a good job with the company; nobody was going to the top floor until he first checked with Senhor Rigg.

The Americans entered the penthouse elevator with the two Venezuelans in tow.

"Look," Preston whispered impatiently as the doors closed and they started to rise. "Jose said he had the guy face down on the floor, didn't he? Why in hell—I mean, he has the *gun*, for Chrissake."

"I don't know," replied the younger man.

"Why didn't he—"

"We'll find out, sir. It's no problem. It's just a slight hitch." He tilted his head to the South Americans.

"I *must* get to that plane, Walt. Bottom line. You know where I'll be afterwards."

"Yes, sir."

"And look, whatever it is," the chairman hissed, his face a scant two inches from Rigg's, "just *do* it. And get rid of the body. I'm not taking any more chances on this deal." The elevator came to a cushioned stop, and the doors opened.

They crossed the marble vestibule and the spacious reception area, turning left down a carpeted hallway decorated with paintings of hunting scenes in rosewood frames.

They entered the executive suite. Preston called out, "We're here, Jose." He took a few more steps forward before Walter put a hand on his shoulder and drew him to a halt.

Walter said nothing until he had sent the Venezuelans noiselessly into flanking positions and pulled the chairman behind him.

"Jose?" he whispered. "You there?"

There was no reply. Walter moved Carlos, the man to his right, forward and hurried down the other wall toward the dim light spilling from the inner office, his .38 high in his hands.

Preston's teeth clamped. It was too dark to read his watch, but it was getting close. The plane wouldn't wait.

Walter knew how close it was getting, too. He caught the eye of the man behind Preston, the one they called Navarro, and pointed toward the reception area. The man shifted, the barrel of an Uzi appearing from beneath his raincoat, as Walter slammed through the lighted doorway with Carlos right behind him.

When Preston got inside, even in the muted light cast by the desk lamp over the wide room, he could see that Jose's big bull neck had been broken.

With a tremor of shock, he realized the dead man's .357 Magnum was gone, too.

A piece of note paper lay near the body. Walter picked it up, took a look, and handed it to Preston.

It read "Try harder."

Jose's eyes were frozen wide open in shock, the angle of his broken neck grotesque.

"Goddamn it, Walt," the chairman snarled, "*find* this Brody sonofabitch. He's got to be up here. The stairwell is bolted shut." He headed toward the safe. "I'll start getting the stuff into the valise."

Walter took Carlos with him.

Three, four minutes went by. They found no one in any of the rooms. Just to be sure, they checked the stairwell door at the end of the suite. It was still locked.

Preston was stacking bonds, cash, and disks of database records into the suitcase when Rigg came back. "No sign of him?" Rigg shrugged. "All right, forget it. Let's just get out of here. There's no *time*, Walter."

Walter helped him close the suitcase, and the four men made their way back down the hallway.

Then Walter had an idea. "You take Carlos down to the lobby with you," he said aloud as they approached

3

the elevator. "Meanwhile, Navarro and I'll go back. This guy's got to be out on the terrace somewhere."

"Good," said Preston.

Walter waved a finger at the elevator door and stepped in front of Preston as the Venezuelans took aim.

He checked their positions, reached out, and touched the elevator button.

The door didn't open. Instead, a burst of white light exploded from the elevator with a blinding flash, and the sheer force of the voltage sent Walter flying through the air like a puppet. He slammed against the marble wall five feet behind him and slumped to the floor.

The two Venezuelans, nearly blinded by the haze of gray smoke and burning insulation, were already bringing their weapons around when a ceiling tile above them moved aside. The dead man's .357 went off with an ear-splitting clang, catching Navarro full in the chest and kicking him over screaming as he fell.

Carlos swung his weapon at the ceiling and started to spray it with automatic fire. He didn't hear Brody drop to the floor ten feet away. Carlos was lowering the automatic when the .357 went off twice more, hitting him in the head and ripping the side of it off.

Preston had his briefcase open.

"Stop dreaming!" Brody commanded. Preston froze and saw the big barrel of the revolver pointing right at him.

"Get away from the briefcase." Brody motioned with the gun. He was six feet three and broad in the shoulders and didn't look like he wanted to argue.

Preston did as he was told. Brody glanced at the small-caliber pistol in the briefcase, left it there, and lifted Walter up by the elbow. "Move," he said to Preston. "To the terrace. *Move*."

They paused to unbolt the stairwell door with Preston's key as they passed by. Brody stretched Walter out on the terrace couch with a cushion under his knees. He showed the older man to a comfortable chair, poured a couple of straight bourbons, handed one to Preston, and called the police.

"Let me speak to Da Silva. This is Steve Brody. Tell him it's urgent."

Walter was still in shock. Brody fixed Preston with cold green eyes before adding, "You're busted, my friend. It's over."

Preston took a deep breath. "Look, there's a couple of million in that suitcase. Can't we make a deal?"

"Sure," Brody replied. "You stop talking, and I take my finger off this trigger. How's that?"

"Fuck you."

"I'm touched." Brody lowered the gun, picked up his glass, and took a sip.

"They'll never get it to trial. I'll take down half the government first."

"Take, take," Brody replied calmly, and turned his attention to the phone. "Da Silva? You'd better get here quick. . . . Oh, yeah, there's a suitcase full of it, and a small automatic in his briefcase. . . . As a matter of fact, yes, there is somebody who could use medical attention. And three who can't. And don't use the penthouse elevator. I had to hot-wire the button while I was waiting. Take the other one, and come up the stairs from there."

Inspector Da Silva of the Rackets Squad was an anonymous-looking man with slicked-down hair and thin eyebrows. After he finished supervising the arrests, listing the locations of the bodies, and cataloging the evidence, he told Brody not to worry, that everything would be turned over to the accountants when they got there—and to kindly get his ass out of Brazil as soon as was reasonably convenient.

Brody was very glad to oblige him. When he returned to his hotel, he took a long hot bath followed by a short nap and cleared out of his room. He had a Jack Daniel's neat in the bar downstairs, then took a cab to Rio International Airport to catch an early morning flight.

He was leaning against a ticket counter watching the

sun come up when he turned to the ticket clerk and told her that he had changed his mind.

She glanced up past his broad chest and met his eyes. "You don't want to fly to New York?"

"No. Can you get me on a Miami flight?" His candid face conveyed a sense of easy confidence to anyone who did not notice a certain guardedness in the eyes. They were the most startling feature in a generally striking face. In different lights they could look blue or green and could rivet a person in place or melt the frostiest heart.

At that moment, they were pale blue and weary, like the rest of him. It had been an ugly few weeks, and he was glad to be leaving Rio—but New York in the middle of August, though it was home, suddenly did not appeal to him.

The young ticket clerk began punching buttons on her keyboard. "There's a seat on the seven A.M.," she said after a few moments.

"An hour from now. That's perfect." He smiled gratefully and lowered himself a bit closer on his elbows. "Can you book me through to Key West?"

She hit a few more keys and ran a pencil across the lines of data that came up on her screen. She was eager to be of service. It wasn't the platinum card he had handed her to make the reservations, or the front-page news story about Preston—Brody's name had mercifully been suppressed. It was simply that he seemed so nice. "You'll have a half hour wait in Miami, Mr. Brody. Is that all right?"

"Sure," he replied, "as long as it isn't in San Juan."

She laughed and began to write out the ticket.

He was happy to have thought of Key West. It would be hot and humid but blessedly quiet in the off season. There would be the ocean to swim in, and he would get to see Katie.

He was at the edge of exhaustion by the time Key West appeared out the airplane window many hours later. A few palm trees hung like a mirage in the blur of diesel exhaust. Beyond them, he thought he could catch a hint of blue sky above Flagler Beach. Brody rubbed his eyes—they were long past the sandpaper stage—and took another look at his in-flight magazine.

After the air-conditioning (what passes for air-conditioning in a DC-4) shut down, a few people got out of their seats and stood awkwardly in the aisle, mopping themselves.

Brody figured the exit ramp wasn't in place. What else could it be? He would have liked to stand and stretch his legs, but DC-4s were not designed for people his size to be comfortable in. Easier to stay put.

He flipped back to an article on sea turtles—Brody loved sea turtles—and made a mental note to go to the turtle farm if he got the chance.

At last the line of passengers began to move. Brody took a slow breath, waited for an elderly gent with a big panama hat to pass him by, then grabbed his flight bag and brought up the rear to the exit.

The stewardess, darkly pretty, Latin—"nailed tightly in place," Brody would have said—smiled appraisingly at him. Yes, he thought, smiling back, squeezing past to avoid brushing against her, I'd be glad to get to know you better sometime.

Actually, she was not thinking how *hermoso* Brody was or anything like that. Her lips were working on automatic.

He grinned. "Tired, huh."

She shrugged. "You look a little beat yourself."

"Been flying since seven. But hey, I'm here."

"Vacation time."

He kissed his fingertips.

She sighed knowingly. "Enjoy the beach. *We're* going back to Miami in half an hour."

"Jeez."

"Tell me about it. These heels are murder."

"Glamorous life."

She found her pocketbook and followed him out.

Out of habit he asked, "Live here?"

7

"Sort of."

As they came off the ramp onto the tarmac, he turned to her. She had a fabulous figure, he thought, the kind that loses nothing to harsh light. "Well, I hope it's an easy flight," he said, meaning it.

She laughed and brushed a strand of long dark hair from her face. "Thank you. Enjoy your stay."

She strolled off toward the staff area, and he watched her for a moment or two before entering the Land of the Lotus Eaters.

He collected his luggage, placed a quick phone call, then found a cab. He gave the driver an address on Catherine Street.

"So? How's it going down here?" Brody asked as they pulled out of the airport and headed along the shore.

"Just fine. Water's been out."

Brody grimaced. "Is it fixed?"

"Early this morning. You a lucky man," the driver added with a chuckle. "Vacation?"

"My kid sister lives here."

"Ah."

The ocean looked glorious, deep green and, farther out, that blue of the Gulf.

His sister saw him getting out of the cab and rushed to the porch to meet him.

"Katie!" he shouted.

"Hiya doin', handsome?" she shouted back.

He ran up the path and, dropping his bags, embraced her. She pressed her lips against his cheek.

"Let me look at you," he said when they had parted. "Hey, you're starting to get big."

She nodded. "I'm not even shy about it anymore."

"No shit. When are you due?"

"November."

"God, that's wonderful."

"Isn't it?"

"Mom would have been proud."

Katie nibbled at her lip and nodded again. "I know. I

8

tell you, though, there were times I didn't think that man and I would make it.''

He shrugged. "Neither did I. But here you are. What was it? Love get you through?''

"Love?'' she said with a smile as her husband, Jorge Castillo, burst through the screen door in work pants and undershirt, puffing at a small cigar. "What's love got to do with it? This here character knocked me up! Make him marry me, Stevie.''

Jorge slipped his arm around her and grinned. "Jes, daz me. I jam de papa. Bud I already *habing* six wibes. Hiya been, man?''

Brody embraced him.

"Good to see you, Jorgelito. You're looking pretty fine.''

Jorge stroked Katie's back. "Better believe it, *hombre*. It's going good. It's going to be okay from now on.''

"And you're going to be an uncle!'' Katie added. "Think your image can stand it?''

Jorge grabbed Brody's valise. "Hey, what the fuck,'' he said before taking another puff of his cigar. "If my image can stand it, so can his.'' He appraised Brody for a moment. "You ought to try it sometime, *hermano*.''

Brody shielded his face in defense.

"See?'' Katie said to her husband. "What'd I tell you? He's too scared. But it wouldn't be such a bad idea.''

"Sure, sure. I'll order up a nice little wife from L.L. Bean.''

"Hah,'' replied Jorge. "She's right. Come on in.''

The house they were renting looked much the same as it had the last time he'd paid his more or less half-yearly visit: Florida homey, yellows and oranges prevailing on the furniture and walls, and a profusion of indoor plants that quickly identified the couple as transplanted northerners. Jorge heaved Brody's bags up into the loft, assuring him that they would leave the air conditioner on at night.

"Look,'' Katie said, her arm around Brody's waist,

"we're just getting dinner together. What do you feel like doing? Taking a swim?"

He winked. "You bet. I feel like I've been traveling for years."

He changed into trunks and an old gray T-shirt, found the can of Brazilian coffee that he had brought as a gift, and went down to find his sister in the kitchen. She was sitting at the table before the glass doorway that led out to the back deck, shelling shrimp with a paring knife.

She whistled at him when he reappeared. "You're looking pretty good for a broken-down ex-marine," she remarked. "Those girls are gonna love you."

He grinned devilishly. "Hope so. Listen, I'll go over to the liquor store on the way back, buy us a bottle of wine for dinner. Nice bottle of red to go with whatever that is?"

Jorge, immersed in his cooking, nodded with enthusiasm.

Brody handed his sister the can of coffee. "Sorry it isn't wrapped," he said. "I had to leave Rio in a hurry."

"That where you got the tan?" she wanted to know.

He told her as much about the case as was proper with food on the table.

"No kidding," she said when he had finished. "So Preston was out to really screw your client."

"Well," Brody pointed out, "I wouldn't put it quite like that. The bank was out to screw him, too. They told me so up front. But they weren't committing grand larceny to do it. And he couldn't have been extradited."

"Nice piece of change you made, though."

"It comes and it goes. I only have me to look after, you know."

"Yeah, well . . . Tell me the truth. You never found anybody who mattered enough, huh?"

He shrugged. "Something like that. Besides, it's not the kind of life—"

"You have to *let* a woman matter, Steve. You never dared to."

He'd heard it all before. "You could be right. Maybe someday. And you? How are the two of you doing now?"

Ladle in hand, Jorge turned from the marinara sauce. "Pretty good. I'm working steady now for a couple contractors. Hey, got a kid coming, right?"

"You still, you know, doing your thing?"

Jorge waved the ladle at Brody. "Why you talk to me like that, man?"

Brody squared his shoulders and scowled back at his brother-in-law. The heat was still oppressive, thick as butter, but it wasn't the heat that was getting on his nerves. "Come on, Jorge," he said calmly. "It's a question, isn't it?"

"Can it, Steve," said Katie.

"I'm just asking."

"I said, *can it!*" Her dark blue eyes were cool above the light sprinkling of freckles that covered her pert nose and wide cheeks. "So he gets a little high."

"A little high? Jesus Almighty."

"Yeah, man," Jorge added placatingly. "So I blow some—what's it to you? You want?" he asked, breaking into a wide grin. "It ain't like you're a regular cop or nothing. You want, man, I give you some."

Jorge put down the ladle to wipe the perspiration from the bald spot above his wrinkled forehead. He started cleaning his hands on a dish towel that hung from the refrigerator.

Brody sighed and glanced at Katie again before replying, "No, I don't want some." He shook his head slowly. Listen to me, he thought, suddenly pissed at himself. I'm talking like a football coach—like a goddamn *father*.

There was a long pause. Katie went back to cleaning the shrimp, and Jorge, shrugging, stuck the ladle back in the spaghetti sauce, which had started to bubble.

"Listen, Jorgelito," Brody finally said in an easier voice, "I don't mean anything by it. But we've been there, all three of us, and you know it and she knows it and she's pregnant now. You don't want to get caught again. I just want to know what's coming down."

11

"He understands, Steve," Katie said. Brody could hear the impatience in her voice.

"That whole scene," he continued anyway, "that's building a house on shit."

"He knows," she repeated. She wasn't the sort who whined. He hated himself for persisting. "We both do, Steve. Really. It's not as if he's dealing anymore. He's got a good job. And he'll shake this, too. You wait and see. He's shook worse. Right, baby?"

"You bet," Jorge said.

For a moment, she glanced back defiantly at Brody; then she giggled. "Oh, my God. I couldn't've actually *said* that! I sound like some forties flick."

Brody grinned. "You sure do." She had a theatrical sense of the absurd, a gift for making dramatic statements that didn't quite fit her demure image—on the surface, at least. He remembered the June day she'd left home for good at the ripe old age of eighteen, how she'd marched off to the bus stop, hair bouncing loosely around her shoulders, suitcase in hand, hips swinging in her jeans, leaving the whole Milwaukee suburb speechless. She was still a toothsome twenty-nine.

"God. D'you think it really could be all the dope I've smoked?" she asked.

"Shit," he said, laughing. "Smoking these days, too, are you?"

"No. I got fussy with a kid coming."

"Hey, babe, there's a time and a place."

Her eyes began to glisten. "I can feel him kicking all the time, Steve. You're going to be an *uncle*. Can you imagine?"

"I'm looking forward to it, Katie."

"And I'm telling you, Steban, I got it together," Jorge said. "That's the truth."

Brody more than half believed his brother-in-law. He had faith in people. It was hardly a common trait among his work associates, some of whom considered his optimism a real drawback, if not a downright threat.

Though the truth was, he thought as he nodded in

12

brotherly acquiescence, Jorge had only been able to shake smack four years earlier in New York because he realized it would kill him. With coke, he wouldn't realize.

"And you better believe I want to be an uncle," he told his sister. "Anyway, I'm sorry I spoke out of turn. I'm going to take a swim in the ocean now, if the two of you don't mind."

"Hey, do it," Jorge declared from his post at the sauce pot, waving the ladle for emphasis.

Katie nodded, continuing with the shrimp. "That's what you're here for, honey."

He walked out the screen door, past the front yard and its sad ratty grass, turned down the street and over to Duval. He wasn't sure the trip had been such a hot idea after all, but maybe they'd all get over it if he could remember to keep his stupid mouth shut.

Turning up toward the Sands, Brody stretched gratefully and took a few deep breaths of air.

Look at the bright side, he told himself. Jorge knew plumbing, had even broken into the close Conch trade, could be civil when he had to be, even polite, though one look at him and you could see he wouldn't be messed with, either. A plus when half the businessmen in town are gay and everybody knows how to screw you.

Brody ducked under the thatched entrance of the beach bar and strolled past a few clumps of people sitting at the rough round tables over drinks and backgammon.

Entering a place or walking up a flight of steps, he moved easily: for a big, tall man, his step seemed effortless, and his shoulders rolled up and back just a bit, as if he were riding a horse.

He liked to tilt his head slightly to one side as he climbed the steps, too. And his eyes moved a lot—not only sideways, but up and down, patrolling a perimeter without conscious effort, marking lines of sight, deflections, architectural masses that could stop a slug if they had to.

He dropped his towel onto the sand and stretched out on it with a sigh. The Preston case had taken a lot out of him, he realized as he felt the muscles in his back relax.

He took a little snooze, finally got up and waded into the water like a buffalo. He flopped sideways, causing a fine splash, and swam straight out along the shallow bottom, holding his breath to see how long he could last without air. He counted slowly to thirty before coming up, then floated blissfully under the glaring sun.

He thought about what Katie had told him, how he should Find a Nice Girl and Settle Down. Maybe she didn't understand what it meant to be a private eye whose specialty was offshore cases. Going to Hong Kong, darling. Be back in a month or so, if I haven't been murdered.

Or maybe she did understand. Despite the twinge of irritation he still felt, he suspected that she knew what she was talking about.

He started swimming out to where the water turned colder.

Two or three hours later, he was strolling around the corner of Catherine and Duval on his way back to the house in the gathering twilight. He'd blissfully lost track of how long he had been out, giving in to the luxury of judging time in the water by the setting of the sun. He was carrying the bottle of Orvieto he had chosen with care, feeling content, his hair pleasantly sticky from the salt water, when he saw two men leaving his sister's house.

Medium-sized Cuban carrying a black plastic trash bag and a tall South American with short hair and dark glasses. Loping. Talking to each other. They climbed into a rose-colored van with a driver waiting and pulled slowly away from the curb.

Son of a *bitch*, Brody nearly screamed. I'm down here, Jorge's still hustling. He slipped into an alley and watched them drive by. The driver looked more like a native, with the heavyset face of a Conch. Thick arm leaning out of the window. Gold pinky ring pressing into his fleshy finger.

Brody got the plate number easily enough, peeked around the corner of the building, saw them turn right on Duval. What if he busted Jorge right this minute and then went after them? Right now? He could just picture it. Katie'd never speak to him again. Well, maybe. He had half a mind to get the next plane out and be done with it.

But where would that leave Katie? In the middle. Well, she's *in* the middle, goddamn it.

Pondering this, deciding finally it was none of his business, he found himself back at the front gate before he knew it. Swung it open in resignation. Blood's thicker than water. I promised Mom. Like hell I did.

He heaved himself up the front steps and entered, shouting, "Booze's here! Come and get it."

The smell of gunpowder stopped him in his tracks.

"Katie?"

No one answered. All he could hear was a palm frond scraping against the back of the house.

Stricken with a sense of awful foreboding, he ran down the hall to the kitchen.

Chapter

2

Less than an hour later, Detective Lieutenant Corky Reddon grunted, pressed his palms against his knees, and rose from his crouched position between the toilet and the tub of the Castillo residence.

"Didn't go in for big bathrooms, did they?" he said in an embarrassed murmur. Then, sighing, "Sorry about all of this, Mr. Brody." Another plainclothes cop, a spare, slow man in his late thirties, stuck his head in the open doorway. "Mr. Brody," Reddon said, "this here is Detective Baar. He'll be working with me on the case. Okay, let's move him."

Detective Baar hitched up his pants and backed away from Brody, who nodded and left the room. Baar took a look, pressed his lips together thoughtfully, and slipped his arm around Jorge's waist. Lifting the man's head out of the toilet bowl, he turned the body over on its back.

People get murdered in all sorts of ways. Reddon was always on the lookout for the particularly unusual, which got difficult after a while if you called yourself a successful old sheriff and half of what you saw you maybe couldn't put in the report. Drowning in a toilet bowl he did not find unusual. "When do you figure?"

Baar glanced at his watch. "It's seven-forty now. Hour and a half tops?"

"See how close they can make it. And look, you make sure you ask the lab boys to type whatever the hell is in the bowl there, too."

"Type it?"

"Type if there's any blood. I want to know if it was his own excrement he drowned in, Kevin. Tremendous things they can do in the lab." Reddon smiled paternally. "Say, pull his undershirt up, will you?" Three purpled hash marks, about three inches long, had been cut into each side of Jorge's chest just above the nipples. "You ever seen cuts like that on an upper torso?"

"Could be he wasn't too keen on being shoved head first into a toilet bowl."

"Could." Reddon glanced at the glass shelf torn from its supports beside the medicine chest, bottles smashed in the sink and on the floor, the eerie scent of White Shoulders lingering in the air, and returned to the body. "Looks to be more some kind of ritual thing, though. All right, wrap it up, my boy. What else're you gonna do to earn the taxpayer's money tonight?"

"Catherine's a pretty quiet street late in the day. Somebody must have heard *something*."

"Hard to imagine somebody didn't. Check out the ladies in the neighborhood—she was a pregnant woman, fer Chrissake. Maybe one of 'em'll say something. Otherwise, it's damn near amazing what a Conch can tell you he don't know."

"Looks like a drug hit, Lieutenant."

"You didn't find that much of it."

"Enough."

"Yeah," said Reddon, "all right. I'll have a talk with Tiny when his boat gets in."

Reddon eased his way out of the room. Brody was

17

leaning on the thin wrought-iron Dutch door that led into the parlor.

"They must have done him after her," Brody said in a lifeless monotone. "She would've wanted it the other way." He was rubbing the tip of an aloe, broken off an overturned plant, between his fingers.

"Mr. Brody, am I right in thinking you showed Officer Parker a New York State detective's license when he first talked to you?"

Brody nodded.

"Y'here on a vacation, are you?"

"I was. I came in on the four o'clock out of Miami to visit. Them." He glanced at the kitchen again, where Katie's body lay sprawled, arms apart, head jammed at a cockeyed angle against the bottom of a cabinet, blue eyes fixed in stunned disbelief. The gaping wound in her stomach was unspeakably red against the light green housedress she had been wearing. Someone had turned off the flame under the marinara sauce. The cleaned shrimp were still sitting in a glass bowl on the table. A few unshelled shrimp lay on the cutting board.

"Where's your luggage?" Reddon asked him.

"Up there in a cubby in the loft. Hasn't been touched. They must have missed it. I didn't unpack."

Two men in blue uniforms and baseball caps started to rubber-bag her. Reddon waited until they were through. Brody had started, convulsively, to cry.

The lieutenant's glance fell to the floor. This was never an easy moment for him. "S'cuse me a bit," he whispered, and hustled out the door to the waiting lab truck. They were just locking up the back.

"Henry?"

"Yes, sir."

"Tell 'em I want to know if they can tell me what position she was in." Henry frowned dubiously. "Yeah, yeah. Tell 'em I don't say it'll be *easy*—just ask them, from the path the shells took, could they take a guess. You do that for me?"

"Yes, sir."

"See, Henry, it ain't every day you get a pregnant woman killed like that, shotgun wound to the stomach. So maybe this here *was* some kind of jungle murder, but maybe it wasn't."

Henry shrugged, unconvinced. "I—I don't know, sir."

"Well, you're probably right. Ugly any way you turn it, that's for damn sure. This kinda murder, you wonder will the flowers grow here again." Reddon mopped his face with a handkerchief and lit a cigarette. "But stick around a while and you'll see more of 'em."

"Off and running," said Baar, who had come up behind them. "Don't hold your breath, though."

Reddon shrugged in agreement. The lab truck pulled out of the driveway, and he watched Baar drive off down the block before returning to the house. The Key West quiet had once more descended; Reddon could hear a kid riding a tricycle around back of the houses. He found Steve Brody slumped on a chair in the front room.

"You look like you could use some air," Reddon remarked. Brody raised his hand to wipe the sweat from his mouth. "Let's go out to the back porch."

Brody leaned on the porch rail and looked up at the overhead banyan tree as if he had never seen it before. Behind it, stars were already appearing.

"Pretty brutal thing in there," Reddon began, removing his panama hat and studiously wiping the liner with his handkerchief as he settled himself on one of the aluminum deck chairs. "Mr. Brody, I'd like to ask you a few more questions. You up to it? Could wait, but it looks to be there's some serious felons running around out there."

Brody nodded, clearing his throat.

"Called it in, did you? At seven-oh-eight, I believe it was?"

Brody nodded.

"And you say you flew in on the four o'clock flight."

"That's right. Took a cab here, make it four-forty or so."

"Narrowly missed getting killed yourself, then. Where did you happen to be when the crime occurred?"

Coming out of Corky Reddon's mouth, the question sounded like the rustle of silk.

"At the Sands," Brody replied. "I went for a swim ten or fifteen minutes after I got here."

"Pretty big hurry you were in."

Brody's jaw flexed in disbelief. "I'd been flying all day. I was grimy."

"Anybody see you take your swim?"

"Plenty of people—local kid with a Labrador, coupla secretaries on vacation, older man sitting on a deck chair. What exactly are you suggesting, Lieutenant?"

"Just having a chat here, is all. Man flies into town, he's here fifteen minutes, barely misses getting killed along with two other people, comes back just in time to see three mysterious assailants leaving the scene of the crime—wouldn't you find it curious, Mr. Brody, how all that fits together so neat?"

"Sure I would," Brody snapped, "but that's the way it happened. What are you planning to do about it, aside from making some half-assed insinuations?"

"No need to talk that way to me, Mr. Brody," Reddon replied in the same silky voice. "You *were* the first on the scene."

"I called you right away, Lieutenant."

"So you did, so you did. And everything's exactly how you found it?"

"I didn't touch a thing. I was in *shock*, I'm not *stupid*."

For a long moment, Reddon stared hard at him. Then he said, "Okay. You seem to be leveling with me."

"Gee, thanks. I could have told you as much."

"Be remiss if I didn't find out for myself, though."

Reddon lit another cigarette and offered one to Brody, who shook his head. "Gave them up six months ago."

"Good for you. Wish I could. That van'll be long gone by now anyhow," Reddon observed confidentially.

"Like as not, we'll find it tucked away in a stand of mangrove up Marathon or some damn place."

"Maybe."

Reddon lazily drummed his fingers on the arm of his chair. He broke the silence by saying, "All right. Seeing as how you're a trained observer, what do you make of it?"

Brody widened his stance. "Too much blood," he forced himself to say. Bodies, he told himself. They're just bodies, they're not people anymore, and you're being debriefed now because the man thinks he needs it now. "I thought whoever it was *wanted* to make it a real mess," he went on. "Pretty large gauge, close range. Doesn't add up—unless they were sending a message to somebody else. The guy knew what it was going to do to her. Maybe he got a kick out of it."

Reddon was studying the rippled-glass top on the table beside him. "You figure that, do you?"

Brody nodded and added, "I thought they did her first, too, as I said. I don't know why. Make him suffer more? But they knew just what they were doing. If they're maniacs, they're trained ones."

The lieutenant exhaled slowly. "Notice anything else?"

"Paring knife's gone—the one she was cleaning the shrimp with. Ordinary knife."

Reddon ran three fingers down the side of his chest. "Your brother-in-law had cuts on him here, three on each side, like service stripes. Coulda been that knife. . . . Tell me, how well did you know them?"

"Well enough." Brody told him about Jorge's narcotics convictions in New York.

"Yeah," Reddon replied after he'd heard the story. "I figured as much. Thing I care to know, was he dealing down here?"

"Come on, Lieutenant. Hard to believe he wasn't, isn't it? Didn't get blown away like that for true love. Besides, if they *were* sending a message to somebody else . . ." Brody shrugged. "What the hell do you know about a

21

brother-in-law? The last time I saw the two of them was nearly six months ago. I knew he was a user. But if you're talking serious possession with intent—well, I've had my suspicions, but I never had any proof.'' He waved his hand in the air. ''She kept quiet about that, didn't confide. And he wouldn't have said.

''This was supposed to be a new start,'' Brody added bitterly. Noticing it, Reddon leaned back in his chair.

''Proud lady.''

''You bet.''

''You a little proud, too, are you?''

''Why do you ask?''

Reddon narrowed his eyes. ''Don't do to get all wound up at a time like this, start kicking in the place, you know what I mean.''

Brody shook his head. ''Lieutenant, you just find the sons of bitches who did them like that,'' he said in an even voice.

''To you it's just another drug hit. You'll make a bust when you make one, if ever. To me it isn't. To me, it doesn't matter what the odds are. You do understand that, don't you?''

''Oh, we'll make a bust all right. Need a bit of time, but we'll get to the bottom of it. The whole thing don't quite add up, I'll allow you. Case like this, not like what you're used to in the way of a trafficking murder, could break pretty quick. I've seen them happen like that.''

Reddon rose to his feet as he was talking, tapping his pudgy finger on the table as he stared into Brody's eyes. ''It's the really ordinary ones that're tough to crack. But maybe it won't go like that. You just keep your nose clean while you're in this jurisdiction. This ain't New York City, and that license of yours don't cut no ice with me.''

Corky Reddon was especially charming when he got to talking real hillbilly just for the hell of it. Brody rose from his slouch against the rail. ''Listen,'' he said in a voice as mellow as morning coffee, ''I'm not looking for trouble. But if you can't find those men, I will. Period. And I'd like to see you try to stop me.''

Reddon let it pass.

"Now, if you'll excuse me, I've got some mourning to do.''

The lieutenant nodded. "You planning to stay here?'' he asked. "Be all right, I think, if you'd like.''

"I'll let you know.''

"You do that, case I need to ask you something. I am sorry for your loss, truly. You don't seem the kind of man deserves a thing like this to happen to him.''

Brody shrugged.

Later, just after nightfall, he left the house and registered for an air-conditioned efficiency at the Santa Rosa Motel from which he did not emerge—except for a few meals at the Cuban place down the block when the rooms were being cleaned and a visit to the undertakers—for the next three days.

When the third day had nearly ended, he was again sitting on the bar stool with the red vinyl seat in the open-air snack counter, leaning into the rice and black beans before him—not pointing his thumbnail at himself as he ate, like a stevedore, but just as polite as could be. His mama's son, he was sure.

And what had Katie been?

He was wearing a loose pair of shorts and a green cotton shirt he had picked up in Macao. At least his clothing didn't feel strange to him. Plenty more did. He'd managed to shave, to call the local church and his New York answering service again.

He'd slept the rest of the time away, or thought he had. And awakened, finally, to take a fearful look around him and spot a nearly empty bottle of Jack Daniel's. Impressed there was any left at all, Brody had recorked it and, in the first of the deep gold evening light, had come by the Cuban place for *ropa vieja*, needing the feel of the stewed meat in his stomach.

The woman who ran the place came over to clear away his empty dish.

"*Un café con leche, por favor,*" Brody said.

The light coming from over his left shoulder was turning her face a burnished copper.

"*Es bello,*" he murmured, swiveling his seat, when a stocky younger man—her nephew, he guessed—handed her the cup of strong coffee and she brought it to him.

"*Sí,*" she replied. "Is very beautiful." She said it as if to say the sky was blue, knowing it was and having seen no other.

He paid her when he had finished the coffee and another for good measure. "*Hasta la mañana,*" he said, rising from the stool.

"*Muchas gracias,*" she replied. "*Mañana* you come, *vamos a tener dorado al especial. Muy gustoso.* Very good."

He nodded in appreciation; though *dorado* was his favorite fish, he was still finding it hard to imagine it would ever be tomorrow. He walked toward the afterglow, down Simonton and across to the pier. Was not going to go out looking for killers. No, sir; had read himself the riot act, muttered a few choice words about the kind of schmuck who meddles in his own business. He was no lawyer or shrink (he didn't have the stomach, he felt, for either occupation), but he knew how conflicts of interest could make a person lose his head—act without acting, as a former sensei of Brody's used to put it. Over the years, Brody had seen disaster strike many people because they had lost their heads. In his work, as he had in Rio, he tried to *force* them to whenever he could.

He stopped for a fruit punch at the foot of Malory Square and walked out onto the pier resolved to keep his nose clean—so long as Reddon didn't start stringing him along with his clever bullshit.

As usual, half of Key West was sitting around on the pier watching the last of the daylight play itself out over the Gulf, the great masses of clouds, white and black and peach, riding up from low on the horizon.

24

Someone had started to play a blues harmonica. The tourists were snapping photographs, kids wandering around with melting ice cream in their hands, blond lovelies of both sexes in minutely abbreviated costumes coasting through the crowds on bicycles or lazing against the pilings where they met the broad expanse of the pier on that flat southern end of these United States.

He felt good being among people again, people who didn't know him but whose flesh recalled him to the daily life that had been abruptly and completely torn apart. He browsed a few tables covered with leather goods, brightly colored shirts, crystal beads on silver chains that turned now apricot, now lime.

When he saw her, it took him a few seconds to remember who she was. It might have been the shirt she was wearing, white, with a low-cut, tailored collar and big buttons down the front, over a pair of gym shorts that looked like they'd been poured on and left to dry.

Then she spotted him and waved in recognition.

He strolled over.

"Hello again," she said.

"Hello to you again. I have to tell you," he said, "for a minute there, I didn't recognize you. You sure do look different in fatigues."

"Darling man," she replied, turning sideways. "Look! No heels!"

Her lipstick was fire-engine red.

He nodded approvingly. "Name's Steve Brody. Nice to meet you in the real world."

She shook his proffered hand, and her smile grew a little wider. "Luz Almeida."

He felt the awkwardness of a man who has just left isolation. "Were you walking over that way?"

"And back. It's a law in Key West," she said with a local's nonchalance. "Care to join me?"

They said nothing for a while, enjoying the deep light fading slowly from the Gulf. "Boy, does this renew you," he finally remarked. They had walked to the end of the pier.

"Sure does."

"Good for the soul. Finally gave you a break, did they?"

"Air Florida?"

"Mm."

"Till tomorrow. And did I need it. This time of year they're always short on staff."

He nodded again. The last traces of salmon pink vanished above the gray of the clouds. He wondered how long he could survive on nodding. "Been with them a while?" he asked.

"Two years. Seems like five."

"Why stay?"

"Used to it, I guess. I majored in art history," she added by way of explanation.

"Burgeoning field."

"You got it. Not as if my dad didn't warn me."

"What's he do?"

She smiled. "Sales director for an appliance chain. We moved to the States when I was four. I was born in Caracas."

He stretched and leaned, arms folded, against one of the pilings. "Anyway," she went on, "I get out of school and I make the big discovery—like, wow, I can be a secretary for the next hundred years, think of it. Working for an airline seemed a whole lot better."

She studied the pillows of water breaking open against the dock. "How come you didn't try the major airlines?" he asked. "Pretty obvious you have the looks, you don't mind my saying. And the brains."

She laughed and looked up at him. "I didn't have the nerve, I guess. Not then. Key West, Charlotte, New Orleans, out and back, round trips like that, I didn't have to be away for long. It was kind of the best of both worlds."

"And now?"

"Mm. Now I'm not so sure. I must be the only flight attendant in the country who's never been outside it. Not even Paris. I've always wanted to go there, but not, you know, like a tourist. I see so many of them. I'd like to buy a one-way ticket and not know when I was coming back, maybe never." She wrapped her arms around herself and squeezed. "That's the way to do it. This place isn't very conducive to making big changes, though." As if to emphasize her point, her lovely eyes roamed over the old buildings and the moon brightening above a stand of Christmas palms.

"No," he said, "I guess not."

"Make any sense to you?"

"Sure. Something like that happened to me, too, actually."

She hooked her thumbs into the pockets of her shorts. "It did?"

"Well, sort of. After 'Nam, just hanging out seemed to fit for quite some time. Then I got into gear again," he added with a shrug.

"What are you doing now?"

"I'm a private investigator."

Her eyes widened. "Really?"

He showed her his license. "I sort of specialize in international cases. Pretty wild for a boy from Milwaukee."

"You look looser than you did then," she observed.

He studied the photo under the New York Department of State legend and agreed. "The edge gets sanded off," he added. "I was a real tiger in those days."

They started walking back. The vendors had departed, and there wasn't an ice-cream cone in sight. "So you're living in New York now?" she asked.

"I've got an apartment in Chelsea."

"And I bet you miss it when you're not there."

"Hey," he replied. "Always."

"How's your vacation been?"

"Different."

"Not what you expected, huh?"

"No."

"You do seem kind of low." The first stars began to

emerge above the silhouette of a freighter moored to the pier.

"The truth is," he said, "I've had a pretty rough time. My kid sister died the day I came in."

"Oh, no . . . oh, you poor man." She studied his face.

"I don't really mean to—I mean, you're a complete stranger. I don't—"

"Hey, that's okay," she said, resting her hand on his arm for a moment. "Is the rest of the family here?"

He shook his head. "I'm it."

She struggled for the right phrase. "Was it, you know, sudden?"

"Very. My sister and her husband were both murdered."

"My God." Luz crossed herself.

"Look, I really feel awkward—"

"No, it's okay," she assured him. "Would you like to go sit down someplace?"

"I—it's just that I haven't spoken to anybody but cops and telephones since it happened." He looked away. "Not that there's a whole lot to say."

"How about buying me a drink and we can just sit?"

"I'd like that very much," he said, meeting her glance. "You point the way, though. I've never gotten to know this town much."

They headed back toward the square. "There's a nice place a few blocks over, if you'd like. I go there pretty often. Mostly locals, but you can hear yourself talking."

"Is it always this pretty here at night?"

"Oh, yes. Except during hurricane season sometimes." She turned right and headed toward Whitehead. "When the cloud bank hangs too low, there's not as much to see. But it's good for the eyes, all that color."

"So are you." She looked at him, and he smiled. "I'm not trying to come on to you. It's kind of hard not to notice, that's all."

"I don't mind. You're not a breather. You wouldn't

believe some of the clowns I run into when I'm working.''

They turned into a trellised alley hung with bougainvillea that led to a bar with a nice sweep of flagstone terrace, Christmas palms, and an assortment of wooden tables and chairs. There were orange candle pots on each table. Pleasant buzz to the place, nothing fancy. They took a table off to the side.

''So you've never been to Paris,'' he said, getting settled.

She shook her head. ''Have you?''

''Oh, yes.''

''Is it really like what they say?''

''I don't know. What do they say?''

A waitress came over, and they ordered two beers.

''Well,'' she said, trying to sum up, ''like it's not just romantic old buildings and stuff. People say it's real wild.''

''It always has been. They've even got Burger King,'' he offered.

She winced. ''They've got a lot more besides,'' he confessed. ''They've got at least a little bit of anything there is. It's a great place when you have the time to appreciate it.'' He grinned, thinking of an afternoon he had once spent in a bedroom on avenue Foch. ''Maybe you won't believe this, but I actually hum 'The Last Time I Saw Paris' every time my plane lands. That's the God-honest truth.''

The beers came, and they both took a long sip.

''So you've been there a lot, huh,'' she said enviously.

''Mm.''

''I want to see . . . Pago Pago, you know? Helsinki. Berlin. I want to see the Berlin Wall and ask myself, 'What's a nice Venezuelan girl like you doing in a place like this?' ''

''Do it, then.''

''Someday.''

Brody had been lounging on his chair, ankles crossed

under the table. Suddenly his shoulders tensed and he leaned forward.

There was a man with his elbow against the bar who looked familiar, though in the dim light Brody couldn't be sure. Nothing striking about him. Beefy but solid, with thick shoulders and arms and a face that sloped down from the eyes like a ski run; like half the others there, a Conch who looked nautical.

"What's the matter?" Luz asked.

"Oh, nothing. You hang out here a lot?"

"Yeah. It's one of my favorite places. Why?"

"Don't look now, but there's a guy over there in a dark blue shirt, smoking a cigar. You know him?"

She shifted on her seat, lifted her beer, and glanced over casually.

"Uh-huh. His name's Chuck Rio," she replied. "I thought you mingled with a better crowd."

"What's he do?"

"He works on one of the boats."

"You don't sound like the two of you are very friendly."

She made a face. "He's a pig. He's been trying to get into my pants for months. And," she went on, leaning forward so she could lower her voice, "that's no laughing matter. Chucky's a mean son of a bitch. Nobody wants to mess with him. He's strong as an ox."

"And he didn't get the message."

She nodded. "Right. Well, finally, after I don't know how many times I'd told him no, I didn't want to have a drink or anything else with him, he says, 'Hey, I could make you do it if I wanted.' " She looked ready to spit.

Brody stared at her. "What did you tell him?"

She blinked once and glanced again at the bar. "I said, sure he could make me, and if he did, my two brothers, when they found out, they'd come here and feed his balls to the fish. He believed me all right," she went on defiantly. "He'd better. What I do with my body is my own business."

Brody pursed his lips in appreciation. "Sounds to *me* like you're ready for the majors."

She fingered her glass. "People like him don't scare me, Steve. I scare me. Not knowing what to do with my life scares me."

"You know which boat he works on?"

Anger spent, she considered for a moment. "I think one of Roper's. Why?"

"Who's Roper?"

Luz hesitated for a moment. "Roper Gance. Nobody talks much about him, but he's *muy jefe* in Key West. He's like the Carimo brothers, like Elmore Johnson—guy everybody calls Tiny 'cause he must weigh over three hundred. They all have fingers in everything. Gance owns a lot of businesses around here, down at the port, mostly."

Brody rose from his seat and strolled over to the bar, finding an empty space next to Rio. The man had both his hands spread out on the bar. The way the gold ring on his left hand pressed into his pinky was practically unmistakable.

Brody asked the bartender for a pack of Marlboro, paid for it, and pulled off the outer wrapper, lost for a moment in thought.

"Hey," he heard Rio say to him. "You looking at something?"

"No," Brody answered, surprised.

Rio had already turned to face him. "Oh, yeah? What is it? You some sort of smart-ass?"

It sounded to Brody like the man had had a few. He shook his head and held up his hands. "Sorry," he murmured, "didn't mean to disturb you," and strolled back to his seat at the table.

"What was that all about?" Luz whispered.

"I'm not too sure you'd want to know."

She didn't seem pleased.

"It's about my sister, Luz. I think I recognize that man."

"You mean *Chucky*—"

"They had a van. He might have driven it. I'm not sure. And I'm not looking for trouble, either," he added, taking another sip of his beer. His eyes crinkled at her over the top of the glass. "Certainly not when I'm with someone I'm trying so hard not to come on to. Tell me more about Roper Gance."

Luz shrugged nervously. "I don't *know* much more about Gance. I don't *want* to."

"Ah."

She glanced down. "You have to be crazy to get involved in some of the stuff that goes on around here."

Nearly blushing, he rocked forward on his elbows and lightly kissed the downy smoothness just below her ear. He could feel her shivering, just as he was.

She raised her face to rub the tip of her nose against his. "That was lovely," she whispered.

He slid back onto his seat, and they spent a while looking at each other. She asked him about his tan, and he told her about Rio and then about the streets of Sorrento and the shop windows in Rome. The Conch left. They had another beer before Brody paid the tab and they walked out.

They were halfway down the alley when Rio emerged from the shadows at the other end, hefting a piece of lead pipe. "Okay, smart-ass," he grunted. "You want to look at me some more, go ahead."

Brody fixed his gaze on the man's eyes. "Look, I'm sorry if I caused you any offense back there, Mr. Rio."

"Oh, you know my name, do you? This what you're hanging around with lately?" he barked, staring at Luz.

"Leave us alone, Chucky," she said. "We're not bothering you."

Rio came closer, swinging the pipe from side to side like a nightstick. "That so. Well, far as I'm concerned you are. I don't care for no fucking tourists coming around where I drink, thinking they can act tough. Goddamn teach you to keep your eyes to yourself, you cock-*sucker*," he shouted, lunging at Brody, the pipe like a baseball bat in his grip.

But Brody was already moving down and to the left. He came up with his elbow just as the blow whistled past him, catching Chucky in the armpit. The man howled in pain, the pipe falling with a clang onto the flagstone, Luz wincing, getting out of the way.

"You crazy or something?" Brody shouted. "I said I'm not looking to *mess* with you."

"Fucking bastard," Rio snarled, straightening up, and slid a knife from his waistband.

"Put it away, Sinbad. You've had a few."

Brody caught the glint of the blade in the moonlight and jerked backward as Rio backhanded it and swung. He felt the edge slice through the front of his shirt and threw himself between it and Chucky's body the instant he could, breaking the arc. He landed a right just above the man's beer belly, then brought his wrists together and swung them up, catching the tip of Rio's chin. The fat man collided with the trellis behind him, and Brody sent him down with another hard jab in the ribs and a short, brutal chop to the side of the head as he was coming forward. Feeling bone give, Brody stepped back.

"Son of a bitch," he said to Luz. "Let's get out of here."

"Steve, he cut you."

"I know." The front of his shirt had begun to stain. "I'll be okay. You have any peroxide at your place? Any gauze?"

She nodded. "Will he b-be all right?" she stammered, looking at Rio's jaw as he lay crumpled in the shadows.

"Oh, he'll be just fit as a fiddle come morning," Brody answered grimly, reaching into his pocket for the pack of Marlboro and flipping it onto the flagstone next to Rio. They edged around the entrance to the alley and walked quickly to the apartment Luz shared with two other airline employees.

"It stings, huh," she said, her nose crinkled, when she had stripped off his shirt and dabbed a soaked wad of cotton across the long red streak on his hard abdomen. A first-aid kit lay open on the hamper beside them.

He winced. "Whatever gives you that idea?" He looked down at the cut. "No, really, I'll live."

She proceeded to paint it with Mercurochrome, her hand shaking slightly, and cover it with a gauze pad strapped in place with adhesive strips. "There you go," she said. "Compliments of Air Florida. How about a drink?"

He nodded and followed her into the kitchen. She retrieved a pair of sheer blue panty hose from the drying rack next to the sink and threw it onto one of the chairs. "Rosalee," she observed. "She left for Orlando yesterday." Luz shook her head and poured out two shots of gold tequila.

"Thanks," Brody said, taking a sip. She lifted her glass in reply.

He reached for her hand. She touched his fingers, then moved closer and kissed him hungrily, pressing against him. "Boy," she said, catching her breath. "Isn't it great you're not one of those men who comes on to a woman."

He reached around the small of her back and lifted her closer, kissing his way down her throat to the ripe breasts inside her loose shirt.

"Oh, I want you," she murmured. "I want you so *much*. Now. No, don't wait. Now."

He set her down on the edge of the counter, and she slid her shorts off.

"God, you're gorgeous," Brody said, entering her. She shivered, and her hips rose as he unbuttoned the shirt and spread it open. "Gorgeous," he said again, and ran his hands over her breasts and waist. She fell against him with a sigh, and he started to carry her into the bedroom.

She opened her eyes a slit. "That wound," she whispered. "Is it all right to carry me?"

"I'll manage."

"There's something—"

She didn't finish what she was going to say. As if a

wave had caught them, churning white and rolling them against itself, there was no up, no down, only his effort to stay upright long enough to fall sideways on the bed. She slid on top of him with her eyes shut tight, and he coaxed her on, clutching her hips in his large hands, stroking her thighs and her back.

And then time seemed to disappear, and her body with it, and his, released, soaring upward until the mounting surf pounded her into a blinding flash and she threw herself forward to kiss him with an urgency she had never known. She thought that it would never end, until she heard him cry her name and felt him explode.

For a long while, they neither moved nor spoke. When he opened his eyes at last, he shook his head and murmured, "God, I've never. . . ."

"I know," she whispered.

He hugged her more tightly against him. "It happened to you, too?" he asked.

"Oh, yes."

Chapter

3

When she awoke the next morning, the first pink light of dawn streaking through the bamboo blinds, he was already dressed in his sandals and shorts and was looking out the bedroom window at the fig trees and the tangle of fences that marked out the surrounding houses. She gazed approvingly at his back and his snug waist.

"Good morning," she said. "Who *was* that guy from New York, anyway?"

He turned. "I'd have got some breakfast for you, but there's nothing in the refrigerator."

She sat up and raised a pillow behind her naked back. "No," she agreed. "I'm flying to Miami at ten."

"You really are gorgeous."

"Likewise."

"How about we go out to eat?"

"Sure."

"We can take a cab to the Marriott. It's on the way."

"Great," she said, stretching, and leaned over to look at the travel alarm on the night table. He lost himself in the deep tan curve of her smooth leg across the sheet, letting his eyes move up over her hip and around her breast. "But my flight isn't for another four *hours*. Come hold me. By the time I get back, you may not even be here."

"Oh, I'll be here, I think."

"Come hold me anyway."

They made love again, slowly, finding places they hadn't found the night before, and were sitting down to ham and eggs at the Marriott by eight. Luz was wearing her blue flight uniform and tie, and a blue leather flight bag was draped over the back of her seat. She had found Brody a black T-shirt someone had left in the apartment after Rosalee broke up a hot affair with him. It fit Brody pretty well, only a shade tight across the chest.

"Luz," he said, folding a bite of ham over the end of his fork, "last night you mentioned something about this guy Gance?"

She paused over her coffee and frowned. "All I know for sure is he's dangerous—and not the way Chucky is. You don't mess with him, Steve. He has too many friends."

"I'm not planning to mess with anybody. But I have to go see the police today. I'd like to know how the land lies."

"If you mean the island, flat. If you mean the people on it, it's roller-coaster turf."

He nodded and gently pulled open a steaming biscuit. "Everybody knows everybody."

"And they can't get out of each other's way, either."

He took her hand in his, rubbed his fingers over it. "When *are* you coming back?"

"Two days from now, on the one o'clock flight."

"Where are you staying in Miami?"

"At the Sheraton. Are you really going to be here when I get back?"

"I sure plan to. Do me a favor, though, will you?" He asked her for a paper and pencil and wrote down his

number at the Santa Rosa. "Two days, that's Thursday.
If you can, call me before you leave for the airport."

"Why?"

"I don't know. So I can hear your sweet voice?"

He dropped her at the airport and walked all the way
back to his room on Simonton.

A few hours later he was ushered into a small, dishev-
eled office at police headquarters. Brody had changed to
shorts, a white cotton shirt, and a pair of old moccasins.
The heat had already built mightily, though the whole
building was situated in the deep shade of old trees.
"What can I do for you, Mr. Brody?" asked Lieutenant
Reddon, looking up from a pile of folders. He had his
jacket off and his suspenders down.

Brody removed his sunglasses and folded them. "I just
thought I'd stop by, hoping maybe you could tell me
what's been happening on the case."

"I believe I suggested this might take some time."

"So you did."

Reddon sighed. "I hear Mr. Castillo maybe owed a
favor and didn't come through on it. Old favor. Not very
convincing, frankly. Maybe he was out of the game already, maybe not—nobody seems to know for certain. I
haven't heard any talk about your sister, if that's any
consolation to you." He cleared his throat and flipped
open a file, bringing a pair of half glasses up to his eyes.
"It wasn't your brother-in-law's shit in that toilet, neither. Type-O blood, though, so it could've been damn
near anybody else's. Still, I have never heard of an M.O.
like that. That ain't no ritual, that's a goddamn Ayrab
insult."

For a long moment, Brody didn't know what to say.
"You know a guy named Chuck Rio?"

Reddon pursed his lips and leaned back in his swivel
chair. "Yeah. How do *you* know him?"

"He tried to knife me last night."

The lieutenant snapped a cigarette from the pack on
his desk and lit it. "Why?"

"He's the one who drove the van, Lieutenant."

"What?" Reddon exploded. "I thought I told you to stay the hell out of this case."

Brody shook his head. "He didn't know I recognized him. He was looking for a fight, that's all."

"And you gave it to him."

"I wasn't trying to. He jumped me coming through the alley in front of a bar on Emma Street. I hear he works for a guy named Roper Gance."

"Yeah, well, never you mind about that. That's my business. Besides the evidence of your own eyes, you got anything can put Mr. Chuck Rio in that van? Any proof?"

"No."

"Well, it ain't enough. Local jury, it wouldn't stand up, not coming from an immediate member of the family and a stranger to boot."

"I'm just saying maybe you could lean on him a little. I didn't see *him* coming out of the house."

Reddon appraised the well-built private eye whom he had found, during a not-so-discreet conversation with a friend on the New York P.D., to be highly regarded in various police circles. "So? He'd be an accessory to a murder one anyway. What's the difference? You don't fool me. All you want is the one with the shotgun."

Brody nodded.

"Well," Reddon continued, "then you got a blind spot about it, ain't you? I don't care a damn if they fry him on A.C. or D.C. Listen, Brody, a doctor don't cut on his own family. I hear you're a pretty sharp P.I. You're not thinking like one now. Don't get yourself hurt, you hear me? Where in the hell are you staying, anyhow?"

"The Santa Rosa."

"Under an assumed name?"

"You bet. Want to lock me up?"

Reddon frowned. "Go and enjoy the water sports, will you? And leave me alone." Brody raised his hands and started to leave. "And thanks for the lead."

"Anything for a fellow servant of the law," Brody

remarked, but the lieutenant had already gone back to his reading.

Hands in his pockets, Brody skipped down the steps at the front of the station, rented an old two-wheeler at the store around the corner, and took a slow ride through the quiet back streets to the turtle farm.

He climbed off the bike at the end of a lane on the west end of the island, some distance beyond the old cemetery. He parked it at a stand in the deep shade and stepped through a gate into an open shed with a thatched roof that stretched down toward the water.

What breeze there was seemed, like the flies, to have been drugged asleep by the intense, almost gauzelike humidity. Though he was not in pain, Brody could feel the wound near his ribs beginning to draw, nagging at him. But that did not affect his movement.

An elderly Cuban gentleman, a true ancient, garbed in a broad straw hat and an outrageously vivid tropical shirt, rose from his seat against one of the wooden pillars that were holding the roof up and came over to sell Brody his ticket. Courteous in an old-world manner, he was nevertheless burdened by poor eyesight that thick glasses in massive tortoiseshell frames did little to correct. And, Brody suspected, from a little looseness in the brain as well.

He had some trouble breaking the twenty Brody handed him, had to hold a few bills up to the light, after removing them from the cigar box in his cashier's table, before he found a ten. He did not rush, nor did he seem to care to. Brody knew immediately that he was going to like the place. The old Cuban presented Brody with his change and waved him forward, politely but with great dignity.

A perfect warm-up, Brody thought, for the turtles sitting impassively in enormous pens that ran the entire length of the shed. Snuffling to themselves or grunting forward on the fulcrums of their claws, the turtles' stench was overpowering in the soggy dirt, but he ignored it.

He strolled down the side of the pen, crouching a few times to get an eye-level view of the immense creatures with their great helmeted heads and their inexpendable patience.

The only way you could kill them, short of a bullet, was by turning them onto their backs; they couldn't right themselves. But the specimen nearest him weighed four hundred pounds, Brody figured, all of it balanced a half inch off the ground. And all that fingernail-tearing weight saying, Hey, mutha, turn me over an' I'm dead. Brody had seen the great tortoises before, in other places.

On a vacation once, he had watched them waddle out into a hundred thousand miles of open sea without the slightest hesitation, ready for anything. He had lifted his eyes, squinting at the Pacific horizon line sweeping nearly all around him in a vast, 240-degree arc. It was, he still concluded, the most dangerous thing he had ever seen.

The tortoise sneezed contentedly, and Brody looked up. Food was coming; a rangy young man with mahogany skin had creaked open a gate and was dragging a heavy pail into the pen.

An older man in a blue workshirt and pants, his grizzled hair cut short, was watching him quietly, sipping coffee from a Styrofoam cup. He had the name *Mister Bud* stitched over the pocket of his shirt.

The tortoises responded to the creaking of the gate with an assortment of grunts, sounding a lot like pigs.

Biceps straining, the young man cautiously poured the contents of the twenty-gallon pail into a low cement trough set near the middle of the pen. It smelled worse than chum. Brody grimaced.

"Feeding time," the older man explained, gray mustache curling apologetically over his smile.

"Afternoon," said Brody.

The man nodded, taking another sip from his cup.

"They like it that way, do they?"

The young man, who was shutting the gate behind him burst out in a laugh. "They worse than *fish*. But, hell, they want to eat this God-awful shit, we give it to 'em."

41

Brody laughed. ''Well, let me tell you, I've seen them out on the loose, and you keep these in pretty good condition.''

''Oh, yeah,'' the young man drawled, shifting the empty pail to his left hand and reaching into his back pocket for a handkerchief. ''We treat the old folks pretty good hereabouts, don't we?'' he asked the tortoise Brody had been observing, and laughed again as he paused to mop his face.

''You really seen them in the wild, have you?'' Mister Bud asked with interest after the younger man had gone off to hose down the ramp at the back.

Brody nodded. ''The Galápagos.'' He told him the story.

''Well, now,'' the man said quietly when he had finished. ''Ain't they something. Tell you the truth, I wouldn't mind seeing that myself sometime. Sorry 'bout the smell. Ain't much you can do about it.''

''Actually,'' Brody observed, ''looks like you run a nice clean business here.''

The man nodded, finishing his coffee and flipping the empty container into a trash can nearby. ''Well, we try.''

''What do you do,'' Brody asked, ''chop it up and let it go bad?''

The man's gray mustache curled upward again. ''You kidding? Ain't no *expensive* shit these mothers eat. Just smell the way they like it and be plenty of it.''

''I didn't know.''

''Oh, sure. We get it same as the commercial fleet. Truck hauls it in by the barrel from Johnson Marina.''

''That Elmore Johnson?''

The man smiled broadly. ''Well, I ain't never seen Tiny J. come drag it in himself, now.''

''Pretty important man, I hear.''

''Shit,'' agreed Mister Bud, ''ain't much of nothing he don't do in this town, that's for damn sure.''

''Like Roper Gance.''

''That's right.'' The turtle man bent to retrieve an ice-cream wrapper some tourist had left and dropped it in the trash can. "Like Gance and a few other people. How come you want to know?" he added amiably, studying Brody's reaction.

"Not me," Brody said, slipping a folded bill from his shirt pocket. "My friend here. It's got nothing to do with Tiny Johnson. I'm checking into a certain other person's finances and I wouldn't care to have him know about it. It's about an offshore deal. I need to find out what Roper Gance is like."

The turtle man accepted this, if not as genuine, at least as polite bullshit—there is a big difference between discretion and lying—and slipped the bill into his pocket. "Well now," he said, "you take old Tiny J.—now *there's* a live-and-let-live kind of fella. Not just saying that because he's a brother, neither. You take care of your business, even you an old cracker boy, he treat you just fine. But you fuck with him, get on your case real quick."

He paused to choose his words as he and Brody began to stroll around the pen, watching one tortoise turning toward its repast with what Brody thought was considerable gusto. "But Roper Gance is just a mean man, guy you take a pass on, you know what's good for you. I ain't saying Tiny give it away," Mister Bud added, raising a finger in emphasis. "That there's one tough customer. But he do *give*. Roper don't do nothing but take, any damn way he can."

Brody nodded. "Say I wanted a talk with Mr. Gance— a private talk. Where would I find him?"

"Keep a boat name of *Sea Legs* tied up the end of the Pier House. Sixty-footer, hard to miss." Mister Bud ran a hand over his grizzled skull and looked Brody straight in the eye. "Man likes to hang out there with his friends. Not what you call cordial people. But most of them are gone just after the night shift come on in the bars."

"Much obliged."

"Hell, I ain't told you nothing I couldn't tell Tiny I said."

"Nice turtles you got here."

Mister Bud offered him a grand smile. "Well, I'm

obliged for your story 'bout the Galápagos, too. Glad you enjoyed yo' visit.''

Brody left, wondering how much of the man's accent was a put-on, a mild form of entertainment for the tourists, a fondness, like Reddon's, for dressing out the spoken language with hand tools.

He slid onto his bike and pedaled back past the cemetery with its whitewashed sepulchers marshaled irregularly over the terrain like miniature trailers. The massed growth of pink hibiscus in some of the yards was intoxicating. He eased the bike toward the Santa Rosa.

He told himself it was just insurance; Reddon was chewing his way through the case with all deliberate speed. Reddon had also been dead right about the blind spot.

Instead, Brody thought of Luz. Lazily pumping the pedals, feeling the eager pressure in his thighs as the breeze delighted his face and chin, it was easy.

When he got to the Santa Rosa, he tied up the bike at a stand in the breezeway just off the parking lot. He walked through it to the poolside but paused when he turned the corner to his room: the sliding patio door was partially open. He hadn't left it that way the night before. He glanced at the courtyard, looking for the maids. All he could see was a cleaning trolley in an alcove at the far end of the motel.

Suddenly alert, he slid back into the shade and froze in place, listening. He barely heard the silencer go off with a *thwock*. A slug slammed into the edge of the archway before him, and he lunged across the breezeway.

Down on all fours, Brody turned his head, heart pounding. For one frantic moment, he measured the short distance across the courtyard to his room, but he froze again. Eyes glued to the shadows on the grass and the still surface of the pool, he backed away and to his left, noiselessly, barely moving the air, until he was standing exactly where he had been when the shot went off.

Sweat began to drip from his eyebrows. He could feel

the seconds tick. Nothing happened. Then he felt some-one drawing close on the other side of the wall. He slid off one of his moccasins and spun it, underhand, out into the parking lot. As it skipped out of sight, he braced himself and rammed his head and shoulders into the side of the man who came around the corner after it, throwing him forward. He was shorter than Brody but muscular, Cuban, his face pockmarked and taut. They crashed into an old dracaena, and Brody, kneeing him in the hip, was already reaching for the man's wrist, bending it down and away to get at the gun, when the Cuban lashed out with his arm. Brody caught the blow low in the ribs, right across the bandaged cut on his abdomen, but he didn't let go as they went over with the meaty Cuban on top, the back of the guy's gun hand still in his grip. Wrenching muscle on muscle, he was still trying to reach the finger guard.

The Cuban pulled the trigger, and his weapon—he had removed the silencer—exploded in a shriek of chipping concrete and stucco. He lashed out again at Brody's ribs, then, suddenly, lunged to the right as Brody forced the muzzle away and fired again. Brody felt the weight of the slug lift the man up, shatter against his hip, and tear its way out of his body as he tried to scream before col-lapsing on top of Brody like a sack of potatoes.

Brody yanked himself free and, gasping, rose to one knee, gripping his ribs where the wound had pulled open, orienting himself dizzily. The Cuban was so dead, he didn't have to check. One of the maids was shrieking, holding her hands over her ears, and a couple of men were running toward him from the office.

"Holy Jee-sus Christ!" gasped the taller of the two when he had covered the distance from the office to the pool.

"Call the police," Brody said.

The second man drew up, agitated. "What is going on here—oh, my God!" His gaze had fallen on the dead man crumpled at the base of the dracaena, his blood spattered against the pink stucco.

"He tried to kill me," Brody said, breathing hard. "Would you please call the cops?"

"You mean—*oh*, my God."

"Just call the cops." Smarting, Brody stood up and half stumbled the short distance to his room. The place had been ransacked, the bed turned over, the kitchenette cabinets and medicine chest in the bathroom rifled. He opened a can of beer and waited on the patio.

Detective Baar showed up first and quietly had the area cordoned off. The manager, who had taken a seat next to Brody, was nervous as hell. Brody sucked the last of his beer out of the can as Baar came over.

"Mr. Morrison," the detective began, "very sorry about this business. We're trying to get you back to normal here as quickly as possible. Now, this"—he pulled a notebook out and glanced at it—"this Irenia Hernandez, does she work for you?"

"Mrs. Hernandez! Is she feeling better?"

"Yes, Mr. Morrison. Just shaken up a bit. Responsible woman, is she? Comes to work regularly?"

Morrison nodded.

"Ever had any trouble with her?"

"No, sir."

"Honest?"

"Mrs. Hernandez has been working here for at least ten years. She's a *very* responsible person."

Detective Baar nibbled at his upper lip. "And would you consider her judgment reliable?"

"I certainly would. Of course, this is such a terrible upset. . . ."

"Yes, Mr. Morrison. Everything will be back to normal in half an hour. Thanks for your cooperation. It'd be best if you returned to the office now."

Morrison rose, shaking his head, and shuffled off down the poolside.

Baar settled himself on the seat Morrison had vacated and, loosening his taupe jacket, rested his elbows on his knees. "Mr. Brody," he said, "this is the second time in four days you've been present at the scene of a killing.''

"They guy tried to *shoot* me. That's his gun."

"This *is* the second time in the four days you've been in this jurisdiction, Mr. Brody," Baar continued, unmoved. "I think you'd better have a stab at explaining that." His eyes were subdued but earnest, his whole manner splendidly new South. Brody thought he could just as easily have been a homicide cop in Tuckahoe, New York, or in any other respectable suburban town in America. He was efficient, bright, careful, and probably working on his master's. Good solid comer.

"I've been keeping pretty much to myself. Maybe somebody's declared war on Irish Catholics over six two."

Baar sighed. "Do you really want to play games with me, Mr. Brody?"

"Look," Brody said as calmly as he could, "I come down here on a vacation and two sons of bitches murder my sister and my brother-in-law. Now somebody tries to murder me and you're doing an *interrogation* on me? Are you joking?"

Baar shook his head slowly. "I'm not suggesting you murdered anyone, Mr. Brody. But it could have been the other way around. Whoever did your family could have been looking for you."

Brody didn't have a chance to reply. Reddon's car had slid to a stop in the parking lot, siren off, and the lieutenant, who had heaved himself out of it, was marching over.

The first thing he said was, "What the fuck is going on around here, Brody?"

"That Cuban tried to kill me, Lieutenant."

Reddon snorted. "Where have you been since you left my office?"

Brody told him.

"Turtle farm?"

Brody explained about the article in the in-flight magazine.

"And then?" Reddon continued.

"And then I rode the bike back here—I was going to take a swim before dinner—and that superstar took a shot at me with a silencer on the piece."

Reddon patted his forehead with the back of his hand. "And then he came after you and a struggle ensued."

Reddon glanced at Baar, who nodded. "One of the maids confirms the struggle, Lieutenant."

"Dig that first slug out of the archway," Brody added, "it'll give you the other. Your man here thinks they've been after me since I got here."

"Well, it do set the mind to speculate," Reddon responded dryly. "How in the hell do *you* explain it?"

"Somebody must have made me the night I left the house, tied me up with it."

Reddon considered a moment. "You kind of favoring that rib cage. What's the matter?"

"I got cut, Lieutenant."

"You got cut? Where's the blade?"

"There is no blade, Lieutenant. It happened in the fight with Rio last night. It's a superficial cut. I didn't think it was worth mentioning at your office. Pulled open just now. It'll be all right once I get it bandaged again."

"Maybe Rio's the one who sent this old boy to look for you."

"He didn't know where I was staying, Lieutenant."

"Maybe he found out."

Brody nodded. "So? It still had to be somebody that could put me in that house yesterday."

Reddon shrugged. "Brody, besides the Key West Police Department, who else knows you're staying here?"

Brody thought for a moment. "Guy at the funeral parlor. Father Dannon. My office in New York."

"Nobody else?"

"Nobody."

"Nobody?"

"A girl who works for one of the airlines," Brody conceded.

"What's her name?" Reddon demanded.

Brody shrugged.

"You don't know her name?"

"Modern love," Brody said. "Nothing like it."

"And you don't know her name."

"She may have mentioned it. I don't recall. I'd had a bit to drink, Lieutenant."

Reddon grunted. "Well, you are a *good*-lookin' boy." He nodded a shade, scratching the hint of stubble on his chin. "Detective Baar maybe has a point. Anybody else know you were coming down here?"

"It was a spur-of-the-moment thing, Lieutenant," Brody explained, toying with the beer can. "A short vacation after wrapping up a case. I figured I'd take a week or so and then go home. Nothing pressing that couldn't wait a few days."

Baar tilted his head to one side. "What if that case of yours wasn't wrapped up tight enough?"

Brody was momentarily speechless. "I don't leave loose ends," he finally replied. "Besides, why follow me here? New York is a *great* place to kill somebody."

"Still and all," Reddon said amiably, "you got any good reason why I shouldn't hold you here as a material witness?"

"Oh, come on," Brody snapped. "On what grounds? You told me to keep my nose out of this, and I have. Hell of a way for a tourist to get treated."

"Don't get smart with me, sonny," Reddon declared. "Hell of a way to ruin the whole fucking tourist *trade*," he added in a snarling whisper. "Chamber of Commerce ain't pinning no medals on your chest." He rubbed his plump red hands together and shifted the subject. "You recognize this guy? You said there was a Cuban, medium height, come out of the house that day. This him?" Reddon shook his head in the direction of the breezeway.

"No, it isn't," Brody replied. "There's some resemblance, but it's not the same man. I'd swear to it. Why don't you find out who he worked for?"

"And maybe what clubs he belonged to?"

"I'd like to know if Roper Gance paid this guy's salary," Brody said simply.

"Well, honey *lamb*," said Reddon. "Mr. Gance pays a lot of people's salaries. It's a name comes up often in this here town. Listen, you want to get yourself killed, Brody, that's your business. You try to, that's my business. You're a good man, but the next time I see you tap-dancing around this case, I'm going to bust your ass, so help me God."

Brody folded his arms across his chest.

"Go to the Pier House," Reddon suggested. "Go to the *beach*. Lots of pretty girls hanging around there this time of year, just looking for a big boy like you. See the coral reef like any other tourist, why don't you? And after you wind up your sister's business, have a nice safe trip the hell out of here."

Brody nodded obediently, squelching a few questions of his own. Reddon sighed and touched the brim of his panama as he turned on his heel and walked off. From Baar's expression, it was clear he thought of Brody as an increasingly difficult tourist, one step up from the complete slob who had to be carried out of the bar by the elbows for his own good.

And then they were gone. Brody went to buy a first-aid kit at the drugstore down the block. He locked his patio door with a vengeance when he returned, pulled the blinds closed, and took a long hot bath, brooding over the puzzle of Katie's death. There was no denying his suspicion that Luz Almeida had set him up—but he didn't believe it. Oh, really? Oh, really.

He slept soundly for two hours before dinner.

Dorado is the finest fish there is if it is fresh and grilled to a rosy doneness, with a splash of lemon to bring out the flavor. A miracle of a fish, Brody thought to himself, chewing happily.

The woman in the slipper shoes was leaning against the counter, smiling vacantly at him as the evening shadows started stretching down the street. He could tell she was ready for a good night's sleep. He was grateful, too, for the promise of a quiet evening to come, an easy stroll through the August lanes with the great clouds as bright as moonlight scudding across the open sky, and then beddy-bye—'cause tough guys need to sleep, too, he thought.

"Muchas gracias," he said to the woman. He almost hated to disturb her growing placidity. *"Un café, por favor."*

She came awake. *"¿Café con leche?"*

"Sí."

She called the order back. Brody reconsidered the possibility that Luz was hustling him, as he thought any decent man would under the circumstances, knowing how obvious a deception it was to fall for. He shook his head and snorted. He wanted her badly, but he was pro enough to know the difference.

The Cuban in the back came out with the cup of coffee. Brody barely glanced his way—just long enough to confirm the family resemblance—his eye passing quickly to the steaming coffee and hot milk. He loved the smell of it. The woman handed him the cup, and he took it eagerly.

He finished his coffee, then paid the woman and wished her a good night. He strolled off, and when he had doubled back and taken up his post in the lee of a big palm a block and a half from the snack bar, they were just closing up the place. A crescent moon had appeared in the night sky.

The old woman and the man padlocked the door and the wooden awning that came down across the counter, then went their separate ways. Brody tailed the man up Simonton and then out toward the Bight. It took Brody ten minutes to verify that nobody was following *him*, and another fifteen before the Cuban climbed onto one of the charter boats.

Brody found himself a comfortable seat behind a few crates stacked to one side of the dock and extracted a box of cantaloupe-flavored sucking candies from his beach bag. They were expensive but contained no sugar; when he gave up smoking, Brody had decided to try a healthier alternative to sugar for indulging what the clerk in the health food store had quaintly referred to as his "oral need."

He leaned back against an old tire wedged against one of the cleats, studied the clouds, and thought again about the tortoises. He thought about Mister Bud, too.

The Cuban left the boat and started briskly for the center of town. Brody was off after him like a faint shadow. He was as good as an Indian at tracking—half his sense trained on the figure two blocks ahead of him, the other half alert to the unlikely, and therefore deadly, possibility that he himself was being watched. Forty minutes later, when the Cuban reached Duval and turned down toward the Pier House, he still had no idea that he was being followed.

By then Brody was pretty sure he knew where the man was going. The Cuban waved to a watchman at the entrance to the marina, strolled by, approached the motor yacht *Sea Legs*, and climbed aboard. From the shelter of a few Christmas palms, Brody studied the craft with some interest. A couple of people were sitting in the saloon, deep in conversation, and there was a man on a director's chair on the deeply shaded after deck, with what looked like an automatic weapon across his lap.

Brody slipped away through the back alleys around Whitehead and skirted the house where Katie and Jorge had died, climbing over the front fence to confirm that the place had not been entered since he left it. He found no indication that anyone had tried and moved along the east end until he reached Luz's apartment near Emma. After quickly checking the area, he rang the bell.

"Hi," he said when Rosalee Taylor opened the door. "Can I come in? I'm a friend of Luz Almeida's."

Chapter

4

"A friend of Luz's?" Rosalee replied.

Brody nodded, and Rosalee, dressed in a peach-colored teddy and nothing else, moved aside to let him enter. "Yes," he said. "Am I, uh, interrupting something?"

"No. I was just getting my stuff together for tomorrow's flight. What can I do for you?"

He took a breath. "I'd like to spend the night here."

Rosalee raised her eyebrows so high they nearly disappeared under the corn-silk hair punctuating her forehead. "Oooh," she murmured. "I *love* the subtle approach."

"Let me call her," he suggested. "She's in Miami. Then she can explain it to you."

"Oh. Hey, no, that's all right," Rosalee assured him. "I'm not expecting any other guests tonight. Rosalee Taylor. Pleased to meet you."

"Steve Brody. You know, I had the feeling you were

Rosalee. Luz mentioned your name. I really appreciate this." He paused. "But I need to call her anyway."

"Go ahead." Rosalee bent forward to retrieve a pair of folding bedroom slippers from the floor. She had quite a pair of legs, and she knew it, yummy as peaches and cream. And a face to match. "Phone's right in there," she said, pointing.

"Who is this?" Luz asked when Brody finally reached her, taking the phone from another member of the crew. "Steve!"

"Yeah. Look, a guy tried to shoot me this afternoon."

"*What*? Are you all right?"

Brody laughed. "Except for the head wounds."

"Your mother," Luz replied, nodding vigorously for her underthings to get included in the laundry load somebody else was doing that night, in time for the morning flight to Orlando. "Hey, they really tried to shoot you? Where did it happen?"

"At my place."

"You mean where you told me to call you tomorrow?"

"Mm. And I'd lay odds they have it staked out right now."

"Jesus," she exclaimed.

"It's fine, really," Brody assured her. "I'll be okay as long as I can stay here tonight—and maybe tomorrow night, too."

"Ha. That's what you think."

"Why? Does Chuck Rio know about this place?"

Scowling, Luz blew a recalcitrant curl from her eyes. "I'm not talking about Chucky. No way in hell would I ever let Chucky Rio find out where I live. I'm talking about Rosalee. Let me speak to her."

Brody called Rosalee over and handed her the receiver. She took it from him and listened for a while, stamping her foot once or twice. She glanced back at Brody, whispered a few words to Luz, nodded vigorously, and, at long last, handed the phone back to him with a twinkle in her eye.

"It's okay to stay," Luz told him.

"Uh-huh. And tomorrow?" he asked.

"She's not sure who's going to be there, but she's gonna give you the extra key."

"I miss you," he whispered.

"Me too," said Luz, turning her back to the activity in the room. "And listen, Steve—I didn't tell anybody what hotel you were staying in."

"I know you didn't."

"Honest?"

"Uh-huh. I had a pretty good idea who did, though, and I proved it about an hour ago."

She whispered, "Until Thursday, then."

Brody's eyes lit up. *"Por dios."*

"I been thinking about you all day," she said.

"Me too—especially when I was riding my bike. Call me here instead, before you leave."

"I will. Oh, and about Rosalee," Luz went on. "Well, you'll see what I mean. It's just the way she is."

"What are you talking about?"

She gave him one of her exquisite, throaty laughs and hung up.

He awoke the next morning to the feel of Rosalee's hair against his shoulder. He had a little trouble remembering precisely how she'd got there at three in the morning—the silkiness of her skin merging with a dream he was having of Luz. He had been, frankly, speechless.

"It's okay," she had whispered. "You don't have to. Just hold me a little. Luz does, too, sometimes. I hate to sleep alone."

"Is that what she meant on the phone?"

"Uh-huh. She didn't think you'd get the wrong idea. Do you mind?"

Smiling to himself in the darkness, he had draped his arm around her and stroked her hair until she was asleep.

He raised himself carefully and reached for the night table, realizing as he did so that the old cigarette reflex was still there; though he no longer needed to smoke, he marveled at the various unconscious devices his body still had to unlearn. Rosalee sighed in her sleep and turned over. Like an ice-cream sundae with plenty of whipped cream, Brody thought.

He slipped out of bed and stretched. A dank drizzle was coming down, the kind that can last all day without robbing one of the hope that it will soon be over. He peeked through the blinds at the maze of back alleys, the rain forming opaque puddles on the ground.

He showered and dressed, put up some coffee, remembered there was no milk in the refrigerator, and, sipping it black, brought a cup into the bedroom for Rosalee. She sniffed it and opened one eye. "Good morning," he said.

She glanced at the light coming through the blinds and turned her lovely face to him. "Leaving already?"

"Not 'til I've had some of this," he affirmed. "Actually not 'til I have a lot of this. Did you sleep well?"

She laughed. "Wonderfully. I hope I didn't disturb you too much."

"Not at all."

She studied him for a long moment. "She said there was something special between you. I think she's right. Oh! Do you have the key?" He said he didn't. She hopped out of bed to get it.

"Thanks," he said when she handed it to him. "And thanks for putting me up, too. I really appreciate it."

"Oh, hell . . . you're a nice guy, Steve. I like you."

"I'd love to take you to breakfast."

She giggled again. "I can't. I have to meet my boyfriend for breakfast."

He raised his eyebrows.

"I just wanted to ask you . . . is there anything else I can do for you? Luz said something about your sister getting murdered? I'm real sorry."

"No, nothing, except answer a few questions."

"Like what?"

"Okay. The cops figure, and I figure, it had to be drugs were involved. There wasn't much there, no inventory to speak of, some pot, a little coke. But everything else—the way they were killed, the way the place was trashed—was how drug money acts when it gets mean."

She nodded, and he took another sip of his coffee.

"I'm trying to find a link. Is there anything you can tell me about a guy called Roper Gance?"

Rosalee shivered at the mere mention of the name. "I wouldn't touch him with a ten-foot pole. I don't know many girls who would. He's a real smuggler. You know, flight personnel hear everything, especially when it has to do with making a few extra bucks. 'Course, that kind of business is international, so all we ever hear is hearsay, but still . . . Anyway, the point is, none of the people I know want to mess with that stuff. It's money, right? But you can get *killed*—I mean. . . ."

She saw him grimace.

"I didn't meant to say anything wrong, Steve."

"No, it's—I'm just not over it yet. She was my only sister," he said with a sniffle, "and she loved her husband very much, which meant I learned to like him, too, and now—poof, they're dead. I cried for the first three days, and then I stopped crying, and now it's only every hour or so that it hits me. I guess that's the way it is."

She nodded. "Well, that bastard could've ordered it all right. You know, sometimes he even tries with us—asking us to be messengers, drop off a letter for a friend. Bookkeeping for the coke and weed trade coming through here. Most everybody says no, flake off. But he can get very persuasive. 'C'mon, you just fly this to Jacksonville for me.' I heard him say that to one of the girls once, in Miami. He handed her a Jiffy bag, taped up tight, and she slipped it into her flight bag. I got out of that hotel lobby as fast as I could. I didn't want to know about it."

"Hm. You're smarter off not."

"Don't I know it. But like I said, you can't help hearing things."

Brody walked over and kissed her. "Thanks again."

"You too, sweetie."

"Love to do it again sometime."

"Any time you say." She drew one knee up to her chest and reached for her coffee cup again.

He set his down on the table and nodded, slung his beach bag over one shoulder, and left.

Brody treated himself to a big breakfast of eggs, grits, fresh bread, and sassafras tea in one of the cafes off Malory Square, then went off through the rain to look at fishing tackle.

"I'm thinking about doing some bonefishing," he explained to the salesman who approached him at the rack. He had a boron rod in his hand and was flicking it back and forth.

"That's a fine one there," said the salesman. "Pull 'em in fine on that. But a bit steep, if you don't want to spend a whole lot."

Brody took a rod the salesman suggested and hefted it. "Good feel. You have a nice heavy-duty reel?"

"You bet." The salesman began to look for one.

"Know somebody who could take me out around here?"

"Sure. Day charters aren't too busy right now. Lots of places out on the flats. 'Course, there's Islamorada, too, but you don't want to go up that far, I guess."

"No. I wish I could. Can't spare more time this trip."

"Ain't that the truth. Now here's a well-turned job, do you fine." The salesman took a bit of tobacco between his teeth.

Brody examined the reel and said he would take it. "How are they running now?"

"Oh, you might still find a hundred-pounder out there. Little late in the season, though."

"What should I fish, a thirteen-weight outfit?"

The salesman agreed. "A four-aught, three-aught flies. Captain'll carry them, of course."

"Yes, but I live up north. It'll feel good to have a couple tarpon flies in my kit this winter."

The salesman grinned and showed him a few grizzlies.

Brody took two and asked to have the package sent to the Santa Rosa as the salesman began to write up the bill. "I'll have it there by late this afternoon," he said. "You can pay for this at the front desk," he added when he had finished, separating the pink copy and handing it to Brody. "And about the day charters, they'll be able to tell you who's around."

"Thank you," Brody said. "Much obliged."

"Thank *you*, sir. Thanks for shopping at Johnson Marina. And enjoy the fishing, now."

For the moment, however, there was no one at the front desk. Brody looked around impatiently, reminded himself that this was, after all, the South and that he must mind his manners. Finally he called out, "Is anybody home?"

A very tall, immense black man stuck his head out of a doorway, looked around with a trace of irritation playing across his face, and came over.

"Bet-*ty*?" he shouted, glancing through heavy bifocals around the vast supply area. "I'm awful sorry," he said to Brody. "I can't imagine where that girl has gone. What can we do for you?"

"Some things I'm having delivered." Brody handed him the invoice and an American Express card. The man peered at it through the lower half of his glasses. "I was looking to maybe fish some tarpon. Fellow back there told me you could help me with a day charter."

The black man deftly completed the charge and had Brody sign. Rubbing two fingers together, he said, "Now, the day charters. . ." and began searching among the papers that covered the desk. "Aw, hell, *I* don't know what she did with them. I have another list inside. Come on, we'll get it."

Brody followed him around the desk, past a few offices off the hallway where an accountant and a sales manager were talking on phones, and into a wide back room illuminated chiefly by north light coming off the Gulf. Brody slipped into a proffered chair and observed two pelicans meditating in the rain.

The black man settled himself behind the desk as only such a large person could, quickly came up with a list of reliable captains who weren't booked for the next week or so, copied out their phone numbers, and handed Brody the slip. "They're getting two hundred a day," he explained, "or a thousand a week. That's an honest price, by the way."

Brody folded the slip.

"Isn't what you really come for, though."

Brody looked up; the man had instincts. "No, Mr. Johnson, it isn't."

Tiny leaned forward, planting his elbows on the desk. "Well?"

Brody abandoned all pretense and showed his license. "Jorge Castillo was my brother-in-law."

"Ah. I didn't know."

"Did Roper Gance order it?"

"Roper *who*?"

For a moment Brody said nothing. "I can't give you anything but money, Mr. Johnson, and something tells me you don't want that from me. But I *would* owe you."

He received a grim smile by way of reply. "You sure you want to know?"

Brody's level stare was all the answer he needed. Tiny pondered for a moment, pursing his lips. "Did he order it? So I hear." He raised two fingers. "Contract on both of them. But they say he was just paying back a favor. To a friend, they say."

Brody's mouth had nearly fallen open. "*Both* of them?"

Tiny shrugged. "You got it. She wasn't no bystander. Kinda surprised me, too. I didn't meet your kid sister but a couple, three times—come around to drop off some estimates for a construction job. Seemed like a proper young woman. But if it ain't our business, Mr. Brody, we don't want to make it our business. Town does try to keep some semblance of a reputation."

"Mr. Johnson," Brody replied after trying to absorb the idea that someone had paid to have Katie murdered, too, "with all due respect, you aren't bullshitting me, are you?"

Tiny, shaking his head slowly, was not offended. "No, that is the truth of it—I'll swear it to you. I don't have to lie about this, fella. I didn't murder your people, and I don't have a dime to make out of the thing. Come to that, I didn't have to talk to you, either."

Brody said, "I do appreciate it, you understand."

"Yeah, I do. Look, Castillo worked for me, on and off, practically since they hit town. Had one sizable job I give him just last month. He was okay, a little quick-tempered, maybe. Didn't have no reason to get wasted *I* ever suspected."

"What kind of job was it?"

"Plumbing contract."

"For real? It wasn't some kind of a front?"

Johnson chuckled. "A front for what? You know, if you don't mind my saying, you're having a hard time understanding what I'm telling you. Your brother-in-law was a nickel-and-dime dealer who came down here and found out there wasn't any room left in the pond. He would have starved to death trying."

Folding his hands together, Johnson leaned back med-itatively in his chair. "You know how many dreams of glory come rolling down that highway every year? Real tough dreams. It's bullshit between the ears, is all. Give 'em three, four months, most of 'em fold up the tents and go on back where they come from. Castillo got the message. That man earned his pay down here working a trade, and he was pretty good at it."

A pelican flew by in the rain. Tiny Johnson's eyes, as he turned to watch it, betrayed a hint of fatigue, the fatigue of a good linebacker near the end of the third quarter.

"What he did with his money afterwards," he added after turning back to Brody, "that was none of my busi-ness, or anybody else's. Man wants to go blow that hard-earned sweat and blood up his nose, well, there's plenty who do."

"But if that's the case, why—"

"Why indeed," concluded Johnson, and Brody knew the interview was over. "I don't think you're going to find out in this town, I'll tell you. Do you? There going to be a funeral?" he asked, rising.

Warm and dry, Brody thought when he felt Johnson's handshake. "They both wanted to be cremated—ashes scattered, the works. Private service."

Tiny was surprised. "Both Catholics, weren't they?"

Brody shrugged. "They were both afraid of the dark."

"Ah . . . You really planning to go out after some tarpon?" Tiny asked on a lighter note.

Brody smiled, releasing Johnson's hand. "Maybe. Or take a trip?"

"Just remember to set your hook solid and keep your line stripped." He wasn't talking about bonefishing, and Brody knew it.

"One last thing, if you don't mind."

Tiny turned both hands palms up, as if to say the larder was empty.

"Does Detective Lieutenant Reddon know about all of this?"

Johnson laughed. "Of course he does. Oh, by the way—I also hear that Corky pulled a Mr. Chuck Rio in sometime early this morning. Attempted assault charge, disturbing the peace. I hear Chucky's having some trouble explaining himself—seems to have got his jaw wired together."

"Oh?"

"So I hear."

Brody thanked Tiny Johnson and excused himself. The clerk named Betty was back at her desk when he passed it on his way out.

An hour and a half later, he was sitting beside two coffins in a quiet chapel at Dickinson's Funeral Parlor.

With his eyes, he was asking his sister's broken body what in God's name had been going on with her that afternoon five days before, and all the afternoons before that. Oh, my darling Katie, the eyes were saying. My sweet darling Katie.

To Jorge Castillo's body he did not know what to say, except that he himself was too impatient at times, that faith was hard, that he was sorry for having gone on like a fool that day.

He didn't swear he would get even. Only that *someone* would have to get to the bottom of their story. Jorge, if Tiny Johnson were to be believed, and Brody believed him, had kept the bargain he'd made to go straight—his kind of straight, which was straight enough, anyway.

For these and for all the other reasons he had—the pictures of Katie and Jorge that kept sliding in front of his eyes in burning color, not merely the memory of snapshots thrown into hurried letters, but ones going back years and, in her case, literally to the cradle—Brody started, finally, to weep. He didn't stop for fifteen minutes.

But, dear God, he thought, what in the hell were they doing to get somebody that mad?

Clearing his throat, he looked up. *Both of them.* He couldn't figure it, hadn't been able to since the minute he heard Tiny Johnson say it. It meant—what? His eyes swept over the coffins aglow beneath electric candles, his professional instincts beginning once more to take over.

Okay. Point one. Gance blows them away as a favor to somebody up north. Then, four days later, the Cuban comes after me with a goddamn elephant gun. Why? Because I broke Rio's jaw? No way. Because someone tied me to the scene of that crime. That's what I've been saying all along.

But why does it matter to them? Nobody found any drugs to speak of. The drugs weren't there anymore. If it *was* drugs. Say they thought I had them, and the stash. Say the Cuban wasn't just out to tie up a loose end when he came after me.

What if he was trying to search the place?

Yeah. But what was he looking for, drugs that don't exist?

And I'd swear the dead Cuban was that cook's brother, the one I tailed to the charter boat and then on to Gance's yacht—or his cousin, some kind of close blood.

And not a shred of evidence to support any of it, you damn fool, Brody snarled. Show me material evidence, fool. Love to turn those boats inside out. That, of course, was not very practical without causing the hale specter of the law to clamp down on him for cause, he reminded himself. Besides, it violated rule one of his Special Forces training: Thou shalt not frontally assault an automatic weapon.

Just then, Lieutenant Reddon slipped into the room and quietly took the seat opposite Brody, on the other side of the coffins.

Brody, who had been expecting him, crossed himself, closed his eyes for a moment, and greeted him. "Thanks for coming."

"Figured you might care to have a visitor. How are you holding up?"

"It isn't easy, but it's started to come and go now."

"Takes time. You're looking better."

"I hear you took Chuck Rio in."

"Suspicion," Reddon replied without enthusiasm, not bothering to ascertain how Brody had found out. "Somebody found the van up by Pine Key. Hasn't got a clear print *on* it. I told the boys to have another go, of course. Waste some more of the taxpayers' dollars."

Brody grew exasperated. "The man is an accessory to a double murder, Lieutenant. Isn't that what you've been saying to me? Can you get him to talk?"

"Oh, we are trying. Ain't easy. Ain't as if we got anything can hang it on him but *you*. Nobody else saw the men, the van—zero. Must have been noise enough to attract attention. Your people didn't have any friends in the neighborhood, I don't think. Conch neighborhood, of course, and maybe they hadn't been living there long enough."

Reddon raised his pudgy red hand and touched thumb to forefinger. "Still, it's a zero. I think those folks might be telling us something, or else somebody has the lot of them mighty scared."

"What about Gance?"

"What about him? Yeah, I know. You had a chat with Mr. Elmore Johnson, who told you what he told me."

"Do you believe him?"

Reddon snorted. " 'Course I believe him. So what? What's to tie it?"

"Look, Lieutenant," Brody replied, turning up his hands. "There's a couple of things I'd like to suggest that might scratch up some hard evidence." He gave Reddon a description of the cook and the name of the charter boat that had been moored at the Bight the night before. "I don't know what the connection is, but there has to be one. I've never believed in coincidence."

"And now you're going to tell me this Cuban cook went to see Mr. Roper Gance, I suppose."

Brody nodded.

"No kidding," said Reddon, giving him a noncommittal glance. "Been kinda busy, ain't you? What'd I tell you about staying out of this case?"

"Just taking an evening stroll, Lieutenant. Nice touristy thing, write postcards home about how pretty the clouds are at night, digest my dinner."

Reddon had to smile. "Boy, you sure know how to play the game. I've got to hand it to you."

"No point in ruffling feathers, Lieutenant."

"Okay, I guess maybe we can have a look or two."

"Also, do you mind if I go over to my sister's house and start cleaning up the mess?"

"Why? Did you follow the Cuban over that way, too?"

"No, I didn't. I just thought there might be something your people overlooked."

"Like what?"

"Like whatever in hell they thought I took."

"And you know you didn't."

"Maybe that's why they turned the house upside down, and my room at the hotel."

Reddon studied the nondescript carpet at his feet,

seemed suddenly pleased, and Brody realized the lieutenant hadn't thought of it before. "All right. Makes
sense, though I can't imagine there's something there we
didn't find. Anyway, you are the next of kin and all. I'll
send somebody over with you."

"I'd rather not be too conspicuous, Lieutenant."

"If you find anything, Brody, it better be on my desk
quick as you can get your ass over, you hear me?"

"Fair enough."

"You hear me, Brody? Don't give me that 'fair enough'
shit. No games and no excuses. I have shown my respect
for your grief, and I'll treat you like a pro if you deserve
it, but I do not aim to be handing in this badge until my
fabled retirement commences."

"I hear you all right. I know the rules of evidence."

"Good. And here's just one more thing. We only got
Mr. Rio for disturbing the peace and a couple other
chickenshit charges, just to keep him where I can see
him. 'Nother day or two, 'less we come up with some
of that evidence you're going on about, he'll be back on
the street. And *you* will be out of Key West."

"Wait a minute—"

"That's it, I swear. If you're still around, I'll take you
in for your own protection. Can't be playing this game
forever, my boy. In the meantime, don't forget there's
plenty more where Rio came from." He rose, tipped his
hat, and lumbered out of the room.

A few minutes later the undertaker appeared. Brody
stood up. "Is it time?"

"Whenever you say, Mr. Brody," the man replied.
"There's no rush."

"No, it's okay, Mr. Dickinson."

"Would you care to come with me?"

Brody shook his head. "Just tell me what. . ."

The undertaker seemed to understand perfectly. "Two
hours at seventeen hundred degrees. Everything but the
bone ash. We'll hold the remains for you."

Brody nodded. "Thanks. You've been very kind."

Brody made his way over to the house in the gray drizzle. He could have laid odds that no one was following him.

He found a few razor blades and a heavy screwdriver first thing, after he had locked the back door from the inside and quietly drawn the shades. It gave him something to do with himself as he adjusted to the atmosphere of the place, allowing his instincts to take over.

He checked out the plumbing first, throughout the house. Condition of the walls behind which it ran. Boiler. Water tank. He had to admit when he was through that Jorge hadn't used his journeyman's skills to hide anything.

He turned his attention to the rest of the house. Though he recalled that Katie and Jorge had made a fetish of traveling light through life, he was surprised by all they had managed to gather—furniture, clothing, records and files of papers (labeled *Household*, *Auto*, *Checks*, *Misc*, and ?).

Still, it amounted to only so much, and an hour later he had gone through all of it twice. He would take some personal papers home after Reddon had had a chance to look at them, but he doubted that any of them had a thing to do with the case.

He sighed and began to go over the furniture like a surgeon, studying seams, using a razor blade to tease at joints. When he was done, snapping a slow rhythm with his fingers as he wondered what to do next, he tried the floor—from one end of the house to the other. He covered every square inch of the bedroom, went through the laundry room, checked the grouting around the bathtub and the back wall of the medicine cabinet, then returned to the kitchen, stumped.

He found a can of beer in the refrigerator and drank it while poking around in the freezer, unearthing a bit less than half an ounce of bagged marijuana frozen to the bottom—overlooked by Reddon's people, who probably hadn't wanted to bother hacking it out, Brody assumed. Nevertheless, he found a pair of tweezers and a box of

Baggies, lifted the small package of frozen weed with the tweezers, and lowered it into a fresh plastic bag.

He sealed and taped it and wrote "Mark for Evidence" across the tape. Then he tilted the refrigerator out of its nook and went over the condenser coils.

Still nothing. In growing frustration, Brody glanced at his watch. Another hour had gone by. He sighed and climbed up to the unfinished loft—hardly worth the effort—before slipping back down. He examined the closet walls with a practiced eye. Zilch. "This is ludicrous," he muttered aloud. On his way back to the kitchen, he studied the ceilings for any odd patchwork.

He picked up the can of beer and took a sip.

There's nothing here.

"No, there has to be," he said matter-of-factly, and tried to remember what other kind of construction work Jorge was familiar with. He was thinking about opening the sewer lines when he suddenly stopped short.

Shit.

It hit him like a ton of bricks: Why Jorge? Why did it have to be Jorge? What if . . . what if it was Katie? Where would *she* have hidden it, you dumb horse?

A hiding place, champ, not a fucking renovation job.

He was thinking of likely places when he remembered where his mother had hidden things in the house. He set down the beer, grabbed the tweezers and a few Baggies, and hurried back to the laundry room.

In the gloom, on tiptoe, he began skimming his hands across the upper surface of the lines of copper piping that left the boiler and water tank and traveled up and between the unfinished joists. The row of pipes forked in two directions. He took the right fork and followed it as it passed through the joists.

Near the far end of the room, Brody felt something square shoved behind an elbow in the pipes. He wiggled it loose with his fingers and pulled out a package neatly wrapped in black plastic. Sitting on the floor, he opened his pocket knife and slit the clear tape holding the package together.

Inside, he found two United States passports. The first had been issued to Katherine Mary Brody. He glanced at her picture before setting the passport down and gingerly opening the other, issued in the name of one Maria Castillo. A black-and-white photograph of Katie was attached to it. With his tweezers, Brody flipped through the pages. Maria Castillo's passport contained Peruvian, Canadian, and French Customs stamps.

He returned to the first passport. Under her maiden name, Katie appeared to have traveled to France, and to the British Virgin Islands, before returning to the States.

Tucked into the back folds of the first passport, he found two other items. One was Roper Gance's business card. He turned it over and found a New York telephone number, recorded in what looked to him like Katie's neat, schoolgirlish hand. The other was a small sheet of KLM Airlines memo paper, folded twice. On it she had written, less evenly and in pencil, *Jackie. Sunday. Not before 12.*

He slipped the card and note into his rear pocket.

Chapter

5

"This all of it?" Lieutenant Reddon asked when he had finished looking at the passports and the thawed-out marijuana in the glare of the overhead fluorescent fixture. He removed his glasses and tapped the table with them.

"Yes," Brody replied.

"Well, there's enough here to indict her for conspiracy all right."

"Very funny. It's more than that, Lieutenant. This is what they were after."

"Oh, fer Chrissake, listen to you talk." Reddon picked up a phone and grumbled, "Kevin, come in here a minute."

To Brody, he continued. "You setting out to replace coincidence with sheer speculation? Five points to the man."

"Lieutenant," replied Brody patiently, "this is right up my alley. I specialize in international cases. I get around a lot. I know about Customs." He reached for the plastic bag of dope. "Shit," he continued, flipping it back onto Reddon's desk. "When I found that, I said to myself, 'What the hell kind of a two-bit operation is this? Where's the stash?'"

"Figured they took it with them. You said one of them was carrying a trash bag."

"Maybe. I'm not so sure. But they had to be after these, too, and they didn't find them."

Reddon looked at him, and Brody frowned before continuing, "The thing is, it's obvious she was the one. She was transporting drugs. I mean, I haven't sat down to work out the details from the dates on those stamps, but it wouldn't be hard to do."

Baar came in, and Reddon showed him the evidence. "Could be the young lady just wanted to see a little of the world, couldn't it?" Reddon asked the detective.

Baar shook his head when he had finished handling the passports. "Could be if my grandmother had wheels, she'd be a motorcycle."

"Tell the man," said Brody.

"Butt out," Reddon growled.

Brody reminded him, "It's my line of work."

"Then why," the lieutenant said soothingly, "don't you consider this a learning experience for Detective Baar here? How's that sound to you? What do you see there, Kevin?"

Baar replied, "Well, I see Miami, Paris, L.A. And here I see Lima, Toronto . . . B.V.I. ? Hm." He shrugged. "One of them must be forged. Could be a way to move contraband."

"Had to be," said Brody, glancing at Reddon. The lieutenant's closed eyes were fixed on Baar, and he was smiling paternally. "Still don't know the gimmick she used, but that's not the hard part. The hard part is finding the right person to pass it—somebody the agent wouldn't suspect."

He rubbed the bridge of his nose between his fingers. "If the courier looks right and behaves right, all you have to do is pick a good time." He turned the cover of the Katherine Brody passport and pointed to her photograph. "Does that look like a drug smuggler to you? Would anything about that face tip you off? She'd probably be wearing a little blouse and jacket, too. And a goddamn pleated skirt."

Reddon leaned back in his chair. It creaked.

"Still, so what?" Brody concluded.

"Yeah," Reddon agreed. "Look, Kevin, get these here things dusted. Might be they can lift off a usable print." Baar tipped the passports back into their Baggies and left.

The lieutenant rose heavily from his seat and stretched like a self-assured cat before lighting a cigarette and puffing on it as he stared out the window. "Well, all that's plain enough," he said. The rain had finally disappeared and been replaced by clean yellow sunlight that was casting long shadows over the lawn. He returned to the desk and flipped open the Castillo file.

"Something I didn't know the other day, Brody. Curious kind of detail." He slid his glasses on. "It's about your sister. When they killed her, she was lying on her back. The angle of the wound makes that probable, so the boys in the lab say. They also found some powder burns on the inner surfaces of her calves. Never seen that before."

Stunned, Brody whispered, "You mean she had her legs bent at the knees?"

Reddon came around to the front of the desk to put his hand on Brody's shoulder. "I'm telling you because it might ring a bell for you somewhere up the road—and I think you're going to need all the help you can get, son. Whatever it turns out you find, well, I care to think we did what we could for you down here."

Brody leaned across the table. "What about the money? Either of them have a safe deposit box? Savings accounts?"

Reddon sighed in displeasure. "Two accounts. Small change. No safe deposit."

"What about the town clerk?"

Reddon spit a fleck of tobacco into the air. "Castillo's

listed here and there in the variance. Construction jobs.
Drew a blank on her. I checked it myself. Easy to bury
some cash in a corporate way down here.'' He shrugged.
'' 'Grab that paper trail, boy,' I said to myself, 'and you
got yourself a case.' I don't care much for bad routine
work. Well, there wasn't no trail. 'Course, the boys up
in Tallahassee are still looking, and maybe they'll find
something. Something tells me they won't.''

"Me too. I appreciate it, Lieutenant," said Brody,
rising. "And I won't be abusing your hospitality much
longer. It looks like I'll be pulling out of here pretty
soon, the way things have turned out. I'm not taking on
Roper Gance with my penknife, that's for sure."

He slung his beach bag over his shoulder and shook
hands. "Anyway," he added quietly, "it's not him I
want. I want whoever asked him for the favor. I find him,
they'll lead me right back to Gance, and you can have
him and Chucky Rio for breakfast. Those passports are
better than evidence."

"Hell, *I* know," the lieutenant replied with a nod.
"Where are you going to start?"

"New York."

"Why New York?"

Brody chuckled and ran his fingers through his hair.
"It's where they came from. Besides, it's about time I
changed my socks."

Reddon smiled. "Must be a pretty fast place, New
York. Been meaning to take a trip up there for years."

Brody extracted his business card and handed it to the
red-skinned lieutenant, trying to imagine how he'd fit
into SoHo or Chelsea. "Any time you do, Lieutenant,
give me a call."

Reddon pocketed the card. "You see if I don't sometime," he said, and added, "I figured my boy Kevin
there might just as well pick up a few pointers. What do
you think of him?"

"Pretty sharp," Brody replied.

"Yeah, ain't he. Cool as a watermelon pie, but I guess
that's the way they're rearing 'em up nowadays. Knows

his work, sure enough. Good performer. Still, this case is mine—especially the money part, you follow?'' Brody nodded. ''Anyway, if you can give me Gance and that pig-piss operation of his, I'd be much obliged.

''So. . .'' He sighed, raising his voice as they reached the door. ''Not going to get the chance to truss you up and throw you on a plane, am I?''

''No. See you around, Lieutenant.''

''You too, Brody. Keep your brains between your ears.''

Brody left the station with his hands in his pockets. He thought about the ocean blocks away and of how it would be nice if he swam in it a few more times. Hell of a way to spend a week in Key West, he felt. His fading Rio tan still made him fairly inconspicuous—in a place where pale skin is an oddity, few people seemed to notice him as he strolled up Simonton—and that water sure was tempting.

Maybe some other time. He had the phone number in New York and somebody named Jackie. How many Jackies could there be in the world?

He collected his package of fishing tackle at the front desk of the Santa Rosa. Mr. Morrison came to the desk personally to take care of him, and Brody had an opportunity to apologize to the innkeeper, whose native desire to act a proper host was still visibly at war with his sense of shocked embarrassment. He fidgeted with his tie a bit and seemed enormously relieved when Brody told him he was checking out.

Brody took a hot bath when he got to his room. He saw that the wound on his lower chest had pretty much closed up and felt no worse than a deep scratch.

He dried himself with the fresh white towels the maids had left, shaved, combed his hair, and proceeded to hook up the rod just to see what it felt like.

Then he packed, dressed in a pair of beige slacks and a brown sports shirt, and, leaving one light burning on the night table, went out to eat.

There was a quiet restaurant he had passed on one of

his excursions, an open-air place situated in an orchid garden. It offered fish in black bean sauce and tofu dishes.

On the way, he found a pay phone and dialed his partner's number in New York. Marty Solomon's gravelly voice came on the line. "Steve!" he shouted. "You okay?"

"Yes, as okay as I can be. The service called you?"

"Right away," Marty said. "I—I wanted to offer my condolences sooner, but you said not to call. I'm awful sorry, champ . . . I know how much they both meant to you."

"Thanks, Marty. It's never too late to hear." Brody paused for a moment before continuing. "I think she was a narcotics courier, Marty."

"Jesus Christ. Katie? You're kidding."

"No. There was a contract out on both of them, and yesterday somebody tried to kill me, too. Could try again. Anyhow, they were cremated today, and this part of it's over. I'll be back home in a day or two. No point waiting around for some other clown to shoot me. Listen, Marty, two things I want you to do for me."

"Shoot," Marty said, grabbing a pad and pencil.

"Find out everything you can for me about a Key West resident, a U.S. national named Roper Gance."

"Okay."

"And I'm going to give you a New York phone number. Find out whose it is. It might be somebody named Jackie."

"How do you spell that?"

"With a c-k-i-e. That's the way she wrote it." He slipped Gance's card from his pocket and read the number off the back.

"East Side exchange," Marty observed.

"Ah. Well, it may be tied up. Get me as much of a fix as you can, and be careful, okay? And Marty—I'm paying the fees on this case."

"Like hell. You're my partner. Say, is this line clear?"

"Pay phone. Can't imagine it isn't."

"You got any angle on the possible traffic?"

"North and South America and Europe."

Solomon grunted. "Sure you're holding up okay?"

"Managing."

"Good. Call me the minute you get in. Steve?"

"Hm?"

"Just—you know, I'm sorry."

"I know. Take care of yourself."

Brody entered the restaurant and, after a quiet pair of margaritas and a dinner of marinated octopus and tofu in black bean sauce, ordered coffee. The place was pleasantly full but uncrowded, and he was relishing the privacy he had finally attained. Katie, Katie, he wondered, where was your head? Well, it's your case now, kid.

The coffee came, and he took a sip, lost in thought.

So? If it's your case, where *is* the stash? Even if they took the last of it, there were two, maybe three trips before that. Where the hell's that money?

Asking it, Brody realized the question could easily have been a client's sort of question. Well, hey, man, he told himself, this is the client's dead relative you're talking about. Speculate.

Okay. Could have been plenty of cash in that plastic bag the Cuban was carrying out of the house.

Could have, but he didn't think she'd have made it that easy for someone. Better to have some leverage if things went sour. Besides, her first trip had taken place months before.

But there was no safe deposit in her name or Jorge's. Or a company front.

So? he concluded. She plant it in the garden?

He promptly laid his train of thought aside. A simple game to play in the bathtub or on a long flight, but not when he was working on a case. If he managed to discover what had really happened to her, the money would turn up, or the burned residue of it. First things first.

After paying for dinner, he strolled over to the pier at the end of Simonton. The moon was nearly full, and the way its light spilled across the water soothed him.

He covered the short distance to the Santa Rosa and made his way over to Luz's place with all deliberate speed in an easygoing figure eight that thoroughly scoped the terrain—no simple task with luggage in hand.

He rapped on the front door twice and waited. Hearing nothing, he rapped again and paused. Then he let himself in with the key and was closing the door behind him when he saw a moving shadow in the living room alcove and froze. He could feel his heart pound. For a moment, nothing happened. Then the shadow spoke.

"Who is it?"

Brody flipped on the hallway light switch.

A young man in boxer shorts took a few steps toward him from the alcove and, squinting, asked, "Do I know you?"

Brody caught his breath and explained who he was.

"Oh," the young man replied, shaking his head in sudden relief and coming over. "Is *that* what Rosalee meant. You should see the note she left for me. My name's Val," he said. "Pleased to meet you."

They shook hands, and Brody replied, "I hope I didn't wake you up."

"No, no," Val assured him.

A slightly older man emerged sleepily from the room beyond the alcove. "Is everything all right?" he asked.

"This is Steve," Val explained, turning. "He's a friend of Luz Almeida's, Jerry."

Jerry nodded in recognition, waved hello to Brody, asked what time it was. "Quarter past eleven," Brody replied. "Sorry to have disturbed you." Jerry shrugged philosophically and returned to Val's bedroom.

"Do you get up for breakfast?" Val asked.

"I'd love to. When?"

"Oh, I think around nine-thirty or ten tomorrow. I'm picking up Luz's return flight."

"Oh?"

"Yes, she asked me—oops. Didn't she tell you?"

"Tell me what? When did you speak to her?"

"In Orlando this morning. Oh, I hope I haven't spoiled it. She'd *kill* me."

"Spoiled what?" asked Brody.

"Oh, no," Val declared. "It's a surprise. My lips are sealed."

Brody nodded and said that, in that case, he would be retiring.

"Well," Val concluded, "good night, then. The bathroom should be free by nine."

Brody opened his flight bag on the stand at the foot of Luz's bed, undressed, and propped himself on both pillows to read a few chapters of a book he'd brought along before turning in.

He awoke to crystal light streaming through the blinds. He quickly showered, shaved, and dressed before entering the kitchen. Val and Jerry were sipping coffee.

"Morning," he said.

"How did you sleep?" asked Jerry.

"Like a log."

"Help yourself. There's toast on the counter."

Brody took some of the scrambled eggs and two slices of bacon, poured himself a cup of coffee, and began to eat as Jerry completed a discussion of Key West antiques.

"How long are you staying in town?" Val asked Brody when he had the opportunity.

"Think I'll be leaving tomorrow. I had a funeral to attend to."

Jerry and Val were shocked.

Brody nodded. "My kid sister died."

"Dear, dear," said Jerry. "I'm so sorry to hear that."

"I hope she didn't suffer," Val murmured.

"No. It was quick."

"Ah," Jerry replied. "Did she have a good life?"

"She sure tried to," Brody said, reaching into his pocket. He showed them a picture of Katie that he carried in his wallet.

"Such a lovely young woman," said Jerry in sympathy.

"She'd been living here about a year and a half. You may have seen her around town."

Jerry shook his head and sipped his coffee.

The phone rang. Val rose and drifted over to answer. "Luz!" he declared. "How did it go? Oh, good. . . . Yes, I'll put him on— What? . . . No, I most certainly did not tell him," Val declared.

As he handed Brody the phone, Val whispered, "Now don't you dare tell her I said anything at all to you."

"Hi," Brody said into the receiver. "What are you doing this afternoon?"

Luz laughed. "What did you have in mind?"

"I want to take you snorkeling."

"I'd love it."

"There's a reef boat leaving at two-thirty. I'll meet you at the airport and we can ride back here together."

"Great. See you then."

"You too," Brody whispered, and hung up the phone as Jerry glanced at his watch.

"Time already?" Val asked him.

"Destiny calls," Jerry said. *"Así es la vida."*

They both rose. "I'll clean up," Brody offered, rising as well. "And thanks for being so hospitable. I'll see to Rosalee's key. Luz will know what to do with it."

Val and Jerry left, and, after he washed the dishes, Brody placed a call to Tiny Johnson. Then he read for an hour in the sun, sipping the last of his coffee.

After a while, he left the apartment, called a cab, and got out a few blocks from the airport, twenty minutes before Luz's flight landed. To his relief, no one else was waiting.

She hurried toward him as the flight crew broke up, and they met in a long kiss, sheltered by one of the broad columns at the side of the baggage claim area.

"Missed you," he whispered.

She murmured, "Oh. Right there."

He pressed his palm more firmly into the small of her back and kissed her again. Then he grabbed her overnight bag, and they headed out into the clear sunshine and cabbed back to her place. On the way they talked about going snorkeling and seeing the reef fish.

"Queen angels!" she was telling him as the cab drew up. He paid the driver, and they hopped out. "Did you ever see a queen angel?" He nodded. "Oh! The big ones?" she went on in a rush of enthusiasm. He let her in with the extra key and handed it to her awkwardly.

She studied the key for a moment and, raising one finger in the air, walked into Rosalee's room, where she proceeded to tuck it into a small box that contained her roommate's diaphragm.

She returned to the living room, engrossed in thought.

Brody was smiling when she looked up.

"He told you!" she said petulantly. "I knew it."

"No," Brody swore. "He just let it slip that you had some kind of surprise for me." He cleared his throat. "I didn't ask him what, and he didn't tell me, so help me God."

"He means well," she sighed. "I guess it doesn't matter, but I really wanted to surprise you. That way, if you didn't. . ."

"Didn't what?"

"Well, my vacation's coming up."

He was thrilled. "Starting when?"

"Starting now," she said quietly. "Since I got off the plane. But—"

"Are you teasing me?" he asked.

She shook her head and looked away. "But I don't know how busy you are or anything."

He pressed her against him. "How much time off do you have?"

"Two weeks, altogether."

A smile broke across his face. "Two weeks? How about coming with me to Paris?"

Her eyes widened in disbelief. "To Paris? You're going to *Paris*?"

He kissed her parted lips and then sat her down next to him on the living room sofa. "There's something I have to tell you, though. I'll be working. Looking for the people who killed my sister."

She frowned slightly as he laid out the facts, then took a deep breath when he had finished. "So you figure that Paris is the hinge of a triangle scheme," she concluded. "That makes sense. Whoever set it up would want to stay in the clear—away from the origin *and* the destination."

"Right. The truth is," he added, changing the subject, "even if you don't want to come with me, you'd be better off leaving town for the next few weeks. Once Chucky Rio's out of jail, you might not be safe here. He knows you were with me. I was even looking for him at the airport before your plane landed."

"Something tells me Paris might not be much safer," she said.

He was unwrapping a piece of gum. "There's that, too," he agreed. "Look, I'm sorry to put you in this position. You could stay at my place in New York if you'd rather. I have to go there first, anyway."

"I'd rather be with you," she said flatly.

"You're sure?"

She nodded. "Uh-huh. Maybe it's just what I need. I'm sick and tired, Steve. Something happened between you and me before I left. I've thought about it a lot these past few days. And it scares me, too, you know? But I want to take that chance. I don't want to settle for anything less." Her dark eyes, meeting his, were hot and steady.

"Neither do I. That's why I'm asking."

"It sounds crazy. I hardly know you."

"No, it's not crazy. Not the way you make me feel."

She ran a finger over her lower lip. "Whoever you run up against, they'd be expecting a man alone, wouldn't they?"

He studied her. "Most likely."

"So I could help you there."

"Yes, you could. But I'm not going to kid you—you're right about the risk. These people play hardball, Luz."

She picked up a sofa pillow, pounded it a few times, and threw it back. "But you have to get close to them. There's no other way, is there?"

"Nope. They don't leave witnesses. There might be paper trails someplace—to Roper Gance, maybe to other people—but nobody who'll talk. So I'm going to have to break this case some other way. They won't know we're coming, though. I'll work out some plausible cover. If we're lucky, the case'll be over before they catch on."

"What would I have to do?"

"Act like you're in love and we're traveling for fun."

"That shouldn't be too hard."

"And keep your eyes open. From what I see, you read people pretty well."

She laughed her breathless laugh. "I do, actually. *Should* I be scared, Steve?"

"About Paris?"

"No. About falling in love."

He studied her face for a long time. "Not with me."

"Let's go, then."

"You're sure?"

"Don't ask me twice. Promise me one thing, though."

"Name it."

"That you'll tell me when to start worrying."

"It's a deal."

She took a deep breath and, slapping her thighs, stood up. "So that's that. When do we leave?"

"Late tonight."

She paused to calculate. "New York. I haven't been there in a long time."

"I'll get to show you my place, too. Still want to go snorkeling?" he asked.

"Are you kidding? Absolutely."

She went into her bedroom to change and emerged in a black bikini. One look at her took his breath away, and more than an hour had gone by before she had it on again.

Afterward they threw shorts and T-shirts over their suits, called a cab, and caught the two-thirty reef boat with a quarter hour to spare. It was a large craft with a native crew, plenty of cold drinks on ice, and snorkeling gear in good condition. Brody glanced around and saw no one who appeared even faintly suspicious, just a bunch of folks out to witness the underwater splendors. A few serious divers were heaving their weight nets under their seats.

He and Luz found a quiet place on the deck and nuzzled a bit, sitting with their backs against the deckhouse wall, while the boat churned its way out to the offshore reef.

When the boat began to rev down and he could see the green-brown reef edged with sand in the shallows beneath the surface, Brody heaved himself up on his feet and walked over to the rest of the crowd. He pumped a bit of pink detergent onto the glass of the face masks and was cleaning them off in a nearby bucket when Luz appeared with the rest of the gear. A few people finished adjusting their wet suits. Two of the scuba divers were checking their intake valves.

An eager family of five, dressed in identical Key West Perfume Factory T-shirts, descended the ladder a deck hand was holding, and the rest of those on deck moved to follow.

Luz waited until the rush was over before removing her khaki shorts and her oversized shirt. Brody gazed at her for a moment before he followed her down the ladder.

Twenty minutes later, as they were crossing a reef head, Brody pointed up. They broke the surface, found a flipper hold on the coral, and pulled off their masks.

"Isn't it *gorgeous*?" Luz shouted, treading water.

"Did you see that trigger fish?" he shouted back.

"Yes. The one that was swimming near the surface. And the fans just now?"

"Let's get farther in," he suggested. "I saw some

brain coral over that way. Probably has some of the blue ones with the stars all over them."

They returned to the sunken channel and were soon following a school of parrot fish. The glint of aquamarine and indigo along the sides of the fish had begun to show orange as they rose with the sea floor and angled sharply into an opening in the reef.

Brody was about to follow them when he suddenly braked his flippers and pulled Luz to a halt behind him. He heard the speedboat before he saw it coming at them like a shark and the barrel of a rifle with a thick silencer swing free of the windshield. He tore the snorkel from his mouth and screamed, "*Dive!*"

She disappeared, knifing downward without pausing to think, and he lunged after her as a spray of bullets hit the surface behind him.

They kept diving until the pressure on his mask built to a sharp pain and his lungs began to tighten. He listened desperately for the speedboat until he realized it was gone, then came back up. He pulled his head out of the water, his heartbeat magnified in his ears, and started to take deep breaths as he held her in one arm and helped her clear her snorkel. Her face was drained of color.

He took a few more breaths. "You okay?" he asked.

She nodded, shivering.

"Let's get back to the boat," he said. She nodded again and pulled her mask back on.

One of the deck hands had seen the speedboat, but no one had heard the shots. "You know they'll be waiting for us at the dock," Luz murmured as the engines started up.

"Probably," he whispered back.

"Then follow me, cutie," she said, strolling toward the stern. He did. She waited until the boat was a hundred yards from the inlet before diving off. Brody heard a shout of complaint as he went in after her, fully clothed, broke the surface, and began to pace himself against the current. She swam away from the inlet, almost parallel to the shore, gradually closing the distance as she worked her way around to a mangrove-sheltered breakwater. When he hauled himself up beside her, she was wringing out her T-shirt. "You know," she told him, "I'm beginning to enjoy this."

Sometime after midnight, they slipped out of town aboard one of Tiny Johnson's charters, rented a car in Islamorada, drove it to Miami, and caught the next flight to New York.

Chapter

6

The afternoon they got off the plane at Kennedy, an hour before the rush hour Brody had figured to avoid by flying in early, the Long Island Expressway approach to the Midtown Tunnel was nose-to-tail traffic for a mile and three-quarters.

The cab hadn't budged for fifteen minutes. Brody had his arm draped loosely over the back of the seat. Luz was leaning, half-asleep, against his shoulder, and he was considering loose ends left in Key West. The cabbie had an arm out the window, dead cigar in his hand, the other tapping a slow staccato on the shift lever as they waited. He caught Brody's reflection in the rearview mirror and said, ''Ain't this something?'' Brody shrugged in agreement.

Five more minutes went by. Up ahead, a yellow Cadillac Eldorado was pointlessly trying to edge its way into the left lane. Manhattan, little over a mile away, was a vague haze in the distance.

Nothing about Key West weather in the month of August could adequately prepare a person for a trip to New York in the dog weeks that lead grimly toward Labor Day—the air an exhausted brown, clothes sticking to moist skin, the streets full of people doing their best to avoid upsetting the air.

It wasn't the heat. Key West was hot, but more often than not the horizon there widened to a thin stroke of ultramarine against a bitingly blue sky, and the trade wind was always blowing. The only blowing in late summer New York was produced by hookers on Eleventh Avenue and by the automotive engines that considerably outnumbered them.

"Ain't this fucking unbelievable?" the cabbie said again.

"Tell me about it," Brody muttered. "They're probably changing a light bulb." He could feel Luz's thigh against his.

"Ain't it the truth. But Jesus, whoever figured it would be like this at three-thirty in the afternoon? Fucking three-thirty?"

"Hey, why do you think we got here this time of day?"

"It's a goddamn shame what's happening to the road system in this city," the cabbie declared. "But whaddaya gonna do?"

When the traffic finally started to move, Brody discovered that, no, the light bulbs were fine; the stream of traffic had been boxed in by a road crew painting a guardrail.

Luz perked up as they were driving down Second Avenue, and Brody helped her out of the cab when it stopped in front of the Chelsea brownstone he called home. The cabbie pulled their bags out of the trunk, and Brody paid him, adding a tip that included an extra something for the Midtown Tunnel approach.

He handed his bag to Luz and, grabbing both of hers, led the way up the front stoop and into the building. He picked up his mail, and they ascended the flight of stairs to his apartment.

He unlocked the door, flipped on the light switch, and

showed her in. Through an archway beyond the narrow entry hall, she could see a pale gray kimono, framed in black, hanging above a marble mantelpiece. A suggestion of clouds, white yet faintly periwinkle, seemed to float on the dovelike coolness of the robe. Beneath them, a few distant stands of bamboo in a dark shade of bronze were woven into it.

"First thing I look at when I walk in," he said quietly. She had become transfixed. "Isn't it something?"

She nodded, dropping her bag, and went over to take a closer look. "It's so delicate," she whispered. "Where did you get it?"

"Japan."

"You've been to Japan, too?"

"For a few years," he explained. "After the service." An odd look came into his eyes. " 'Old smoke,' they call it. I brought those back, too," he added, nodding toward a table in the far corner of the living room, above which rested two samurai swords on an ebony stand. They were well made but not ornamental.

"They look like the ones on Broadway," she said.

He chuckled. "Don't they? They're not, though. The blades are special, made by a master. The rest is standard equipment."

"You must have paid a lot for them," she remarked.

"I didn't buy them. I was . . . well, given the honor of bearing them." He kissed her hair. "Welcome to my home. How about a shower?"

He carried the bags into the bedroom and showed her to the bathroom.

He was returning to the bedroom to unpack when she jumped on his back, wearing nothing but a pair of black bikinis. "All right, tough guy, don't make a move," she whispered in his ear, pressing her fingers against his temple. "I've got you covered."

He froze obediently as she slid herself around in front of him. "I thought you'd never ask," he said with a smile.

"I've been waiting all day."

"So have I."

Kissing her urgently, he carried her back to the bathroom and made love to her in the glass-enclosed shower stall, standing up with soap all over them and a hot spray of water running down them in rivulets.

Afterward they dressed in jeans and had a great meal at the Spanish place around the corner where he knew almost everybody and the glances at Luz were meticulously polite, before turning in early and sleeping like logs.

The next morning the weather was considerably drier, the light more resolutely autumnal as it came through the blinds in the living room. Brody, yawning in his terry-cloth kimono, padded back to the kitchen to fix the brioches he had picked up after dinner at one of the chi-chi new places on the avenue that he nevertheless felt—shamefacedly—were ruining the neighborhood. The pity was they were good brioches, and once in a while he did like to eat them.

Besides, Marty Solomon was coming for breakfast.

Brody steamed some milk and got the Cuban coffee going. Luz came in wearing a short peach-colored cotton robe, poured a glass of orange juice, took a sip, and offered him some. She was taking another sip when the doorbell rang.

Brody opened it, and Marty grinned broadly when he saw him.

"Hiya doing, champ?"

Brody slapped him on the back and threw his arm around Marty's shoulders. "Okay, okay," he said, clutching tightly.

"You get their affairs settled down there?"

"Everything I couldn't postpone."

"I'm still shocked. I'm totally shocked."

"I know," Brody said. "Me too. But being shocked isn't going to bring anybody to book for it."

"Sons of bitches." Marty absently rubbed the top of his wiry skull. He was short and rather compactly built, with an angular face highlighted by acne scars. He wore thick glasses in frames the color of his brown hair.

He was Brody's partner in the private detective firm of Brody & Solomon and the best research man Brody had ever met—a techie type with a hearty, if not larcenous, soul, a paper genius. "Well, don't worry," Marty said, "we'll get the fuckers."

"It's going to cost plenty. How much is there in the till?"

"After the Rio job? Sixty grand."

Brody whistled. "Come on," he said, turning toward the kitchen. "I want you to meet our new associate." He introduced him to Luz, who hopped down from the stool she was perched on to shake his hand. She had been breaking down Brody's 9mm Beretta; the barrel and slide were lying on the counter, next to an empty magazine and a box of cartridges.

Marty smiled broadly. "*Mama mía.* What's a girl like you doing in a place like this?"

She winked at him. "So glad you approve."

"He been teaching you how to use that thing?"

"No, my father did, after we moved to the States. He's *muy macho gente.* He wanted my brothers to know, not me, but I insisted. He had an old double-action, though, not like this. This is some machine."

"Let's hope you never have to use it," Brody said.

They carried breakfast into the living room, set it all down on the large coffee table surrounded by sofas and chairs, and Marty methodically devoured the omelet Brody prepared for him, two brioches, and two cups of the strong coffee before setting down his cup and saucer with a sigh of regret and turning to the business at hand.

He unsnapped his briefcase and extracted two blue files. "Okay, I've got these reports. But first, fill me in."

Brody did, ending with the final conversation he had had with Lieutenant Reddon. "So there's practically nothing to go on," he said flatly. "You know the score. All we can do is try to slip inside the operation. Follow her trail, get recruited somehow, make the run. Simple.''

"Well, you got the right cover—two good-looking people having fun. Okay, how do you know the passports *aren't* a red herring? Anything is possible in that town.'' Marty was convinced that Western civilization ended about half an hour's drive north of Miami.

"Because he had no other lead,'' said Luz. "There was nothing to distract him *from*, except for Chucky Rio, and they must have known it.''

Marty had a speculative look on his face. "Maybe your brother-in-law *was* involved.''

"Maybe. But he couldn't have smuggled drugs—he didn't look clean enough, and besides, he'd have been running an awful risk with two prior felonies on his record up here. He had to know what she was doing, but other than that, it doesn't figure. I'm sure he never left Key West.''

"Then where's the money?''

Luz, who had curled up on one of the upholstered armchairs, holding her coffee cup in both hands, replied, "Which brings us back to those passports. Even if you assume the payoff from the last trip was lying around the house, that she didn't have time to do anything with it, there were two more before that one, at least. And nobody keeps that much cash at home, not in Key West. So it's in somebody's pocket, and they think they're safe—except for the passports.''

Marty laughed. "Some classy act, aren't we?'' he asked Luz. "A mainframe and a crystal ball.''

Brody shrugged. "Well, that's the way it is. And then,'' he said, getting back to the subject, though he found it hard to talk about, "they really messed the place up, Marty. They really tossed it.'' His eyes flashed with sudden pain. "There was a lot of blood, and some of it was smeared on the walls. Bizarre stuff, you know? Threw me off for a while. Some of these drug killings are like that. . . . Look, for all I know, maybe they're crazy on top of it.''

"Could be," Marty murmured.

"Yes, it could. But Chucky Rio didn't strike me as that type, though I only saw the other two for a couple of seconds. Mulatto, short hair, thin, and a real serious Cuban. Hell, Marty, even if they *were* crazy, there was something else behind it. They were too thorough."

Brody shook his head and leaned back, fingering the piping on the sofa cushion. "No, they were looking for those passports. They were looking to remove the evidence, I'm sure of it."

"What do the cops think?"

"Not a whole lot. The one in charge, name of Reddon, looks like something out of a Robert Mitchum flick, straw hat and all. But he's sharp. If routine work can turn up something, he'll find it."

"Old South," Marty said with a snort.

"Don't kid yourself. There's plenty of new South down there, too. He's got a young man working for him, a Detective Baar, you'd swear could run for Congress."

"Oh, well," Marty began, opening the first of two blue folders. "Then that's that. Let's start with Gance. William Roper Gance. Rope—that's his mother's maiden name, by the way. Tallahassee family, go way back . . . father's out of Houston, fishing business—nothing important." He flipped a page, studied the next one. "Ah. Criminal record. We got one assault and battery charge seventeen years ago. Dismissed. Tax fraud case, 1971, settled without prejudice. . . . Okay, here we are. Suspicion of trafficking in contraband." Marty's eyebrows lifted a bit, and he touched a finger to the bridge of his glasses. "Since the mid-1970s, it is assumed by reliable sources."

He read on for a few moments. "Man has current holdings in seven enterprises in Houston, Tampa, Miami, Key West—fishing, shipping, a cement company, a construction firm operating out of Lauderdale, some real estate interests, even an antiques operation. By the way, that's a T. K. Enterprises on the real estate. Does a lot of traveling up and down the Gulf. Business-related, very legit. Mr. Gance, it would appear, is connected to all the local worthies. All in all, over thirty million a year—man runs some solid businesses.''

Brody shook his head. ''God, why would he want to bother dealing drugs?''

Marty shifted his weight on the sofa. ''That, I think, is maybe a question of the chicken and the egg.''

Brody pursed his lips. ''Really?''

Marty laughed. ''Well, I've never had the pleasure of meeting the man.''

''Neither have I. Luz has.''

She nodded over the rim of her cup. ''He's a slime, even if he does *sixty* million.''

''Well, it wouldn't surprise me,'' Marty replied, and glanced back at Brody. ''Not if he was involved in a murder like that. But you want to go burrowing back to the early 1970s? It'd take forever. Leave it to the Fed.''

''The Fed. You don't say.''

''Mmm,'' Marty replied. ''In 1982, somebody at the Treasury decides maybe Mr. Gance is a little too solid. Not leveraged half as much as he'd goddamn be with a profile like that. The man is cash rich. That always gets the boys to perk up. Of course, there are some folks on the Gulf coast who just like it that way. No crime in that.''

''And, of course,'' Luz observed, ''anybody doing thirty million a year in legitimate businesses is heavily engaged in banking.''

Marty lifted his shoulder a fraction. ''Natch. I've got a list in here I can leave you. *If* the egg came first, it'd be a hell of a nice cover—nothing big, mind you, but somebody could be plastering up his accounts on a nice, regular basis. Making it look just good enough. Hell, the man's been around a long time—they could afford to take it nice and slow. But even so, your man does a lot of retail trade. I'm talking a couple hundred thousand floating through the accounts.''

''So what did the Treasury do?'' Brody asked.

''Nibbled at him a bit. Nothing confrontational—the

man is well placed. Right now, they're keeping an eye on him—at a respectable distance.''

''Nothing else current?''

''Fed's been around a long time, too.''

Brody poured fresh coffee and stretched. ''I don't care about the fine print of it, anyway,'' he finally said. ''So he's a rich man, and he travels a lot. What about the phone number?''

''Unlisted. It's a co-op on Eightieth and York owned by a guy named—'' Marty had set the first folder aside and opened the second—''Theodore Garland.''

''Doesn't sound like he's in cement,'' Luz said.

Marty laughed. ''Never can tell. No, he has an antiques shop off Madison on Sixty-eighth. Deals in fine prints, botanicals, mostly. Bibelots. Quality stuff. A few really good period pieces. Tiny place, actually, but they usually are on the better streets where the overhead can murder you, if you don't watch out, long before the jet set starts to drop by. Your Mr. Garland does very well indeed.''

''Jesus,'' Luz murmured. ''How did you find all *that* out?''

''Access,'' Brody explained, ''is golden. Computers just make it a little easier. This friendly looking fellow here could find out if somebody farted in the Kremlin yesterday, if he really wanted to. What does this Garland look like?''

''Aging preppy. Late thirties, thin auburn hair, plump, understated. Wears vests.''

''So,'' Brody continued. ''Here's this respectable slime businessman in Key West who owns an antiques business, gives my sister the phone number of this other respectable businessman in New York who deals in fine botanicals, and she keeps the card in her phony passport. Where'd you say Gance's antiques business is located?''

''I didn't. It's in Houston.''

''I'd rather go to Paris,'' Brody said, winking at Luz.

''You bet,'' Marty agreed.

"Fuck Houston this time of year. New York is bad enough."

"Fine with me," said Luz, "though to tell you the truth, I'm not as jaded as you are."

"Anything else you can tell me about this Theodore Garland?"

"Not much. He had the same guy in his apartment for two nights. Rabinowitz says if they aren't gay, he'll eat his dork."

Brody's eyes widened. "Rabinowitz? You had Garland staked out?"

"Twelve-hour shifts. The boys were only too happy."

"How are we paying for it?"

Marty raised a baronial palm. "The business will absorb. Besides," he added, "I assumed you'd rather fly to Europe in August." He paused to take another sip of coffee.

"You want me to freshen it up?" Brody asked.

"No," Marty replied sorrowfully. "Coffee's no good for you. So anyway, this other guy, I figured maybe he's a boyfriend or maybe he's an old college chum, but I'm going to check him out."

Brody looked up at the ceiling. "And?"

"His name is Jean-Clair Charlu, and he works for a bank."

"Oh, great."

"Yup. The New York branch of a private Swiss investment firm. He's a loan officer. V. P. for the Caribbean."

"Jean-Clair?" Luz asked. "Not Jackie? Maybe Jacques?"

"Nope. And he's squeaky clean."

"Shit," said Brody. "Well, Jackie'll turn up. It's still early. Have we got anything else in the fire for the next couple of weeks?"

"No, we're clear until the end of September." Marty snapped his briefcase shut, leaving the files on the coffee table, and rose to leave. "Try to take care of this hoodlum," he said to Luz.

"I'll do my best," she replied, walking to the door with him.

Marty paused and said to her, "Whatever it is, keep looking around you."

"I know."

"If they flush you first—"

She nodded again, eyes fixed on Marty's.

"I'm glad I had a chance to meet you," he said. "You're some good-looking woman."

"Well, thank you. I'll try to keep on my toes."

Brody, who had come up behind them, asked, "Where will you be if I want to get in touch?"

"At the shore. Enjoy yourself."

"You too."

"She's a sharp cookie, champ. Cover her ass."

"Don't worry. I will."

Brody returned to the living room and finished his coffee standing up. "Say," he said, catching Luz's eye as she came into the room, "how would you like to take a stroll up Madison and do a little furniture shopping?"

"When? Now?" she asked. "What should I wear?"

"Those eyes."

Theodore Garland's place was called À La Recherche, and it did in fact evoke times long gone when women talked shamelessly to their maids. A bell tinkled discreetly as Brody held the door open for Luz and entered, sniffing the aroma of old varnish. He nodded at a balding young man in a button-down shirt and tie who had his sleeves rolled up and was examining a few pieces of lead glass at a desk at the left of the store, suit jacket draped over the back of his chair.

"May we?" Brody asked, glad that he had chosen a linen walking suit and handmade loafers.

"Please," replied the man. "Take your time."

The walls were covered with gold frames hung one above the other. The engravings were superb, delicately tinted by people who had never seen a railroad.

They moved from one set to another, pausing at a pair of irises matted in emerald green.

"Yes, those are particularly fine," Brody heard Garland murmur behind him.

"Exquisite," he agreed. "Really exquisite."

Luz's eye had been caught by a series of three smaller etchings leaning against the wall near the rear of the shop. "Oh, Steve, look at these," she said, bending to pick up one of them, a spray of bluebells.

"Yes," Garland agreed. "They're late-eighteenth-century French. Just look at the embossing. And the way the leaves are done—you very rarely see work like that."

"How much are you getting for them?" Brody asked.

"Well, the irises are a set, you understand, so I can give you a better price on the pair. They're seven hundred each—say, twelve hundred for both. These are eight hundred each, and well worth it. But hardly to be hung in *pairs*."

Brody looked at him thoughtfully. "I agree. More than one would spoil the effect." Slipping his arm around Luz's waist, he added, "We're looking for a few things for the new apartment, and we're both fond of French accessories."

"Indeed," Garland said in his unassuming voice.

Luz nodded. "You know," she said to Brody as Garland brought the frame up to view, "I don't think we could find something this well done in Paris."

"Oh?" said the dealer. "Are you planning to fly over?"

Brody grinned sheepishly. "We're going in September," he said.

"The best time of the year, except for a real springtime," Garland declared. "You'll love it."

Brody pointed to a slim Sheraton end table against the back wall. "That's a handsome piece of satinwood you have over there, but I imagine we'd get a better break on furniture prices in France, wouldn't we?"

"Well, yes," Garland replied with an ingratiating

chuckle. "To be honest, I suspect you would. How long do you plan to be there?"

"Oh, three weeks or so. I didn't mean to offend you, you understand."

"I understand perfectly. It's the sort of question that comes up quite often. I have, I'm happy to say, a very worldly clientele. The trick is, though, to be very careful."

"Oh," Brody said, nodding intently.

"Yes—you see," Garland continued, broadening his stance, "one needs an entrée of some sort. The French are the sharpest people in this business I have ever seen—all the Europeans, in fact, not only the French. And if you haven't a name to trade on, they'll skin you alive."

"I've heard that about the French," Luz said with an ironic smile.

Garland nodded in agreement.

Brody asked him to hold the burnished-gold frame up for another look. "What do you think?" he asked. "This one, or perhaps that pink one."

"No," she replied, pursing her lips. "It doesn't have as much character."

"Let me take it outside for a moment," Garland suggested. "On a wall with good light, it's quite incredible."

They did. "Look at those shades," the dealer murmured.

Yes, Brody thought. It breathes all right. "Sold," he said with a smile.

"Tell me," he asked in a low voice as Garland was drawing up the bill of sale, "how *would* we go about looking for a few good period pieces over there?"

Garland looked up over his glasses and replied, "I'll give you my card and the names of a few people you can trust. They're always happy to be of service to a . . . well, a serious buyer. They don't have fancy showrooms, but they're highly reputable."

"I'd be most obliged," Brody replied, paying him in cash—he always kept a reserve supply in the apartment—

and waited to see if Garland would skip the tax. He didn't.

"By the way," Brody murmured casually as they were preparing to leave with their parcel, "somebody told me there are ways of avoiding—how shall I put it?—of minimizing the Customs charges on a large shipment of antiques."

Garland nodded. "They can be burdensome."

"We all pay taxes when we have to," Brody added.

"I agree entirely," Garland said understandingly as he turned his back to the door. Brody crept closer. "I do know a shipping expediter," he went on in a low voice, "who's very good at doing the forms, packing, that sort of thing. Has a feel for the regulations, let's say. What you do with him is your business, and it doesn't involve me, but he's trustworthy."

"I won't get into trouble?" Brody asked.

"Oh, no. Believe me, I can't name names, but some of my clients have done very well by him. His name is Dorleac. Robert Dorleac. Frères Dorleac. They're a bit out of the way, but you won't have any trouble finding the place. Just tell him I suggested you see him to see if he could save you a few dollars." Garland winked.

"That's very kind of you," Luz replied, shaking his hand. "We really appreciate it."

He laid his other hand over hers and patted it. "Think nothing of it. I know people there, I have my connections, and, naturally, I try to help where I can."

"It's a complicated world," Brody observed.

"Indeed it is," Garland agreed.

"Very kind of you."

"Oh," Garland assured him with a smile, wagging a plump finger in the air, "it isn't all *that* altruistic. I'll get you sooner or later. Come again."

A few minutes later they were ordering pear *gelati* at Brody's favorite Italian place on Madison. It was wonderful *gelati*, tasting more like pears than pears themselves.

"Oh, it's heaven," Luz said as they walked out onto Madison and began to stroll down the street in the afternoon shade. "How was I back there?" she asked.

"Perfect."

"What did you think of him?"

"Well, if he was bullshitting me, he ought to be in the theater. You?"

"Mm. He seemed pretty straight. You think he had your sister murdered?"

Brody shook his head emphatically. "No, but she came to him. Maybe he was her cover in the beginning, a blind contact. He probably met her once or twice, checked her out to see if she had the right look, and passed her along. I could have steered him around to Gance, but I didn't want to get him nervous. We don't want them waiting for us at Orly."

He yawned and stretched his shoulders. "And then again, maybe Gance's got *him* conned, and he doesn't *know* what's going on."

They glanced into a few shops, studied paintings in windows.

"How could that be?"

Brody smiled and put his arm around her. "Listen, there's a time in every case when nothing makes any sense at all and everybody looks to be a crook."

"What do you do about it?"

"Sex is perfect."

"Animal. No, seriously."

"Nothing. You stop speculating. You pack your bags and you get on a plane. Most of the time, people aren't much smarter than they think you are."

He found a phone and called Marty Solomon.

"Good," he said when his partner answered. "I'm glad I got you."

"I was just leaving."

"Add this name to your search list—Dorleac . . . yes, l-e-a-c. Robert."

"Any direct connection?"

"Direct my ass. No, this Theo Garland just gave it to me."

"Are we in a rush?"

"No, I don't think so. Maybe later. Could we be if we wanted to?"

"Sure. I'll throw a beeper in the beach bag. We got a remote down there, patch in to practically anyplace."

"Good. Enjoy the beach."

Brody hung up and hailed a cab. "You really think something will click?" Luz asked him as they were getting in.

He looked at her with a gray glint in his eyes. "I'll tell you this much—if it doesn't, I'll keep shoving it 'til it does."

Chapter

7

The plane had banked gently to the left, and as Luz watched out the window, she could suddenly see the French hillside north of Paris come into view and houses with red-tiled roofs rush by beneath her. Bright, clear September weather, broken by tufts of cloud, rushed straight to the horizon.

She reached back and tugged at Brody's sleeve. He leaned over in his seat and smiled as he looked out the window.

"It's Paris!" she whispered, barely containing herself.

He brushed his lips against her cheek. "I'm glad you're here with me."

"Oh, yes, me too! Where are we staying?"

"A big place called the Claridge. Nice hotel—not very personal, but it's good cover. The whole world stays at the Claridge."

The plane banked again and started coming in. The blues and reds of cars and trucks on the highways began to grow sharper, bridges to take on height. A resolute look passed over Luz's face, and she asked him, "Steve, is there anything you haven't told me?"

He nodded conspiratorially. "Uh-huh. If a fat guy comes up to you carrying a statue of a falcon, get your ass out of there."

"Be serious. I'm nervous."

He sighed, getting ready to go to work. "Okay, let's see. I'm going to change my name here and there, tell people it's Gallagher."

"Gallagher."

"Mm."

"Sounds just like you. And what do you do for a living, Mr. Gallagher?"

He pulled out his billfold and handed her an engraved card that read *Solomon & Gallagher* in a corporate brown and, underneath, the legend *Communications Consultants.*

"Tasteful," she said, impressed.

"Mm," he agreed as the plane hit the ground and the back engine squeal rose to a shriek, braking, the gray mass of Orly rushing by in the distance far beyond the thin line of blue lights along the runway.

Brody stretched his neck muscles and rolled his ankles, considering at the end of yet another flight how much a tall man sometimes has to suffer to aid the profit motives of people who calculate how little space they can get away with leasing him for four or five hours at thirty thousand feet.

"Oh, yes, one more thing," he added, leaning over to whisper in her ear. "I'm carrying the Beretta in my attaché case. I'll have to show it to somebody in Customs when we get there."

"Oh. Glad you mentioned it," she murmured sarcastically.

By then the plane was taxiing to a stop, and a few travelers had already risen from their seats.

"That's why I'm telling you," Brody explained, keeping his voice low, "so it doesn't take you by surprise. It's a registered international firearm. It's filed with Interpol. They know not to make a fuss. We'll probably be shown into a side room. The thing is," he went on, "if anybody does happen to be watching—"

"They're *watching* for us?" she gasped, alarmed.

"No, no. Just somebody on the lookout for something they might remember later, if anybody asks. All you have to do is act like it was no big deal, like you're going for a drink."

"Ah," she said with relief.

By then, the press of bodies had lessened, and he was able to rise, hand Luz her raincoat from the overhead rack, lift his own raincoat out as well, and help her from her seat.

"The whole thing," he murmured as they made their way off the exit ramp and into a broad hallway, following the signs to Baggage Claims, "is not to draw attention to yourself.

"Reminds me of the time I got stuck in Customs at Kennedy Airport," he went on in a slightly louder voice, "behind a woman who must have been eighty-five if she was a day. It happened during the last week of August. Place was a madhouse—all the tourists coming back, the lines were incredible.

"She was on a flight from Reykjavík. Tiny little woman—*maybe* she was four feet nine—all dressed in black, little white blouse, black sweater, white hair tucked up in a bun, pillbox hat on her head . . ."

Glancing around casually, Brody paused to remember the old woman better.

"So what happened?" Luz asked.

He shook his head. "She was coming to visit her older sister in Queens. The sister was sick, and she was bringing her some kind of plant root wrapped up in a brown paper package she was clutching under her arm.

"The Customs agent is a six-foot hunk of flesh in a tired-looking uniform, and it's been, you know, a long shift? She's got this valise, not much bigger than a weekender, and he goes through it in no time flat. Then he spots the package and asks her what's inside it. When she tells him in her broken English, he explains that he's sorry but he has to confiscate it, you can't bring plants into this country, and he holds out his hand for it.''

They found their bags and a hand cart and began pushing the luggage toward the Customs area. "What'd she do then?" Luz asked as they got on line behind a Dutch businessman.

"She stared at him for a second, as if she couldn't believe him, looked around in a kind of daze, and then started bawling out loud."

"Clever."

"You're not kidding. Out loud. What a sight. Everybody on all the lines started staring at the agent, and it spooked him. There in front of this poor guy was a four-foot-nine-inch grandmother crying like there was no tomorrow, and it was *his fault*."

"How did he handle it?" Luz wanted to know.

Brody smiled, relishing the story. "Like a real public servant, I'd say. He bent down, told her to wait a minute, and hustled himself out of the room."

The line moved, and he slid their cart forward.

"A couple of minutes went by," he continued, "and, you know, it was hot as hell in the room, and everybody on the line started to fidget. Then the agent came back with another guy in uniform, a Japanese with thick glasses and a round patch on his shoulder that read Horticulturist and a small black satchel. Can you picture it? A goddamn resident plant specialist. I never saw anything like it. Anyway, he explained the situation to the old woman, and she finally handed him the package. He wasn't too much taller than she was; maybe she felt more comfortable with him.

"So he opens the package, and there was this thing inside it wrapped in waxed paper, looked like a dried-up bok choy. Color of bone.''

She nodded.

"By then, I was entranced. He started cutting a few bits off the thing with a scalpel—very respectfully, I want you to know—with the old woman and the rest of the immediate world looking on. Then he tested the shavings in different chemicals, grunted to himself a couple of times in Japanese, and, finally, he gave her a big smile and told the agent that everything was okay, he could give the plant to her.''

Brody snapped two fingers. ''She stopped crying just like that. Just like that, and thanked everybody with a little bow, and walked out with her head in the air.'' He shook his head, grinning at the thought of it. ''I wouldn't ever want to tangle with that old dame, I can tell you.''

Luz chuckled and looked up at the high ceiling of the big room while Brody checked the perimeter in his lazy yet thorough way—noticing nothing, but memorizing the sense of it.

Then it was their turn. The Customs agent, a sallow-faced man of medium height who wore his kepi square to the temples, checked through their bags with an air of industriousness that only the first weeks of September could normally provoke in a Parisian's soul.

He glanced briefly at the ID Brody showed him, then at the briefcase. Brody nodded, and the agent pressed a button beneath the counter before stamping their passports. He handed the passports back, wished them a pleasant stay, and they left the area.

Just beyond the counter was a man in a gray suit leaning out of a doorway. He opened it, and they slipped inside. The room, brightly fluorescent, was divided into offices by nondescript partitions, some of them containing large panels of glass. A man in shirt-sleeves, puffing on a black cheroot, rose from behind a desk and approached. He had a long thin face, a thinner mustache, balding hair with moderate sideburns, and, at his side, a .38 revolver tucked into a waist holster.

''*Et voilá,*'' he said, nodding, as he shook Brody's hand.

''*Mais oui,*'' Brody murmured by way of reply. ''*C'est normale.*''

Puffing on his cigar, the man took a long look at Brody, nodded to Luz, and escorted them into the inner office.

106

He snapped the attaché case open when Brody had handed it to him, removed the blued-steel Beretta, and mechanically verified its registration before slipping it back into the holster, snapping the case shut, and returning it.

"Sorry for the bother," he said, looking up. "I have to check it anyway," he explained to Luz, "even if I know the gun. Good to see you again," he said to Brody.

"Likewise." He introduced Luz. "And this," he went on, "is Inspector Massaing. He's with the Sûreté. How come you're here, Henri? You didn't know we were coming, did you?"

The man laughed at the thought. "No, Steven. I only wish. I am here on other business, and I happened to be free when the agent buzzes. Why do you ask?"

"I'm on a case. My sister's. She—she was murdered, Henri."

"Mais non!" Massaing pulled the cigar out of his mouth and stared. "I'm so sorry. Did it happen recently?"

Brody nodded. "Twelve days ago. I was visiting her in Florida at the time. I—I think it was drugs."

He told Massaing about the passports, sketched out the meager trail he had been following, suggested unlikely reasons for examining the possibility that someone was trailing him.

When he'd finished, the inspector made a face, shaking his head, and folded his arms across his chest. "So she probably smuggled cocaine into the country, and you are sensibly paranoid."

"Very. I don't have many leads, either. I have the feeling, though, that she flew the goods right out again."

"Ah. *Le triangle.*"

"Uh-huh. Not much to go on, but I'll break it if I—"

"Two weeks," the inspector interrupted, "is not very long ago, my friend. You think you have, how you say, the head screwed on straight?"

"Well, you're not the first person who's asked. There's

a lieutenant on the Key West police force, name of Reddon, who wasn't sure, either. Yes, I think my head's okay. You know the way I work. I wouldn't take the chance."

Massaing nodded. "Reddon, you say?"

"Good tough cop."

"Very good. I shall call *him* to post the bail for you when we lock you up."

Brody laughed.

"Seriously, Steven," Massaing continued, lowering his smooth voice, "if this case of yours is connected with the drug trade, there will be plenty of danger. . . . You are acquainted with these facts, Mademoiselle Almeida?" he asked, turning to Luz.

"Yes, I am," she said. "I'm helping with the case. Better cover that way, and I might spot a few things he doesn't."

Massaing looked her over and rested his fists on his hips. "A capital idea. But you will try to be discreet, both of you, *hein*?"

She nodded.

"There is anything we can help you with, in a quiet way?"

"Do you know the name Robert Dorleac?" she asked. "A company called Frères Dorleac? Wholesale antiques—"

She stopped speaking when she saw that the inspector, a look of stunned surprise on his face, had stopped listening.

"Dorleac," he replied, reaching for his notebook. "Marlot's employer . . . ah! Here it is," he went on, slapping a page with the back of his hand, knocking the ash of his cheroot to the floor.

He looked at them both and paused. "I am here now at Orly," he explained, "because of a murder, a shooting, committed perhaps ten hours ago, around four o'clock this morning. The victim was a rough fellow, a truck driver from the south. Executed. Two heavy bullets to the back of the head."

Brody bit his lip.

"His name," Massaing continued, "was Marlot, and he was employed by Frères Dorleac."

"Where did it happen?" asked Brody.

"A big construction site in Montparnasse. The body was found a little after eight o'clock by a few steel workers. The local police called us immediately."

"He wasn't named Jacques, by any chance, was he?" Luz asked.

"Non. Pourquoi 'Jacques'?"

"It's a name Steve's sister wrote on a piece of stationery," she explained.

"Ah. No," Massaing confirmed. "He was called Alain. Alain Marlot."

"How'd you find out so fast where he worked?" Brody asked. "They leave an ID on him?"

"No. We found an airline ticket hidden in one of his stockings. He was leaving for Brussels on the KLM noon flight. The killers only took what was in his pockets. It saved us a little time, which we are now wasting. We have been going over this place with a—how do you say—fine-tooth comb all morning."

"For what?" Brody wanted to know.

"For baggage, for someone who appears to be waiting for someone else, for unclaimed tickets, for anything. I even see if any KLM employees didn't come to work today."

"Anything unusual," Luz murmured, "about the condition of the body?"

Massaing eyed her curiously. "As a matter of fact, there were diagonal lacerations, three of them, on either side of the chest. Made with a thin, sharp blade."

"Same as on my brother-in-law's body," said Brody.

"Ah." Massaing scratched his ear. "And one more oddity. Marlot's blood type was O negative. Rare enough, if we locate the weapon."

Luz asked, "What did the company tell you?"

Massaing shrugged. "They profess to know nothing. Marlot didn't show up for work this morning, and so. Is not remarkable. Monsieur Robert had not even been told about it. Is not my department, though, *ces antiquites*. Someone will take a better look at them today. So I come to the airport. Maybe I will find something. *Et voilà*, here you are.''

Brody whistled. ''Do you know where he lived, this Marlot?''

''Yes. He lived alone in a tiny apartment on the fourth floor of a house perhaps two kilometers from where we found him. He had been living there for three years.''

''Anything?''

''You mean cocaine? No. My men are still there.''

Brody murmured, ''You mind if I have a look at the place?''

Massaing was not enthused. ''Now?''

''No. I'd like to give it a little time to quiet down first. Nobody will know. Come on, Henri—it's the same M.O.''

Massaing thought it over. ''All right,'' he said at last, scribbling Marlot's address on a sheet of paper.

''You know where the windows are?'' Brody asked.

Massaing nibbled on his cheroot and murmured, ''The last ones on the left. Try not to climb up the wall in broad daylight.''

Luz laughed.

''Scout's honor,'' said Brody.

''Hm,'' Massaing grunted. ''Meanwhile, I will try to find out what I can for you about this Dorleac. Where you are staying?''

''The Claridge.''

Massaing was surprised. ''No more the Roosevelt?''

Brody smiled. ''No. It's less conspicuous. I'm registering under the name of Gallagher, by the way.''

''How nice of you to tell me. *Alors*, I must return to my work,'' Massaing declared, turning to Luz. *''Enchanté,''* he added with a slight bow, and kissed her hand with relish. ''At least this *type chic* lets me know when he registers in a hotel under a false name, *n'est-ce pas*? Is against the law, *non*? But I don't have to read to

110

you the criminal code. Only, try to keep him careful, mademoiselle.''

"I try to all the time," she said.

"*Bon*. I'll be in touch, my friend," Massaing assured Brody. "Good to see you again."

"I can't *believe* it!" Luz exclaimed as they emerged from the taxi at the entrance to the Claridge on the Champs-Élysées. She saw the Arc de Triomphe three blocks away. "Paris. I still can't *believe* it."

When they had been shown to their room, Brody tipped the bellboy and followed Luz through the dressing alcove that separated the room from the bath.

He came up behind her and, wrapping his arms around her, pressed his body against hers. She smiled and leaned her head back to kiss him, slowly rubbing her backside up and down the bulge that quickly appeared in his pants.

"Oh, yes," she whispered as he kissed her neck and shoulder. "That's the trouble with long plane rides."

He slipped his hands around under her breasts. "God," he murmured. "I never stop wanting you."

She caught her breath, zipped down his fly, and bent forward. "Don't wait," she said hoarsely.

He entered her as slowly as he could, squeezing her hips tightly, then spreading his hands over her pert behind and running them as far down her legs as he could reach.

Her knees buckled, and they fell to the floor. He stayed on his knees and pumped into her faster and faster, lights flashing behind his eyelids, until she spread her legs wider and arched her back, slamming herself into him to bring them both over the edge.

"Wow," he said, gasping, rolling to his side, clutching her breasts, still stroking in and out of her luscious body.

She squeezed her legs together and pressed her hands against his. He fell onto his back, and she wrapped herself around him. "I'm going to take a nice hot bath," she finally said. "Want to come?"

"I have to make a phone call first."

She nodded and walked to the bathroom. Slowly returning to life, Brody stared blissfully at the ornate plastered ceiling. Soon he could hear water running in the bath and Luz quietly humming. He rose to his feet, found an address book in his attaché case, and gave the hotel operator Dorleac's number.

A curt female voice answered on the fourth ring. He asked to speak with Monsieur Robert Dorleac, pronouncing it reasonably well. She asked him to wait, and the line went dead. He was about to hang up and try again when he heard a hiss of static and a man's voice, equally curt. *"Ici Dorleac."*

"Hello, Monsieur Dorleac?"

"Yes?"

"Good afternoon. My name is Gallagher. I've just arrived from New York. I was given your number by Theo Garland. He said that I should look you up, thought you could help me out with some shipping."

"Ah, Theo. Yes, yes."

"I happened to be in his shop last week, looking at a few botanicals, and I mentioned I was coming to Paris."

"I see. Well, of course I be happy to. You know how we work?"

"In general."

"Good. I can come by in the morning. Will be okay with you?"

"Yes. Fine."

"Where are you staying?"

Brody told him and arranged for Dorleac to come by after breakfast. Then he undressed, whistling as he folded his slacks over a heavy wooden hanger in the armoire, and joined Luz for a bath before dinner.

They ate at a place he knew on the Rond Point—a very well prepared turbot *à l'ancienne* that the waiter smoothly deboned at the table, a crisp autumn salad, and a bottle of Sancerre.

Paris really *is* the most romantic city, Brody was

thinking as he studied Luz's face; but that time of year it was even more romantic. He could feel the spark of energy in the air, in the way people moved.

"So what'd he sound like on the phone?" Luz asked, leaning forward.

Brody shrugged. "Like a French businessman. We'll see. You have to remember, we're just riding on a lot of coincidence here. For all I know, this guy is, oh, maybe not as straight as a nail, but totally unconnected to this case."

Luz took a sip of wine and looked at him. "Do you believe that?"

"It hasn't got a thing to do with believing. If I didn't think he would get us someplace, we wouldn't be here. Besides, he's my only lead. No, it has to do with how hard I can afford to push, how much weight I can throw around."

Brody lifted another forkful of turbot and potato to his mouth. "And frankly," he added, "I'm getting a little tired of being so polite. But that's the way I work, even if I weren't the client. Anyhow, if I was figuring to start a war, I couldn't have asked you along," he concluded, covering her hand with his.

"You're so chivalrous." She sighed.

"That's it," he replied with a chuckle. "Just a good excuse not to start shooting people."

"I should have known. Steve," she whispered in his ear after leaning forward to kiss him, "there's a man in a tweed jacket sitting at a table to your left. He's been looking at me an awful lot since he sat down."

Brody knocked a spoon to the floor and took a glance as he was retrieving it. "I don't recognize him. Do you?"

"No. He doesn't look very dangerous," she whispered.

"They never do. Well, chances are he's just been salivating over you. That little dress you nearly have on is something to salivate over."

"You think it's just that?"

"You can't tell?"

"Well, yeah, maybe." She raised her nose and stared at the man, who quickly looked away.

Brody waved his hand to the side. "There's no way anyone could have made us already. We haven't done anything yet. Feel like stepping out tonight?"

"For a walk, maybe. I get tired on planes, even when I'm not working."

"Good," he replied, calling for the check. "I'll show you the Tuileries and the Opéra. That's not far. You'll love them."

They stopped a few times to kiss as they made their way along the great boulevard through the Place Concorde and on into the graveled gardens. Brody showed Luz the trees in their late summer fullness and some of the elegant shops on rue St.-Honoré.

He slipped his arm around her waist and pressed her against him as they were coming back through the Place Vendôme from the Opéra, bought a bag of chestnuts from a vendor, and started to open one.

"How come you look so serious all of a sudden?" Luz asked when he had peeled it and offered it to her.

"I was just thinking of a case I had a few years back. It ended right here."

"You didn't catch the guy?"

"No, I did."

"So?"

"He was my client," Brody explained with a sigh. "I could have made a fortune on that case. He didn't believe it when I turned him in. Neither did I. When he saw the *flics* closing in from every direction, I'll never forget the look in his eyes. It still makes me sad. Had enough of a walk?"

She wrapped her arms around herself and nodded. "I'm ready for a good night's sleep."

The minute they got back to the room, she fell on the bed, exhausted. He did likewise and stayed that way for twenty minutes before saying, "I'm going out again."

"Marlot's place?"

"Yes."

114

"I had a feeling. You're going to find something, aren't you?"

"Who knows?"

"Yes, you will. I know it. Kiss me." He did. "Be careful," she whispered in his ear, and he nodded as he rose to slip his Beretta on under his zipper jacket.

"Don't let anybody in," he warned her. "Anybody but me. I may not be back before morning."

Chapter

8

There was no moonlight falling on the street where Alain Marlot had been living before he was murdered. It was a rather drab street among other drab streets in a blue-collar district. On a corner nearly opposite the six-story walk-up stood a bar. Brody walked past the house and, glancing up, located the dead man's apartment. Then he returned to the bar and ordered a *fin à l'eau* before he slid into a quiet corner, gazing through a window into the street.

A few people entered the building, looking as if they had been entering it for decades—two tired *fonctionnaires*, one male, one female, both somewhere in their late fifties; a young mother and father, wheeling an infant in a stroller that they negotiated through the entry door with a practiced air. Brody watched lights go on in the windows facing him. Marlot's stayed dark.

After slightly more than half an hour, Brody asked himself, How does Rabinowitz do it? He ordered a second brandy, which he slowly finished before strolling out.

He was certain he looked out of place and tried keeping to the shadows. He found an alleyway and slipped into it. Time passed. He glanced at his watch, told himself not to be so impatient, that it was a pretty piss-poor stakeout. It was nearly ten-thirty.

Three more hours went by. He began to feel a chill through his clothes. The street grew quieter, lonelier; lights went out one by one in the surrounding buildings.

He'd just unwrapped a piece of lychee gum and popped it into his mouth when he noticed a young woman hurrying up the street, a scarf covering her hair, hands in the pockets of her thin raincoat. He sprang to attention. She had nice legs, he noticed mechanically, but at first glance seemed otherwise drab. She paused at the entrance to Marlot's building, looked behind her, and quickly let herself through the front door. The angle of the street lamp on her covered head lent her a haunted look.

Brody leaned back against the alley wall and waited in the darkness, eyes riveted on Marlot's windows. The lights did not go on, but after a minute or two had passed, he caught the brief arc of a flashlight as it bounced off the ceiling. He chewed his gum carefully and continued to wait. Ten more minutes elapsed. Fifteen.

Is she looking for something? he wondered. No, he decided; it was taking her too long. He listened for sounds and identified the distant presence of some small creature on an ashcan prowl.

Then the young woman reemerged from the front door, an alert look on her face. She turned left and hurried down the street. He followed soundlessly, like a cat. She hurried away for two long blocks before turning right down a short street into a square with a few old sycamores, then slowed her pace, shoulders relaxing. She lit a cigarette and began to walk away.

Brody quickly narrowed the distance between them. ''Mademoiselle!'' he called out. The figure came to a hesitant stop, then turned, and he approached. In French, he said that he was sorry to disturb her, but that he had to speak to her about Alain.

"Alain?" she said nervously but without subterfuge.

"Mais pas ici," he replied hastily.

She nodded. He came around beside her, and they hurried off toward the boulevard. "It's all right to speak English," she said with a fairly heavy lilt.

He raised his chin. "Did you think you were being followed?" he asked, stopping for a second.

"I—I don't know, monsieur," she replied, slowing down. "I didn't see you."

"Not me. Earlier. There was no one else?"

She started to back away from him. "Please don't kill me," she said.

"Kill you?" he blurted, freezing in his tracks. "I'm not going to kill you."

She began to shiver, blinking back her tears. Brody spread his palms and came up to her. "No, mademoiselle . . . I swear."

The young woman started to cry. He glanced behind him and said, "Please. It would be better if we continued to walk."

They did. *"Did* you think you were being followed?"

"I don't know. I have been terrified all day."

He shook his head and glanced back again. "I think we're okay," he said. "You were . . . perhaps saying good-bye?"

She bit her lip. *"Oui."*

"Did you know him long?"

She nodded. "For two and a half years."

He paused. She could see he meant it when he said, "My regrets, Mademoiselle . . . ?"

"Ebert."

"My name is Gallagher."

He found a cab at a stand that was close enough to the boulevard to be part of the traffic. He preferred the quiet of the back streets to any public place, where noises meant nothing. Noises were usually all he could go by on a tail, if he were being tailed himself. It won't be coming at you from where you can see it, Brody, he remembered being told with more than a trace of sarcasm by a surveillance instructor.

He held open the cab door for the young woman, glanced around quickly, and hopped in beside her. "Port Dauphine," he muttered to the driver, who nodded and pulled away from the curb.

"What do you want from me?" the woman asked in a muffled whisper.

He leaned over and replied, "I'm a private investigator. What is your Christian name, mademoiselle?"

"Jacqueline," she said, feeling a little safer.

He paused before asking in an easier tone of voice, "How did you learn that he was—dead?"

She clutched the pocketbook on her lap. "I heard it this morning on the radio, monsieur. The *radio*. I was alone. I didn't know what to do."

"So you went to his apartment."

"I had to. We were together for . . . a long time. I had to go."

"You weren't looking for something? Something you now have in your handbag, perhaps?"

She shook her head.

"I see. Forgive me for being so blunt. We have little time. Do you know why he was killed?"

She shut her eyes and quickly opened them. They were luminous in the fleeting glare of street lamps through the grimy taxi window. "No. I can guess, but no. He never told me anything."

"Never in two years?"

She shrugged. "I was only his woman, monsieur."

She struggled to speak indifferently, yet a great deal of bitterness lingered in her voice. He knew that "woman" had not been the first word that came to mind.

"Then they would have no reason to harm you," he remarked.

"Yes, maybe I am not worth the bother," she said with a sharp edge of resignation. "Except to you."

Brody shook his head. "I was only waiting to see who would come," he explained. "I've never heard of you." He slipped Katie's photograph out of his breast pocket and showed it to her. She glanced at it, looked away, and glanced back.

"Yes," she confirmed in a low whisper. "The American woman."

Brody exhaled slowly and returned the photograph to his pocket. "How well do you know her?"

Jacqueline looked him square in the eyes and asked, "Who is paying you, monsieur?"

"No one you could possibly know. A gentleman in New York named Solomon. A friend of hers."

She thought. "Once, I saw her in Alain's apartment. And then walking with him on the Place St.-Michel. She was wearing sunglasses, and she had long dark hair and a Spanish name. I can't remember it."

"Castillo."

"Possibly."

"You didn't speak to her?"

A weak smile appeared on the young woman's lips. "Alain didn't like it when . . . He would have yelled at me."

Brody nodded, suddenly realizing she had been taught to know her place. "*Je m'excuse*. . . . Did Alain ever call you 'Jackie'?"

She seemed almost amused. "No, monsieur," she said without enthusiasm. "I am too serious. He called me 'Jacqueline.' Or worse. He was a hard man, from the south, a farmer at heart."

Changing the subject, she asked, "Why are you taking me to Port Dauphine?"

"You don't think I would want to have sex with you?" She shifted on the seat. "Perhaps."

"More than perhaps. But not tonight."

"No, not tonight."

He studied the curve of her cheeks. Her face was heart-shaped, and age was only just beginning to mark its passage. "I wanted to be lost in a crowd," he explained.

"Port Dauphine is the perfect place. What do you know about Alain's work?"

"What he told me. That he drove the freight and helped with the packing. But I knew there was more."

"Why?"

"I knew. Sometimes he had too much money, more than he could explain even if he had tried. And there were people who spoke very little, who came and went—like the *américaine*. . . . He said they were none of my business, some extra work he was doing for the boss. I knew better. I knew Alain would be killed one day."

"What kind of work?"

She threw up her hands. "Can you understand I know *nothing*?" she said in an angry, pleading whisper. "I only saw them in the Place St. Michel."

"Who?"

"Why, Monsieur Dorleac, of course, and Alain—and," she added with a sharp trace of heat in her voice, "this person whose picture you show me."

Brody fingered his lower lip. "Did you think they were lovers?"

"Tsk," said Jacqueline, looking away.

Suddenly he realized what she was talking about. "Oh! You think *she* killed him."

The cab lurched and came to a crawl in the slow-moving traffic at the Port Dauphine terminus of avenue Foch. All around them, polite and for the most part very well dressed couples were offering the pleasure of their company to one another from their cars—for the evening or all night long.

"Mademoiselle Ebert," he said as she was reaching to roll down the window, "the woman in that picture was murdered in Florida a little less than two weeks ago."

Jacqueline's hand recoiled, and she stared at him.

"Yes, it's true. I'm trying to locate her killers—and, it seems, his, too. Do you understand?"

She continued to stare for a moment, oblivious to the

parade of swap sex turning its slow, motorized pirouette. Finally she nodded twice.

"When did you see the three of them together?" he asked.

"Early in the spring."

That certainly tallied with some of the dates on the Customs stamps in Katie's passports. "What were they doing?"

She fell back against the seat. "Laughing. They were all three laughing," she said in an angry whisper.

Brody glanced through the rear window and then, slowly, through the others. He was struck by one extraordinarily aristocratic face and by a pair of exotic eyes on a poised black woman who met his glance from a dark Jaguar sedan.

They rode around in silence for a few minutes. Jacqueline Ebert took a few halfhearted glances out her window and grew calmer. Brody was fairly certain they were no longer being trailed, if they ever had been. Then she said, "It's sad, monsieur, how short are two years."

"Yes, I know," he murmured.

"Did you mean it, about finding Alain's murderers?"

"Yes."

"I cannot pay you well. . . ." She opened her pocketbook and showed it to him.

He shook his head and met her eyes. "The gentleman in New York is taking care of my fee, mademoiselle. If you think of anything else, anything that might help me find these killers, or if you suspect you're in any danger, I'm staying at the Claridge. Gallagher."

"Yes, I understand."

"She was . . . The Castillo woman was six months pregnant at the time of her death," he went on. "I don't think it was Alain's child."

A sigh escaped the young woman's lips. Brody shrugged in understanding and handed a few bills to the driver. "It's safe now. Tell him where to take you—and thanks for your help, mademoiselle."

"Jacqueline."

"Jacqueline."

He slipped out of the cab and strolled up avenue Foch to the Arc and then back to the hotel. It was nearly three A.M.

"How did it go?" Luz asked sleepily when he slid into bed behind her.

"You were right, I did find someone—a woman who can put Katie and this Dorleac together last spring."

"Hm . . . oh, yes, right there."

"Really? Aren't you too tired?"

"Uh-uh. Mmm."

"Oh, my."

"When did you say he was coming?"

"After breakfast."

"Ohh, breakfast."

On that note, their first day in Paris ended.

"Monsieur Dorleac," Brody declared after answering the door to his room at nine-thirty the next morning. Before him stood a man of somewhat less than medium height, plump, sallow-faced, with a high forehead accentuated further by thin, fine hair combed back from his widow's peak.

"Monsieur Gallagher," Dorleac replied with a slight bow after taking Brody's hand. "A pleasure."

"Come in, come in."

Luz had not finished adjusting her makeup in the alcove; the remains of a *petit déjeuner*, still casting a wonderful smell of *café au lait* into the air, lay on a breakfast table between the two armchairs that stood to either side of the window.

Brody slid the wheeled breakfast table with its white linen and heavy pots of steamed milk and coffee out of the way, then offered the man a seat, which he quickly took after removing his blue raincoat. "So," Dorleac began, rummaging for an invoice book in an old-fashioned briefcase that seemed wedded to his body. "You are buying for business?"

"Yes and no," replied Brody. "Mostly for personal

use, although, of course, if we see some unusual items, I plan to pick them up for resale. I know a great many people, corporate types, who are always interested in a fine piece at a decent price. I do a lot of traveling for my firm, and I thought, as long as we're here . . ." He shrugged.

"Ah." Dorleac laid the invoice book on a stand beside his chair. "So you travel frequently. How exciting. You work for a big company?"

Brody spread his hands. "I'm a partner in a consulting firm. We're specialists in communications. Darling," he called out. "Where's my billfold?"

"On the bureau, I think. How do you do," said Luz, poking her head out of the alcove and glancing at Dorleac.

"Monsieur Dorleac," Brody said by way of introduction, "my fiancée, Luz Almeida."

"*Enchanté*, mademoiselle."

She returned to the alcove, and Brody handed Dorleac his card. "Anyway," he went on, "we do a lot of work in Europe, and I thought, why not make a few extra dollars here and there?"

"Ah, *comme ça*," Dorleac replied, studying the card. "Well, of course, why not, to make more money? Is natural."

"Yes."

"These companies that consult you, they are big firms?"

"Some. We've done work for Olivetti, Ciba, Coca-Cola. Some not so big. It depends on what they need."

"I see," murmured Dorleac, flicking the card with his thumb before slipping it in this jacket pocket. "It sound to me like interesting work. And as for what you want me to do for you—where you are planning to do your shopping?"

"Oh, rue Paul Bert, around there. Theo gave me some names."

"*Bon. Alors*, no time to waste, then. What I do, I give you this book," Dorleac explained, opening the four-by-five-inch pack of invoices on the table. "When you find what you will like, and settle on the price, they write everything down here in the book and put your name on the bottom and give to you, and then you give to me, *et c'est tout.*"

"I see," Brody replied, nodding. "And they keep a copy."

"Naturally." As he spoke, Dorleac slipped carbon sheets from the back of the book into their proper places between the copies. "And then I go and pick up the merchandise, and when I have everything crated and ready to send out, I will call you in New York and tell you how much everything will amount to, and you send me the money and I ship. I add ten percent for myself, plus the packing and freight."

Brody nodded again. "Sounds fine to me. And everything is insured?"

"Of course. You have no worries."

Brody fidgeted with the invoice book. "There's just one other thing," he went on. "The Customs charges. . . . ."

"Ah, yes, the *douane.*"

Brody slipped onto the chair across from Dorleac. "Theo said you could maybe help me shave a few dollars off?"

Dorleac nodded slowly. "I can make arrangements, depending on the type of merchandise, you understand."

"You can? I mean, safely?"

Luz approached, fiddling with an earring. Dorleac shrugged and murmured, "Is not too difficult, if you know what you are doing. We send under the right designation, and, you know, nobody is the wiser. I do this all the time for Theo's people. We are quite careful."

Brody leaned forward on his elbow and stroked his chin. "I mean, I'm not looking for any kind of trouble, just to save a couple of bucks."

"No, no, I understand," replied Dorleac. "We all have big expenses, *n'est-ce pas?*"

"But we have heard it's what a lot of people do," Luz said.

"Very many, mademoiselle." Dorleac rose, kissed Luz's smooth hand when she extended it to him, and shook hands once more with Brody. "Then I wait to hear from you," he said, slipping into his blue raincoat.

"Oh, you will, Monsieur Dorleac. You can bet on it."

Brody showed him out and turned pensively toward the alcove, where Luz had gone for her other earring. "Do you think he bought it?" she asked, turning to him.

"I sure hope so," he replied. "Anyway, it looks like we're dealing in antiques. Let's get started."

By ten that morning, they had climbed out of the metro at the Clignancourt station and were making their way across a train bridge and into an enormous open market that covered avenue Michelet from one side to the other. They maneuvered through the crowds already mobbing the market, past dozens of linen stands that stretched up the street as far as they could see. People were haggling everywhere, pressing material between their fingers. One old woman had even bent forward to smell the fabric of a set of embroidered sheets.

"Good quality," Luz observed, pausing to examine a display of pillow shams.

He agreed. "Maybe we'll stop on the way back and pick up a few things."

His eyes were alert, although he knew well enough that he would be unable to notice anything threatening or unusual in such a setting. They turned left onto the rue de Rosiers, an old quarter of three- and four-story stone buildings.

"It's this way," Brody said, pointing. They entered a narrow, cobbled street barely nine feet wide that wound upward past dozens of dealers' stalls spilling haphazardly into it.

They passed a stall packed with woven country baskets, chicken coops, and winepresses. They strolled into another strewn with heaps of sickles, farm colanders, and old bunches of brass keys, all smelling faintly of weeds. Still another contained nothing but sea trunks; its proprietor was sitting outside eating croissants and drinking his morning coffee, calling out, *"Allez-vous en!"* with a wave of his meaty hand.

"You know," Brody said, murmuring into Luz's ear, "there's a story about a Fragonard somebody found in one of these stalls that's hanging in the Louvre now."

"Really?"

"Yes. It's just so much bullshit, of course—good story, keeps the trade moving along. They really understand greed. Can you imagine any of these characters not knowing what something they have is worth?"

"Would you *look* at all of this!" Luz declared.

He nodded. "Let's go up a little farther. There's an indoor area up the street."

Gray cobblestones, gray buildings, peeling gray paint, a fading sign on the side of one of the buildings that advertised Gauloises, and, at the entrance to the Marche Paul Bert, a little restaurant on three levels surrounded by neat rows of flower pots with red carnations, where wine was already being served in clay pitchers. Even in the open air, the area smelled of dust—a couple of centuries of dust—and of varnish and cabinetmaker's wax.

They stopped for a glass of wine—he thought it would be a good idea to carry the smell of it on his breath—and Brody pulled a slim notebook out of his jacket pocket. "Okay," he said. "What do you want to buy?"

"What?"

"You know, what kind of furniture do we want, to outfit the new apartment?"

"Are you kidding?"

"No, I'm not kidding. We're engaged. We're here. I even have contacts among the rich and thrifty, just like I told Dorleac. It's got to look right."

"So Dorleac won't start to speculate. Okay," she declared after nibbling for a moment on the tip of her tongue, "an armoire. A big beautiful armoire, with little brass angels all over it and glass panels and all kinds of drawers on the sides."

"Maybe we could do without the angels."

"Some Catholic you are. Okay, no angels. Sprays of flowers."

He wrote it down.

"How about some side tables? Everybody likes side tables."

"Sure," Luz agreed with enthusiasm. "No home is complete without them. Sheraton."

He laughed. "Now you're getting the hang of it. And a couple of nice chairs, maybe."

"Now I know why I went to college. And a mirror. I love mirrors in fancy frames. Wait a minute—make that a cheval glass. That's perfect. Just a faint suggestion of the risqué. He'll eat it up."

He wrote it down, studied the list for a moment. "I wouldn't have thought of it," he observed.

"Well, he's seen us. He can put two and two together. Let him imagine what we plan to do with it, right?"

"Right," Brody replied with a grin.

"I don't believe it!" she said. "You're blushing!" She broke into a laugh and tried to hide it behind her hand.

"Seriously," he asked, changing the subject, "you having fun so far?"

She smiled. "It's wonderful—you, everything."

He squeezed her hand. "I'm glad."

"And we know she was involved with Marlot. We're getting somewhere."

He finished his wine and paid for it. "Well," he replied, "let's go to work."

Work consisted of acquiring a positively stunning art deco armoire with ebony details and a mirrored panel of exquisite dimensions which they fell in love with the moment they saw it. They did a good job of concealing their interest, too, enough to seem barely inclined to buy. Brody kept glancing around him as they moved from one stall to another, his nerves on edge.

He tried to pick up the armoire for half the price he knew it would bring in New York, then settled for a bit more.

After that came a set of Louis XVI armchairs whose giltwork alone (the saleswoman had assured him in a rapid, unforgiving dialect) was worth what they were asking for the set. Brody acted as if he couldn't understand her, and they finally settled on what he'd expected to pay—a third of the New York price.

"Who wants Louis Seize armchairs anyway," Luz had whispered as they entered the main hallway afterward.

"They're an excellent investment," Brody had replied.

"Six of them?"

"Well, that's true. You need a big room. How about if we put one in the john?"

They were studying two Sheraton side tables and a cheval glass in a fairly large gallery down the hall, near a pair of dealers from Provence, when an aging gentleman with soft blue eyes and a cardigan draped over his spare frame approached.

"May I help you?" he inquired.

"Yes," Brody replied. "We're having some trouble deciding. Is that the best you can do on the little tables?"

They were priced well. Brody knew enough about Sheraton, and the graceful pieces he was looking at were ideally sized—hallway perfect, in New York terms. Luz was holding out for a chest of oyster-spotted lignum vitae that went for a small fortune and had but two things to recommend it: it was gorgeous, and Brody had never seen wood like it in his life.

"You are looking at other items as well?" asked the old man.

"Well, yes," Luz explained. "That beautiful chest over there."

The man smiled wanly. "Ah. Is something, no? Very rare quality, like zebrawood. And so big," he added, raising a finger. "To dominate a room."

"It's very beautiful." She sighed. "But it's just too much for us to afford."

"A shame," Brody agreed sadly.

"I assure you, is a good price. You don't find such a thing on every corner."

"Oh, no," Luz exclaimed. "I'm sure it's worth every penny."

"Centime," Brody reminded her.

"Centime," Luz went on. "You can tell just by looking at it. And we're thinking about the cheval glass, too."

There was a pause as they waited him out.

"You are buying for business?" he finally asked.

"Yes," Brody explained, "but not the chest. That would be for us. We're engaged, you see."

"Ah, *comme ça*. Well, perhaps then I can try to do something for you. Say, forty thousand?"

"Twenty-nine," Luz countered.

"Mademoiselle," the old man replied, shocked, raising his palms with a chuckle. "And the little tables?"

She nodded. "And the glass."

"Thirty-two fifty."

She shook her head. "Twenty-nine."

"An even thirty," the old man pleaded.

"Sold."

On the way back, they bought two sets of linen sheets and paid for them in cash. "Well?" Luz asked when they were done. "Do you think it'll convince Dorleac?"

"Who knows?" he said. "I hope so. We'll see, I guess. I wonder if that old guy is tied in with him."

Chapter

9

They had been gone nearly five hours. There was a message at the front desk to call Henri Massaing.

"You heard me," Brody was assuring the inspector a few minutes later. "She said she saw them together last spring."

Massaing sniffed. "Well, they were breaking no laws being seen together. Ah, well, I have a little information for you, too."

Twelve years before, Massaing told him, Robert Dorleac had been implicated in a drug smuggling operation, had been arrested—he had given an address in Marseilles as his permanent residence—but had been released for lack of evidence in the enormously complicated *instruction* that followed.

"Twelve years ago, you say?" Brody asked.

"Oui."

"That's the early- to mid-seventies. It would put him in Gance's ball park."

"Qu'est-ce que c'est?"

"Ball park. I mean, maybe it's all connected."

"Ah. Why not? They will be perfect together. You can add a bay leaf, a little rosemary—"

"Henri," Brody grumbled, "she was with the two of them."

"So, I am confident, were many people. Look, my friend, Madame Castillo's case is yours, not mine."

"But the M.O.—"

"I cannot even tie Dorleac to the Marlot murder."

"Maybe not, so far." Brody rubbed his nose. "How did they break the heroin case?"

"Ha," Massaing replied. "That was pure farce. They were smuggling it into New York City in the hollowed-out legs of antique chests. A driver delivers the furniture to a store in Manhattan, and they start to uncrate one of the pieces in the street—in the *street*, you hear? Suddenly, they put it down the wrong way, and a leg cracks open and white powder commences to spill onto the sidewalk." Massaing uttered a satisfied grunt. "And less than four meters away is standing a cop directing *la circulation*."

"My God."

"Mine too. Can you picture it? By the time they are finished, there are big arrests. Splendid police work, smile for the camera, handshakes over the sea, the whole shit."

"But you couldn't nail Dorleac."

"Pah."

"Do you have anything else on him, anything recent?"

"No. Not for years. We keep an eye out, but no one has accused him of any crime, and so . . ."

"It sounds familiar."

"*C'est ça*. And there is nothing to implicate Dorleac in the murder of Alain Marlot. Nothing. Not a shred of evidence."

Brody said good-bye and hung up. Luz put down her copy of *Elle* and looked at him.

132

He shook his head. "Heroin smuggling. Twelve years back, and they couldn't make it stick."

"Too bad," she replied.

"This is some case. There are too many people who can't get nailed. I'm beginning not to like it at all."

"So what do we do?"

He rubbed a hand across his eyes. "I don't know. Draw to an inside straight, it looks like. Create the impression, spread as much cash around as we have to, and wait for a shark to bite."

Luz made a face and picked up the magazine. "It doesn't sound like much."

"It isn't. Whoever they are, we're dealing with a bunch of careful people."

She went back to her reading. He called Dorleac and asked him to come by at six.

They changed into more casual clothes and were preparing to go out when the phone rang again. He looked at her, shrugged, and lifted the receiver. "Yes?"

It was Jacqueline Ebert. He could hear the screech of the metro behind her as she spoke. "I have to speak to you, Monsieur Gallagher. Can you meet me somewhere?"

"Of course. Now?"

"Yes. There is . . . yes, I must."

He thought for a second. "Are you near the Invalides?"

"I can be there in fifteen minutes."

"Good. We'll find you. I'm bringing my assistant with me." He hung up the phone. "The woman I met last night. Let's go."

Luz glanced impatiently around the darkly subdued marble mezzanine overlooking Napoleon's immense rose sepulcher. Except for a bored guard clomping his thick-soled way around, the place was practically empty. "She's going to level with us. I know it."

"How come?" Brody asked.

"She's had time to feel it out, enough to realize that,

if she really loved him, she can't leave it unsettled. I couldn't.''

He had opened his mouth to speak when they saw the thin blond woman emerge from the gloom on the other side of the staircase. They hurried over.

If Jacqueline Ebert was surprised by the look of his assistant, she had more important things on her mind. He motioned to a bench in an alcove off the main staircase.

''Why did you want to see me?'' he asked gently when she was seated between them. He had placed himself between her and the stairs, knowing without conscious thought that, if he had to, one shove would remove both women from the line of fire.

''I don't know how to begin.''

''Just tell me.''

She glanced at him. ''I—what I told you last night, Monsieur Gallagher, I was lying to you.'' She was clutching the straps of her handbag.

''It doesn't matter, mademoiselle. People do it to me all the time. All I want is the truth. I don't care how many lies it takes to get there.''

''Alain—I knew what was happening with him. He told me. He told me everything.''

Unwrapping a piece of gum, Brody nodded. ''I thought so.''

She looked at him. ''You did?''

''You seem the kind of woman a man would rely on. Did it have to do with Robert Dorleac?''

She nodded. ''It started before he met me,'' she said, looking out through the marble balustrade at the tomb. ''A few years before. At first, he never mention anything. We argued about that, I remember,'' she added, turning back to Brody with a tremulous look in her eyes. ''I could see the way he was living. It was, as I told you, too much money for a man who drives a truck. He didn't spend like a sailor on the town, but still . . . I couldn't live that way. I absolutely couldn't. It didn't matter what or how, I said, but I had to understand how he gets this money.

"We parted. A few weeks later, he came to me and we talk about our being together. Finally, he told me he was making this money working for Dorleac. I asked him why, and he said, 'For the future, of course.' So I asked him what he has to do for this money, and he told me to deliver packages from one place to another, and sometimes to help with the shipments. I knew what was in the packages."

Jacqueline accepted the tissue Luz pressed into her hand. "You see," she said, looking up at her, "Alain was a man from a small farming town in the south. He was cautious, but transparent. He was a little proud of himself, to have been so clever. But he was also ashamed to tell me. I asked him anyway. Then we fought even more."

Luz asked, "Was it cocaine? Heroin?"

Jacqueline smiled sadly. "They weren't particular."

The guard came by and nodded to them distantly as he passed. They waited until his heavy footsteps disappeared. Luz finally said, "But he was telling you the truth, so you took him back."

Brody asked, "How long ago was this?"

"One year and a half. A little more, maybe. For the packing, they needed someone strong. That's what he said. Someone strong. But he insisted that I continue to live in my own little place, so that"—she shrugged—"well, you know. For that, I must be grateful. They haven't known where to find me."

"So it went along like that for a time. Until . . . ?"

Jacqueline began to play with the buckle on her handbag. "Last winter, in January, he told me he saw a way to make much more, to become a kind of partner between Dorleac and—I don't know, 'the others,' he said—and then we could buy a farm somewhere and go away." She shrugged. "But he said it would take months. I beg him not to do it. I told him he was crazy. But he wouldn't listen."

"And then," Luz said, "spring came. The first time you saw him with Mrs. Castillo."

"Well, you know, I just saw them together with Dorleac. They said they were showing her the city. She had never been to Paris. They ask me to come, but it was my lunch hour, and I had to go back to work. Besides, I knew she was involved in the drug business."

"But you had no reason to suspect her of anything else."

Jacqueline agreed. "But then, the second time, in early June, she call him late in the night, and he became very agitated."

"He told you who it was?" asked Brody.

"Yes. He said he had to go out and meet her, and started throwing on his clothes. He didn't come back until nearly the dawn."

The young woman ran a hand through her hair and shook her head. "After that, he seemed always nervous—he was like that for nearly a month. He wouldn't talk about any of it. I was beside myself. Then—it could even have been early in July—I saw her again. Again, it was late in the night, in the middle of the week. She came to his place and hurry in when he open the door. He asked me if they could speak in private, and so I returned to the bedroom, and they are starting to whisper. It sounded very urgent."

Brody pursed his lips; the young woman was staring hard at the floor, the fine skin around her eyes taut. "Then they began to talk louder, and I heard him tell her that the whole thing was becoming too dangerous. She said, 'Great. Well, it was your goddamn idea,' and what was he going to do about it?"

Jacqueline looked up. "This after a month of me living with him, worrying about him. I cried the rest of the night. I didn't go back to sleep. I pleaded with him to stop doing what he was doing. He kept repeating that it would be all right, and that she would be sorrier than he if she lost her nerve."

The woman's shoulders dropped. Luz said, "And that was the last time you saw her."

"Yes. And then, a few days went by and Alain became more relaxed, as if a weight had been taken from him. It surprised me. I couldn't believe it. He was like his old self. You can't imagine how much relief I felt."

She turned suddenly to Brody and fixed her eyes on him. "We were like that all through the summer. Then, four days ago, the agitation started again—but worse, much worse. Finally, he told me he had to go away, he had to run. He said Dorleac's people were after him. He made me buy him a ticket to Brussels. He said that from there he would go to Greece, and to meet him there in the airport after one week."

Hesitantly, she began to cry. Luz offered her another tissue. Gently, Brody murmured, "And there's nothing else you know."

"I already know too much, don't you think?" she asked, composing herself, blowing her nose with another tissue.

"What about the police? I have to tell them."

She shook her head. "No, monsieur. I will give no evidence. All I ask of you is one or two hours. Alain warned me. I am going away, as far away from here as I can. I am leaving now."

He paused momentarily, then shrugged.

Luz nodded. "You have the money he left, don't you."

"Whatever there was," Jacqueline replied.

"But the big bucks never came through."

"No."

"Anyway," replied Luz, "what there is won't talk."

"No."

Luz sighed. "Good luck."

They all rose, and Brody offered the thin young woman his hand. She took it. "I hope," she said, "that you find these killers, whoever you are working for. I hope that they die."

"I know. They will. I'd like the law to do it, though.

And for that to happen—if they can make the arrests, if it becomes safe for you—you must come forward.''

She searched his face. "If. But I don't think they will.''

They watched her descend the staircase and leave the great chamber.

"I think he must have heard what happened to your sister," Luz said, breaking the silence, "and that's what made him run.''

Brody nodded and began to whistle softly.

"Anyway, the link's really there. Unless you don't believe her.'' She looked at him.

"Do you?''

"Oh, yes.''

He nodded again.

They took a long walk down the boulevard St.-Germain in a nippy breeze. Luz started to shiver, and Brody bought her a dark blue wool beret that framed her face very well and a silver pin in the shape of a gazelle to wear on it. They had a *café crème* at one of the bistros on the place St.-Michel and walked around Notre Dame before turning back to the hotel. They said very little as they walked, holding hands like anyone in love.

So, he was thinking, what do we have? Twice, on separate continents, he had come upon people who, except for skirmishes years before, were beyond the reach of the law. He felt like a man entering a ski chute late in the day, after the run has been ruined.

He glanced at Luz as they were entering the hotel. She seemed absorbed in thought. He wondered if she was as afraid as he'd be in her shoes.

He called Massaing as soon as they were in the room. "No, I *don't* know where she is now," he replied when the inspector began to press him. "I figure she went south. Somewhere south of here. Henri, the point is, she could nail Dorleac for the death of Alain Marlot. It shouldn't be impossible to find her, though it may be harder than you think. . . . Oh, hell, get off my case, will you? Sure I tried to reach you, I just couldn't find a phone that was working. I'm calling you now. Isn't that good enough?''

Promptly at six, Dorleac showed up to collect his invoices. ''You sure this'll work?'' Brody asked Luz as he rose from his seat to open the door.

''I saw the way he was looking at me the last time,'' she replied. ''It ought to. Besides, Garland did send us. Maybe they have their own little plan.''

Brody greeted him with enthusiasm and said they had had a good day in the market.

Dorleac nodded approvingly, removed his raincoat, and took a seat. He glanced over the papers Brody handed him, raising his eyebrows when he saw the charge for the lignum vitae chest. ''Must be quite a piece,'' he observed, pointing to the item. ''How big?''

Brody told him. Dorleac puffed out his lips, eyebrows raised. ''Good price,'' he allowed.

''Good enough,'' Luz said from her chair. ''I bet you'd have paid less.''

The plump man smiled. ''Well, but is not your business. They are clever people, these dealers.''

''So we gathered. Steve darling, what do you think of this one?'' she asked, pointing to a page in her magazine.

Brody bent over her chair to look at the photograph of a model wearing a black crepe de chine evening dress with a neckline that plunged all the way to the waist.

''For you? My God,'' he replied. ''That's pretty revealing.''

''That's the whole idea, silly. It's the latest look.''

''Well, you look great in black all right. What do you think, Mr. Dorleac? You must know how the women dress around here.''

Dorleac rose and came over.

''Such a lovely drape,'' Luz explained as he bent to examine the picture, inches from her. ''And I certainly have the waist for it.''

He finally said, "Is quite *élégante*, mademoiselle."

"Isn't it?" she agreed, flashing him a smile.

"Oh, absolutely. You will look ravishing in it."

She glanced at Brody. "Can we get it, darling?"

"Of course," he said expansively. "Only, where are you going to wear an outfit like that? It's awfully dressy."

Luz furrowed her brow. "That's true. It needs the right setting, doesn't it. Something, um, *racy*," she added throatily.

"Oh," said Dorleac, "There are wonderful parties this time of year, now that the *vacances* are ending."

She turned her enormous eyes on him. "Yes, exactly! I hate feeling like a tourist all the time." She reached up and touched his wrist. "Where would *you* take me?"

"Well," Dorleac replied, looking at her lips, "I don't know."

She winked at him. "I bet you do. Hm?"

He cleared his throat.

"A man like you *must* be able to tell a woman like me where to wear a dress like that."

"I'm not sure, mademoiselle, really."

"Oh, Mr. Dorleac, please don't disappoint me."

He fidgeted for a moment, his eyes never leaving hers.

"Well, I do know of one place you might find amusing."

"You *do*?"

Dorleac smiled expansively. "That's awfully kind of you," said Brody.

"Well, we are working together, *n'est-ce pas*? Is my pleasure. And the dress," he said to Luz, "will be perfect for it. It is a very romantic place, a gaming house in Enghien, an hour from the city by car. I give you the address."

Brody offered him a sheet of Claridge notepaper, and Dorleac scribbled down all the information. As he was finishing, he asked, "You like to gamble, Monsieur Gallagher?"

Brody chuckled. "Now and again."

"Yes. You look like you would. *Alors*, you can be there at nine o'clock tomorrow evening. All manner of people will come—lovely people, *la crème*. Black tie, and I hope you enjoy. I think you will find your host very sympathetic, very charming.''

"This is his name?'' asked Brody.

Dorleac nodded. "*Oui*. M. Alexis Graf.''

"You know him well?'' Luz asked.

Dorleac raised his shoulders and smiled. "We have always some dealings together.''

Luz hopped up and kissed Dorleac on the cheek as he was pulling on his raincoat. "Thank you *so* much,'' she exclaimed with the eagerness of a cat about to dine.

"Mademoiselle—my pleasure.'' He bent to kiss her hand, murmuring something about having to rush, and Brody saw him out with a hearty shake of the hand.

"Well?'' Brody asked when he returned. "What do you think?''

"The guy has a wet mouth,'' she replied, rubbing the back of her hand.

"And?''

"I don't think he tumbled to it. Do you?''

"No. I thought you played him like a harp.''

She shrugged. "Maybe. But it was a little bit easier than I figured it'd be.''

Brody folded his arms across his chest. "So?''

"So I think I was right before. I think he may be playing us, too.''

"And that means we're a notch closer.''

"Uh-huh.''

He sighed. "Let's see what you think of this Graf character.''

"Yes, those 'dealings' he has with Dorleac. And he runs a gambling operation.''

"Kind of all the same shade of slippery.''

"We'll see. Maybe he'll just be a nice sweet guy who likes to play cards.''

"Ha.''

Luz stood up and stretched. "There's too many maybes to be sure of anything.''

"Oh, I know that," he replied. "But I wonder if Katie did get involved with these people."

"If she did, my guess is we will, too, soon enough. If not, you got yourself a lot of expensive furniture. Hungry?" she asked.

"I sure am. What would you like?"

"Three dozen oysters and a steak."

"My God."

"And you for an aperitif."

What with one thing and another, it was after eight by the time they managed to leave the hotel. Brody asked the concierge for a reliable oyster place in the vicinity, and they had a dozen and a half, followed by steak *pommes frites* and two espressos each. They took a stroll around the block afterward. Then he hailed a cab and told the driver to take them to rue Claude-Tillier.

The neighborhood, a business stretch in the far reaches of the Douzième, was dead at that hour. They got out and walked around for a while, adjusting to the dull ranks of warehouses and shuttered storefronts.

Brody had a fondness for such places, backdrops to the glitter of a great city, only to be found at its edges— those unscenic blocks of turf the casual tourist never gets to see, where walls have been painted the same indeterminate buff and green for a hundred years, and the furniture turns to dust before anyone thinks to replace it. How different from the aristocratic glow of Port Dauphine, he thought, and mentioned it to Luz as they moved cautiously through the streets.

Sometime later they slipped through a cobbled alleyway and came upon a loading platform dimly illuminated by a single bulb in an ancient brass reflector. He could just barely make out the legend *Frères Dorleac* scrolled beneath the number 15 in fading gold paint on a black sign.

"Stay here," he whispered, leaving Luz in the shadows, and slipped across the alley. There was a heavily barred window on the platform, a massive, padlocked steel gate beside it, and, farther down, a double-locked door. He listened to the absolute silence for a minute before pulling a penlight from his pocket to examine the locks. It took him a little longer to locate and disarm the alarm wires in the maze of conduits that ran to the side walls of the old building. Then he waved to Luz.

She came up noiselessly behind him as he was picking the first of the locks.

"Is it hard?" she whispered.

"No," he whispered back, lifting the tumbler of the first one. "Not so fancy at all. Probably never leaves anything here, or else he figures nobody'll want to check. This is an ordinary deadbolt. The second looks even easier."

It was. He hooked the alarm wires back up, handed her the high-intensity penlight, and, pulling out his gun, slid the door open and entered. She came in after him, and he locked the door.

They began to make out shapes—wooden crates in varying states of completion stood against the far wall; pallets, stacked shoulder high, occupied the back of the long room, behind two rows of tables upon which stood a few clocks, a figured valence in sections, and a set of wrought-iron garden chairs.

To the left of the pallets stood an office. He motioned her to follow him.

The door was fully open, and he left it that way. There were three steel desks inside. Two were fairly small; an electric typewriter sat on the first; a calendar, two feet wide and serving as a blotter, lay on the second.

He asked her to point the penlight at it. The exposed sheet for August was a maze of scribbles.

The third desk, considerably larger than the first two and provided with a cushioned swivel chair, was obviously Dorleac's. Behind it, the penlight revealed a broad steel closet and a set of filing cabinets, all locked for the night, Brody could tell at a glance. There were no photographs on the desk and few papers. He had the feeling Dorleac didn't spend much time at it.

143

He took a handkerchief from his inner pocket and tried the desk drawers. They all opened, and there was nothing remarkable inside any of them.

He slipped over to the filing cabinet and whispered, "Here. Shine the light on the floor, though. Lower button." The channel lock picked easily. She pointed to the "G" drawer when he freed the mechanism, and he slid it open noiselessly. "G" he breathed in a low growl. "G . . . Gironde, Gironde . . . ah! Gras." He flipped backward. "Gras, Gras, Graves," he murmured. "Misfiled. Marvelous. Okay—Graf."

He had pulled out the folder and was starting to open it when he heard a noise on the landing platform.

Luz froze. He waved a finger at the floor behind Dorleac's desk. She doused the penlight and sank into the space.

Brody touched the front of the drawer, and it slid closed.

He heard a key turning in the lock. Bringing out his weapon, he rolled forward onto his elbows behind the leading edge of the secretary's desk. From there, they'd need a flamethrower to reach him.

Two men, silhouetted against the dim platform light, came in. The first, clearly Mediterranean, had spotted something. He flipped a switch to the right of the door. On came a light, even dimmer than the one out front. Thank God Dorleac likes to save money on electricity, Brody thought, barely breathing. For a fraction of a second, the alarm sounded, but by then the burly Frenchman had reached a coding box farther down the wall and turned it off.

The second man, a thin, lanky North African, murmured hoarsely that it might have been a passing headlight. His teeth were perfectly regular, but yellowed. Both were dressed in work clothes. The Frenchman told him to shut up and started strolling up the room. Brody lowered his head and aimed, but they turned to their right at the end of the second long table, about twenty feet from where he was lying. He pivoted with them. The

Frenchman poked his head into a storage room, disregarding the other's impatient complaints. Then he turned and started toward the office. Elbows balanced, Brody raised the gun a half inch and slid his finger off the trigger guard.

The stocky workman came five feet closer before he seemed to think better of the idea, and the two men left after resetting the alarm and locking up.

Brody rose to his haunches and, breathing out slowly, slide the weapon back into his waistband.

"I've got to hand it to you," Luz whispered, shaking her head as she got up.

He found the Graf file where he had dropped it, and she threw a beam of light across it. It contained more than a hundred invoices, copies of manifests and declaration forms, and correspondence going back two years with Graf et Cie., whose billing address was in Lyons, smack in the middle of the north-moving traffic. But big deal—the man could have a million other reasons for locating a business there.

Dorleac evidently handled much of the company's shipping: ceramic tiles, plumbing fixtures, some antiques, including a number of motor cars. References to New York and Los Angeles, all looking bland and legitimate. No South American transactions, except for a Caracas reshipment; none with Houston or Dallas. "Son of a *bitch*!" Brody exclaimed, pointing to a yellow copy of an invoice for fourteen thousand dollars' worth of plumbing fixtures, delivered a year before to T. K. Enterprises, Key West.

They spent another half hour hunting through the files in Dorleac's office. Luz found a file marked "Avion" that contained a few airline schedules for North and South America and a number of memorandum sheets scribbled in pencil. One of them contained a brace of arrows doodled in a lower corner under the words *À Lyons* and, twice underlined, the legend *Toronto, 12, Catherine*.

"What do you think *that* means?" Luz asked.

"One of her passports was stamped Toronto. Maybe

that's what it's about. I wish Marty were here—there must be things I'm missing.''

''You want to go through the files again?''

''No, let's get out of here,'' he replied after glancing over the memo again, his eyes drawn to the sharp arrows. ''I've had enough exercise for one night. Besides, we have a big date tomorrow night.''

Early the next evening, they were ready to see how big a date it would be.

Though Brody hadn't been expecting a shack, the scale of Alexis Graf's place in Enghien, viewed at a distance through an iron fence at the foot of the property, was still stunning.

''This is it?'' Luz asked.

''Uh-huh.''

She whistled.

They were still enjoying what remained of a day spent in profitable leisure, making a few calls, doing a little shopping—after which she had gone to have her hair done and he had met Inspector Massaing at the Jeu de Paume.

The man had looked so suburban in his corduroys and weekend cap, Brody'd barely recognized him.

''What are you saying?'' the inspector had hissed when Brody sidled up to him beside one of the bronzes on exhibit and told him the news. ''You think Dorleac is involved with Alexis Graf? Where did you hear this?''

''A little file cabinet told me.''

''Oh. *Parfait*,'' he muttered dryly. ''But look here, Steven. If this is so—''

''Who's Graf?''

A short grunt. Didn't everybody know Graf? ''Suddenly,'' Massaing explained, ''I am becoming more interested in this Dorleac of yours.'' A swift, cool glance had passed between them. ''Who is Graf? Alexis Graf controls rather a large percentage of the crime in my country.''

''Ouch.''

"A killer, Steven. A major figure. We have been pursuing him for years."

"Connected?"

"Pah."

"Where? The syndicate?"

Massaing shrugged, as if to dismiss the naiveté of the question. "Steven, if all this is a surprise to you, you are becoming a big danger for me. You could upset my own surveillance."

"And he's clean as a whistle?"

"As a virgin's teeth."

They strolled toward a Giacometti, Brody hesitating a moment before he asked, "Well? Do you want him?"

A slow clenching of the jaw, and then, with a dismissive snort, "Of course I want him. For racketeering, extortion, intent to conspire. Bribery. Stolen vehicles. Illegal sale of arms. Murder."

"Have you found Jacqueline Ebert?"

"Not a trace of her. Perhaps if you had called sooner . . ."

"You'll find her, when she wants you to. Look, this guy Graf could turn out to be the one who wanted my sister dead. All we can do is work a sting on these fucks. If we get the chance to, we're going to make a run."

Massaing snorted. "You're talking like an idiot, Steven. I want him. I don't want two foolish Americans who get themselves killed."

"Not so foolish. We're going to get him, Henri. If we get the chance, we're going to try."

The inspector's eyes had remained fixed on the emaciated bronze. "Are you crazy? Do you know how easily he could have you chopped into pieces and thrown in a river?"

"Only if he thinks he needs to. He won't, until we're ready for him."

"Is that so?"

"It's the game plan. It's the only one I have."

A despairing shake of the head. "So this is what you really came to Paris for."

"Henri, I have to know why my sister died. I have to settle it."

A certain silence passed that shared much with the timeless shriek on the statue's long face.

"Is a stupid risk."

"I've taken worse."

"What about your pretty friend? Has she?"

"She knows. She'll be okay."

"You really think so?"

"Yes, I do."

Massaing folded his hands before him and nibbled on his lower lip. "All right, Steven. Jacqueline Ebert I will find, somehow. As for the rest, I do what I can. Officially, we condone nothing. Get word to me when it will happen—if you are still breathing." He tipped his cap, ending the polite chat between strangers, and left.

On the way back to the hotel, Brody had stopped into American Express and used a public phone to call Marty Solomon at his place down the Jersey shore. He added his growing crowd of Paris luminaries to the list Marty was playing with that included Chucky Rio, Roper Gance, and Theodore Garland and told him to find out what he could as quickly as possible.

A late lunch had followed, and then a nap while Luz took a bath. When she'd finally woken him up, the sun had started to set. Washing up, then changing into his evening wear, he'd watched the sky turn bloody orange.

By the time they reached Enghien in their rented Audi, the stars were out. Brody cut the wheel to the right and drove onto a broad road that wound through a wooded park and led to a limestone château three stories high. Young men in tuxedos were waiting in the circular driveway, hurrying across the fine gravel to assist arrivals with their cars.

He gave his name to one of them when he and Luz emerged into the sharp night air and handed him the keys. The fellow glanced at a small pad in his hand and said, "*Ah oui*. M. Gallagher. Mademoiselle, monsieur, please to enter?"

Luz took Brody's arm and smiled at him. She was wearing a hooded black cape; beneath it, her eyelids were glimmering with faint hints of gold. She hoped the knot of fear in her stomach would go away, yet realized she was ready, maybe even eager, to face the danger before her.

She flipped back the hood as the front door was drawn open, and they entered the place.

Chapter

10

A beige marble entry hall in subdued light; a Venetian escritoire venerably occupying one side wall; a fine Tabriz; candles in sconces. Luz's lips parted slightly in awe.

Two people were waiting for them in the entry hall—a tall black woman in a wine-red glittering sheath and a broad-shouldered gentleman with silver hair and pale eyes. The man was using an ebony cane for support.

Brody said hello, and gave his name.

"Oh, yes," the black woman replied, eyes lingering on Brody. "Mr. Gallagher. Welcome."

"Oh. *Ja, ja!*" the older man exclaimed in a joyful Austrian baritone. "The divine young couple Robert has met." He flashed a smile. "Hallo. I am Graf."

A servant approached; Luz slipped out of her cloak and handed it to him. In the low-cut black dress and silver heels, she looked sleek and gorgeous. Brody shook Graf's hand and presented her.

Unexpectedly she curtsied, as if to suggest a tantalizing innocence at variance with her attire.

"Enchanté," said Graf, allowing his eyes to briefly roam down her body and then meet hers as she lifted her head.

"Thank you," she replied, holding his glance for a moment.

"Mademoiselle Almeida," he said, "permit me to introduce Mademoiselle Leila Moore."

"I'm pleased to meet you," said Luz.

The black woman smiled, holding out her hand to Brody. He lifted it to his lips. "Yes, a pleasure," he murmured.

"So," Graf said to Luz. "Dorleac tells me you are here to have a good time, *ja*?"

She smiled, her eyes sparkling. "It's impossible not to have a wonderful time in Paris."

"I can see why he was so charmed," Graf went on. "Lovely. Perfectly lovely." Brody thought he had the eyes of a pirate—rapacious yet distant, glazed almost by a second corneal layer. "Enormously pleased to meet you both. Please, feel free to circulate, enjoy yourselves." He ended with a flourish of one hand, the other remaining poised on the ivory head of the cane, and cast his eyes back to Brody, who wondered how much he had had to drink.

"What will you play?"

"Roulette, I think. The lady likes dice."

"Ah. I see. Different temperaments."

Brody shrugged. "Brings out the best in both of us."

Graf thought that was funny.

Turning to the woman, Luz whispered, "Such a wonderful place you have here."

She glanced at Graf, who seemed to agree.

"Oh, look!" Luz exclaimed with a high, lilting laugh as they passed through a set of doors into a room glittering with candlelight and the accumulated finery of a few hundred people in evening dress. *"Dice!"*

A waiter came by with tulip glasses of champagne on

a tray, and Brody grabbed two by their rims, handing one to Luz. "Shall we?" he asked.

She took his arm, and they strolled across the room, pausing for a taste of caviar canapes.

"That man radiates power," Luz observed in a low voice.

"A million volts. I can feel it."

"She's something to look at, too," Luz said quietly.

He took a second canape. "Sevruga," he murmured impressed. "Yes, she is."

"Who was coming on to who?"

"I wonder if it's part of her job," he speculated. "You, on the other hand . . ." He planted a kiss on the nape of her neck.

"You can register any complaints with the firm," she said, flashing a smoldering glance his way.

"The hell I will."

They squeezed their way through the crowd of polite people, all of whom seemed long ago to have acquired the knack of gliding past each other like molecules of oil in water. He was conscious of men's eyes and women's laughter.

Someone passed him a joint. He took a hit and offered one to Luz, who declined. He took another hit and passed it on.

"There sure is a lot of snow in the air, too," she whispered.

"You bet," he said, exhaling.

On the other side of the room was a pair of doors that opened onto a long, wide ballroom where the gambling was going on—roulette, craps, chemin de fer, blackjack. Graf enjoyed it all, thought Brody.

He strolled over to the cage at the side of the room, gave a stack of francs to the teller, and handed Luz half the chips he received in return. "I gather you'll be at the craps table?"

"*Mmm.* Gambling's a contact sport. Anything you want me to do?"

"Don't win too big," he murmured as he drew her

close, trying hard to keep his mind on business. "See you in a bit."

He slipped his own chips into a jacket pocket and watched her stroll off toward the far side of the room. As she walked, she seemed to radiate her own electricity, no longer conscious of trying, and he realized he was seeing all of her unleashed for the first time.

He made his way to the roulette table, watched the game for a while, nodded politely here and there to other guests. A number of people at the table were betting even money and two-to-one odds, pretty heavily in one or two cases.

The roll ended. Brody excused himself from the others in his little group and took a seat as bets were settled with commendable rapidity.

For a while he played even money, doubling up on the win.

Depending on the flow of the table, it was a good system for hanging in. He intended to nickle-and-dime the house to death, as if he had long since figured out what all the hustles were, and life was a little boring, and those were the only odds he was concerned with.

It was a good line of bullshit, and he hoped it would serve.

It also made money—cheaply, to be sure, not stylishly, but well enough. He watched his stack of pink tiles take a modest upward spurt and glanced at the chandeliers, promising himself he would try to keep track of his table luck and Luz's—Marty liked to give a full accounting of "Monies Earned While Wagering" as a subset of "Expense of Doing Business."

Brody sighed and started to bet a third of the board. Three women in evening gowns, diamonded to the hilt, were betting their instinct in square chips.

Number 11 came up. Brody let it ride on the red, moving a few chips to the third nine.

The ladies, their petit-point bags beside them as they lounged on their chairs, leaned forward to study their situation and cast a further cargo of square chips to chance—on 1 and 35.

Brody whistled to himself. A guy at the far end of the table with a thick neck and heavy sideburns called out, *"Passe,"* and laid a stiff bet on the high numbers.

The croupier closed the bets, flung the wheel around, and snapped the ball into the chute at the top of it. It finally clattered into the 16 pocket.

The ladies bet 2 and 22 in a flurry of gold; the athlete, scratching his sideburns, slapped ten thousand down on odd.

A tidy gentleman with a small red flower in the buttonhole of his tuxedo took the seat next to Brody and bet the third column, covering himself on the black. Brody rode his winnings there, too.

Twenty-two. The ladies broke into laughter, and one rose from the table with a nice pile of chips. Brody smiled as the chips were passed.

The ladies followed with 0 and 31—incomprehensible to Brody, for whom roulette was a revealing pursuit—but who could argue with success?

He went back to nickle-and-diming and lost for a while to odd, to black, to low numbers. Yawned. The game ran on, chipping the percentage away. A few players left, a few new ones took seats.

When the thick-necked player laid another heavy bet on red, a smile involuntarily crossed Brody's lips; he wiped it off with a shrug when the guy caught his eye and scowled.

Brody tried black and the last quarter.

"Rien na va plus," murmured the croupier, the ball spinning again in the chute. When it stopped rolling at 31, the ladies shrieked.

Brody picked up his pink chips, slid a tip to the croupier, and strolled off to look for Luz.

She was a lot better than even, and proud of it.

"How did it go with you?" she asked in return.

"Pretty well," he replied. "Down and then up. We

must be ahead a few grand by now. I was thinking of trying baccarat. Boy, do you look beautiful.''

She was glowing with energy. ''Can we eat something first?''

''Great idea.''

They strolled back to the front room. ''I've never seen so many diamonds in my life,'' Liz whispered.

''I think,'' he observed, ''most of them would be glad to look like you instead.''

She laughed and squeezed his arm. ''That just shows how much *you* know.''

They had smoked salmon and a ragout of lamb, served with crusty rolls, at a little round table in a corner of the front room.

''Can I come with you?'' she asked.

He beamed at her. ''Yes. Any place.''

''I mean for the baccarat.''

''Sure. Anything happen while you were playing?''

''Not much. Graf came by and nodded to me.''

''Oh? I didn't see him on the floor.''

''Maybe he didn't get over to your side. He was talking to some of the guys at the back of the room.''

Brody nodded. ''Well, there's nothing says he'll bite.''

''No.''

''Come on,'' he said. ''Let's try the iron road.''

She asked for another glass of champagne, whispering intimate suggestions into Brody's ear and laughing her sparkling laugh as they returned to the action.

They were making their way around the craps table, Luz describing a run of naturals, when they found their path blocked by the roulette player with the athletic shoulders and the sideburns.

''Well, well,'' he slurred. ''The laughing American.''

''Excuse me, monsieur,'' Brody replied.

The man didn't move. ''You think you can treat me like the *dirt*?''

''I don't know what you're talking about.''

The man's eyes were glittering violently. ''I am talking," he said, "about *this*," and swung a fist at Brody's face.

Brody raised his arm as if to block the punch, then snapped the man's wrist back in a paralyzing grip, turning out and down, fingers on the central nerve.

The man grimaced in pain. "I think you must be mistaken," Brody murmured. "This is a public place, monsieur. We should behave ourselves."

"Bastard."

"My regrets. I didn't mean to laugh at you. It was a foolish play you made."

He let go of the man's wrist and was shrugging his jacket back in place when the man lunged forward, pushing. Brody blocked him, blocked him again, and then, in growing exasperation, heaved him bodily out of the way.

He crashed into a group of people leaning against the craps table, bringing two of them down with him. He jumped to his feet again to land two solid rights to the stomach before Brody, grunting, decked him with a short left to the chest and a sudden uppercut.

In the flurry of shocked outbursts that ensued, Brody searched for a manager.

"Are you okay?" he asked Luz, putting his arm around her and flexing his wrist.

"Sure. I just—didn't expect it," she said, shivering a little.

The managers weren't long in coming, hustling the man out of the room by his elbows, helping people up, apologizing profusely. Alexis Graf appeared quickly behind them.

"This is disgraceful!" he said. "Absolutely disgraceful. Please accept my apologies. Is everything all right?" he asked Luz. "You were not injured?"

"No," she replied. "A little shaken up. I could use the powder room."

"Ah, please permit me to show you to the private quarters instead. The least we can do. So much more comfortable. Your knuckles are bleeding, monsieur."

"So they are," Brody affirmed.

"Come, please. This way," Graf continued, stretching forth his arm. "I assure you, the fellow will never enter this house again."

He showed them to another set of grand doors at the far end of the ballroom, flanked again by fluted pillars, and asked the floor manager who was standing there to show them upstairs.

"Pardon me, but I must leave you," Graf declared, hands pressed together over the head of his cane. "My responsibilities, you know. We may perhaps meet later."

He was looking at Luz. She returned a nod in which gratitude appeared to have won out over distress. "I hope so. I'm fine, really. It's just—his hand," she added weakly.

Graf nodded understandingly. He seemed burdened.

"I am confident that you will find whatever you need. Once again, so very sorry."

"My thanks, Monsieur Graf," Brody said.

Graf touched a finger to his forehead as if returning a salute. *"À bientôt."*

"You have *got* to look at this," Luz called to Brody after they had been shown to a room with a capacious bath, all white tile and sturdy metal, and she'd found a bottle of alcohol and a chrome-plated cotton jar.

"Looks like it came off the *Queen Mary*," he replied.

"I seem to remember doing this once," she remarked as she started cleaning his bruised knuckles. "Not too long ago, either."

"Well, those gut punches are what *hurt*."

"Was it where Chucky cut you?" she asked, concerned.

"Yes," he went on. "Anyway, we're here, right?"

"We sure are. Now let's make it count."

"I only hope."

She finished bandaging his hand and returned to the bathroom. He stood up and followed her in. "That man

157

really went for you," he murmured, lowering himself carefully onto a white slipper chair across from the bidet.

"Who?" she replied, busy with her eye shadow. "Graf? Why, does it bother you?"

"I'll kill him first."

She stopped fussing and looked at him. "This is a pretty funny time to start being macho, darling. You came here for you sister, remember? Look," she explained, exchanging the eye shadow for a blush, "airline personnel and corporate wives have a lot in common. We all know how to act with people."

For a moment, she studied his honest face.

"I'm just moving it up a notch," she went on, hurriedly applying blush. "What are we here for, anyway? Do you want to nail this guy or what?"

He grunted.

"Do you or don't you?" There was an edge to her voice.

"Of course I do."

"Well, then?" She dropped to her knees beside him. "You think there's going to be some other way?" she asked tenderly. "Okay, so that guy who tried to floor you was a little drunk. But maybe Graf was staging it to test you out, see how you'd respond. And maybe we can infiltrate this smuggling operation because of it. Only, I think there'll be a price to pay, and I think I know what it'll be. So if he doesn't make a move on me, great. But if he does—and, believe me, he will—I'll coffee-tea-or-milk that bastard to death if I have to. I'll do whatever it takes to make him happy."

"But—"

"But nothing. Don't be a fool, Steve. I *love* you. If it makes the difference, if it helps us get all of them—Roper Gance included, and Chucky—what does it matter? I'm not a baby. I can handle it. And so can you."

"You mean with her."

Luz rose and went on powdering her face. "Yes, I mean with her. And no, I don't like it, any more than you do. But don't forget, darling, we're working a con here. There's no other way."

For a moment, he didn't know what to say. "Okay," he finally admitted. "I guess you're right. I guess we can't avoid it."

He studied her as she shook her head and stood back from the mirror to appraise herself.

"You know," he said, "it absolutely amazes me—it's like you're a totally different person."

"No," she replied with a smile, "just a whole lot more of the same one. For the first time in my life, I know what I want. I'd kill for you. Compared to that, this'll be easy."

"Listen," he said, "you still have Marty's number?"

She nodded.

"Okay. If you happen to leave here and I don't—"

"What?"

"Just if."

"What do you mean, 'just if'?"

"You know what I mean. I don't think it'll happen, but if it does, I want you to get to the hotel and call him. He'll tell you what to do."

"All right," she said.

"Just in case." He shrugged his jacket into place, and they left the room.

The hall was spacious, paneled in an antique Chinese silk. It led into a high-ceilinged drawing room with a fire in the grate and Bill Evans jazz in the air. The lights were low. A number of people were lounging around the fire on deep sofas.

Luz sighed, slipping out of her heels and sliding her legs onto one of the silk cushions beside the fire. Her eyes sparkled. "May we?" she asked.

"Please do," replied a handsome blond on the couch.

Nodding, Brody took a seat on the sofa beside her. She bent forward and cut two lines of coke out of the tidy pile on the table before her. She did a line, and he did the other.

It was good coke. He leaned forward to catch the scent

of her hair as she rested her head on his knee, enjoying the music and the fire.

After a while, people began to drift off. A houseboy materialized and asked if they would care for coffee. When it came, they took a few sips, and Brody put his arm around her shoulder and returned to the fire. She nibbled hungrily at his lip. "Marvelous," he murmured.

"Mm. Isn't it? Sure beats carrying trays."

Then came a murmur of voices in the hall, and Leila Moore appeared. "You two seem to be enjoying yourselves," she said.

"Absolutely," Luz declared.

"I'm so glad you stayed." Her eyes flicked like a hummingbird at Brody. "*Finally* we can take a break." The wide smile was breathtaking.

"You don't look much the worse for wear," Brody observed in a low voice.

Alexis Graf appeared a few moments later, only slightly preoccupied, and took a seat as Leila helped herself to the coke.

He loosened the knot of his tie and asked, "The hand is all right?"

"Fit as a fiddle," replied Brody.

"You handle yourself very well."

Brody shrugged. "I didn't have much of a choice. Sorry for the commotion."

"Ah, but no, it was hardly your fault, Monsieur Gallagher. I can only extend my apologies once more. A crazy fellow, to get carried away like that. Have you won tonight?"

Brody grinned sheepishly. "We're up a little. But, you know, comes tomorrow . . ."

Graf laughed. "Do you gamble often?"

"Here and there. I do a lot of traveling."

"Indeed. Robert said you are with a consulting firm in New York?"

"That's right. But this is a vacation," Brody explained, glancing at Luz.

"And do you travel as well, mademoiselle?" Graf murmured.

Luz pursed her lips over the double entendre before smiling back appreciatively. "I sure do," she replied. "I'm a flight attendant, on a domestic airline."

"And you, Mr. Gallagher—may I call you Steve?"

"Please do."

"Where does your work take you?"

Brody shrugged. "All over. Europe, the Far East, South America."

"You don't say. It must be fascinating."

"Has its points," Brody said with a smile. "I met a guy once, though, who had me beat. He was a product consultant for an oil company. He covered the Caribbean ten months a year—five days on this island, five days on that island, and about three hours of work each place he hit. I met him at a hotel pool in Curaçao." He chuckled. "I asked if he was on vacation, and he couldn't remember."

Graf laughed, and Leila shook her head in amusement. She rose in one fluid motion and put more jazz on the stereo.

"Is that your ambition?" Graf asked with a trace of humor in his voice.

"Not quite, but hell, who likes to work hard?"

"And you, mademoiselle—you agree?"

"It depends on the work," Luz replied, her gaze playing over the man's chest and mouth. "I mean, as long as it doesn't become a *job*, you know? Life is too short."

"How true," Graf agreed.

"Mm," added Brody. "Too short and too sweet to miss."

Piano music began to fill the dark spaces in the room, and Leila Moore returned.

"Thanks, by the way," Brody said to her, nodding toward the cocaine.

"Anytime," she answered.

"Yes," Graf repeated thoughtfully, "you handle yourself very well, Steve. You have served in the military?"

"In 'Nam."

Graf nodded. "Regular army?"

"Special Forces."

"I'm impressed. Why do you shrug?"

"It's easier, usually, if people don't know. Not much pride in it anymore."

"Ah."

Luz leaned forward, touched a fingertip to the coke, and sucked on it. "You must be well supplied," she said.

"All the time," the black woman assured her.

Luz sighed with envy.

"You are not?" Graf asked.

"Well," replied Brody, "now and then."

"How would you like to have as much of it as you want, both of you?"

Luz giggled. "Sure. We'll win the lottery!"

Graf laughed, and Brody smiled broadly.

"But I am serious," the Austrian said, and paused to take a sip of champagne. "As much of it as you want. Or the money."

Luz's eyes narrowed. "For real?"

Graf nodded and appraised Brody for a moment. "I have a proposition to make to you."

"A proposition?" Brody asked, alert.

"I know where there is plenty of cocaine. Bring it to me, and I give you thirty thousand dollars for you trouble."

Luz sat up. "Thirty *thousand*? Just like that? Where is it?"

"In South America." Graf leaned forward on his cane. "It is very safe. We know how. We have a great deal of experience. The whole business will take three days, and you get thirty thousand dollars when you deliver the shipment."

"Why us?" asked Luz.

"Because you are perfect for the *part*. Clean-cut Americans, polite, not in the least suspicious. Dorleac saw it the minute you met him. He was certainly right, my dear,'' the man said to Leila.

"You don't look like you cheat on your taxes," she said, smiling at Brody.

"I *don't* cheat on my taxes," he declared.

Graf slapped his cane in approval and went on. "None of our people have ever been caught."

"Never?" asked Brody. "How come?"

Graf smiled. "They have to suspect you first. We arrange matters so they don't."

Brody slipped a piece of chewing gum into his mouth and studied the fire. "Thirty grand for three days, and it's safe." He looked at Luz for a second before saying, "You got a deal, Mr. Graf. When do we start?"

Graf's palms began to knead the head of his cane. "Tomorrow. Can you manage it?"

"Yes."

"Good. Then it's settled. You will fly to Lima on passports we will provide for you. A man will contact you when you arrive there. I rely on him. He will explain everything to you then."

"Okay. Just one thing, though . . ."

"Yes?"

Brody let his breath out and stood up to stretch. "This man I read about who got killed—this Marlot?"

He said it casually enough, working a kink out of his neck.

Graf's face clouded over. "What about him?"

"They said he was working for Robert Dorleac."

"So?" Brody heard the impatience and the lurking threat in Graf's voice. "That has nothing to do with *this*. Robert Dorleac knows a great many people."

Brody raised his hands and chuckled. "Now wait just one minute, my friend. You're making me an *offer* here. The story was all over the papers. I mean, I'm not a fool, you know?

"Hey," he went on, turning to the black woman, "it's no skin off *my* ass. Whatever went down, that was before we walked in. But this is the guy who *sent* us here that the man was working for.''

''Didn't I tell you this might happen?'' Leila asked Graf.

He clenched the head of his cane. ''That damned *américaine*,'' he muttered, rising.

''What *américaine*?'' asked Brody.

''No one. It doesn't affect you at all. Marlot tried to double-cross me. They made trouble. They paid the price.''

''They? You mean they're *both* dead?''

Graf glared at him.

Brody stood up. ''Let me tell you something,'' he said. ''I do business with you, I'm the kind of man you can count on. I don't bullshit you, and I'm damned if I'll let you bullshit me. You say everything's just safe as can be, and here's two people dead? How much of a risk are we really taking?''

Graf sighed. ''No risk at all, I tell you. You have nothing to do with that. The less you know about it, the better for you.''

''Okay,'' Brody said at last. ''You're calling the shots.''

Graf's hand relaxed. ''Good. Wonderful. You will see, I assure you.''

He rose to his feet. ''You can pack a few things when you go back to your hotel. But is still early. Come, my dear,'' he concluded, reaching for Luz's hand. ''Let me show you the rest of the house.''

''I'd love to see it,'' she replied, allowing him to help her up.

When they had gone, Brody leaned back and listened to the music. A few minutes later he looked at Leila, who was sitting on the arm of the sofa across from him, keeping time with her crossed leg. He wondered how far he could push her. ''He your favorite?'' he asked.

She seemed to come out of a trance. ''Who? Alexis?''

''No,'' Brody said with a smile. ''Bill Evans.''

She smiled back a little wistfully. ''Oh, yes.''

"Tell me something," Brody said after a pause. "You aren't just a little bit scared to be playing around with this stuff?"

She laughed. "Honey, it beats the shit out of a lot of other places."

He nodded, said nothing.

"You like Bill Evans, too?"

"Oh, yeah. A lot. Tough life."

She smiled. "Alexis takes good care of me. So he's into what he's into. Anyway, if you don't mind my saying so, *you're* the one who's taking the chances."

He scratched his jaw. "I guess I am. Is it really as safe as he says?"

"Hey, the man engineers a lot of stuff. The man is big. He buys and sells."

"What were those two people doing for him, Leila?"

"Same thing you are."

"Oh, great."

"Hey, they *fucked* with him. They didn't play the *game*—whatever it was. Just do your job, everything'll be cool."

He shrugged. "Hell, *I'm* not looking for trouble. This is a fast bunch of bucks, that's all."

"Care for a swim?" she asked with a smile.

"Here?"

"Of course."

"I didn't bring a suit," he said.

Her full lips parted. "Why bother with one?"

He smiled back and stood up. She rose from the arm of the sofa, brushing her leg against his knee, and led him through the hall and down a staircase, to an Olympic pool set into what had once been a ballroom. It was silvery dark. A long row of ceiling-high windows punctuated the far wall. She left the lights off, unzipping her dress as she showed him the way to the changing rooms.

When she emerged and dived into the perfectly still water, her skin glowed in the dim starlight.

He followed her in. She came up under him and slid between his legs, brushing her thigh against his groin, and captured him in her mouth as he hardened quickly to her touch. After an eternity, she broke the surface and kissed him fiercely on the mouth, twining around him as they drifted toward the shallow end of the pool.

She gasped when his feet touched bottom and he churned against her. "Do me," she whispered in a hurried voice. "I've been waiting all night."

He touched her hair in the silvery light.

"No!" she said, shaking his hand away. "Hard. Do me hard. Hurt me."

So that was it.

He yanked her hair back, thrusting her face up, biting the small of her neck as he dragged her to the side of the pool and mounted her breasts, thrusting toward her mouth. She screamed in delight and pressed them against him. "Oh, yes. More. More."

Suddenly he slapped her, just hard enough. "Oh, you bad girl. Is this what Alexis likes?"

She ran her tongue over her upper lip. "You know it is," she gasped.

"But you're not all he likes."

She said nothing. He yanked her hair again. "No," she finally said.

He grabbed her hand, twisted it behind her, and flipped her onto her stomach. "And otherwise you're just coming along for the ride, huh," he said sharply.

"Something like that."

"But you're not too pleased," he said with a smirk. "I bet the chick who bought it turned him on. What was she, a nice little blonde?"

"Fuck you."

He grabbed her neck and forced her chin back. "Yeah," he said with a leer. "One more nice little—"

It was her turn to smirk. She twisted her head loose and stared at him. "She was an Irish Catholic bitch who acted like a fucking librarian. Such a sweet, innocent thing. Butter wouldn't melt—and hustling dope. Who did she think she was kidding?"

Brody gritted his teeth, suddenly realizing the jam Katie had gotten into. "So she didn't want to play his game. And that drove him nuts, didn't it?"

Enraged, the black woman tried to twist her legs free, "He can do what he likes," she snarled. "Cheap Florida trash."

He laughed again. He could tell she was lying—the jealousy still showed. "Didn't it?"

"No."

He forced her knees apart with his legs and waited.

"Yes, goddammit, you stuck-up bastard. Now *do* it."

Chapter

11

Brody squinted in the overcast morning glare of Lima airport and followed Luz down the ramp and across the tarmac. She was wearing slacks and a light sweater and had a leather jacket slung over her shoulder. He had dressed in a gray suit, the knot of a blue tie loosened at his collar. He paused to stick a fresh piece of gum into his mouth and study her walk.

"Jesus," he murmured, catching up to her. "Sixteen hours."

She shrugged and glanced around. There were no tall trees and almost no green to punctuate the low, dusty buildings, their cinder-block walls covered with murals. "It *was* a long flight. I guess I'm just used to it," she replied. "Fewer landings, anyway."

"But Jesus."

They found their bags and passed slowly through Customs. The agents wore khaki shirts and pants but didn't, despite their badges, look very official.

The agent who glanced at their passports (fake ones

Graf had handed them early that morning and told them to use) and who briefly examined their luggage eyed Luz and Brody for a moment before stamping them in. He did not ask to see Brody's briefcase.

An *ayudante* came over when they were through. Brody nodded to him, and he took their valises out to the taxi stand.

The next cab in line was a 1971 Bonneville. Brody tipped the *ayudante* a few thousand sols, and Luz gratefully entered the broad vehicle, sliding back against the upholstery with a sigh while Brody gave the driver the address of the hotel Graf had recommended.

The driver nodded, and Brody asked how long the drive to the south side of town would take.

Twenty minutes, the driver replied grudgingly. Brody guessed what the New York fare would be—there was no meter in the cab—doubled it, and settled for mild robbery.

Off and on throughout the interminable flight, in low whispers, they had been analyzing the way things were going.

"I don't believe it," Luz had said for the tenth time. "I just don't believe Graf would have had her killed just because she wouldn't sleep with him."

"Maybe not for quite that reason. I didn't dare ask Leila right out."

"I just don't believe it. She was hooked into Marlot somehow. *That's* why she died. Graf wanting her could have made it worse for her, but come on, this isn't a Greek tragedy."

"We keep at it like this, it'll drive us nuts," he had replied. "I think maybe it's time to start turning this around, though."

"How?"

He had snapped a swizzle stick between his fingers. "It'll depend. But, sonofabitch—Graf told you he was going to meet us personally. I wish we knew for sure if he meant it."

"Oh, he meant it."

"Why would he do a thing like that?"

"Beats me. He wants me to wear a short skirt, though. Remind me, will you? And if he *is* going to meet us, where?"

Grimacing, he had glanced at his watch, realized they still had three hours to go before landing.

Brody smiled when the cab drew up to the staid hotel that was part of the Lima Country Club, an upper-class enclave that catered to the families of the wealthy while businessmen in suits and ties clinched deals in the Tiffany-glass dining room or in the bar—which, with its wood paneling and brass railings and fixtures, resembled the Oak Room at the Plaza.

The club stood opposite an immense golf course, though the greens were hidden behind a screen of trees so that the place had the look and feel of a country estate spreading upward from beautifully manicured and lovingly cared-for gardens. The faint hint of approaching spring rose to soften the dusty air.

Only the row of cabs waiting out front and the two kitschy souvenir carts hinted at the club's true function; otherwise, it was a turn-of-the-century château not unlike the one they had just left in Enghien, with perhaps thirty rooms (of which less than half were being occupied) and an entrance facade that arched upward like a tiara.

They were welcomed at the small front desk, set discreetly into an alcove to the left of the marble lobby, by a Spaniard whose accent sounded vaguely French.

"We have a charming room for you, facing the pool," the man at the desk remarked.

"That's nice," Brody replied, signing in, "but do you think we could maybe get one overlooking the course?" He glanced benignly at the man, who seemed a trifle surprised but quickly exchanged the set of keys in his hand for another and rang for a bellhop. Three of them were waiting at the side of the room.

"He simply loves golf," Luz murmured in Spanish. The man nodded sympathetically.

The bellhop led them to a lovely second-floor room with a high ceiling and two tall windows looking out on the greens. Once they were alone, Brody locked the door and searched the place for a bug.

"Anything?" Luz asked, carrying a toiletry bag into the old-fashioned bathroom.

He shook his head by way of reply and stood up. There were half a dozen places a fool would hide a bug and a dozen more somebody who thought he was smart might think of. "I doubt the other rooms would have been bugged, but there's no point taking chances."

She smiled. "What next?"

He grinned and drew her toward him. The phone rang. He shook his head and lifted the receiver. "Yes?"

"Steve Gallagher?" asked a rather reedy voice.

"Uh-huh?"

"Gilberto Rey." He pronounced it with a soft "g." "Alex's friend. Welcome to Lima. How was your trip?"

Brody rolled the kinks out of his shoulder. "Long and boring."

Rey laughed. "I told them to let me know when you got in. Sorry about the flight. It's the biggest drawback in this business."

"Goddamn right. Well, we're here."

"I'll be closing the deal by morning. How about dinner tonight? Drinks up here about eight o'clock?"

Brody could have sworn the man came from someplace in Chelsea, the way he was talking. "Fine. Let me have your address."

"I've got a place right here at the club. You can't miss it—it's the only third-floor suite. Take the staircase up."

"Great," Brody said, checking the time. "See you then."

"Was that him?" asked Luz.

Brody nodded. "We're getting together tonight. Shall we sightsee or sleep?"

"Any other choices?" she replied, slipping back into his arms.

"Choices," he murmured. "Well, there's polo . . ."

She started to unbutton his shirt and pressed her lips against his chest. He ran his hands over her slacks, cupping her behind and bringing her closer. "We could rent roller skates. . . ." He moved his hands around her hips, and she sighed and leaned backward.

"Roller skates sound wonderful," she agreed. "You ever try it on roller skates?"

"Nah," he replied, sinking to his knees. "That's only for the pros." The room began to spin. They were falling over the border between jet lag and urgency. "You're the best," he said, hurrying with her clothes. She was almost violent, wild, as if they had traveled to a different planet.

They slept all afternoon, her head resting against his chest.

At eight o'clock sharp, Brody pulled the door of their room shut behind him, fixed a thin strip of clear tape to the inner edge of the lintel where it wouldn't be noticed, and ushered Luz along the second-floor hallway until they found the narrow staircase.

"Man must like his privacy," Luz remarked.

Brody shook his head ruefully. "You'd need a helicopter to take him by surprise."

They hurried up the steps and rang the bell. When the door opened and their host appeared, Brody's stomach turned to ice and a terrible throbbing began to move up the back of his neck, forcing his teeth to clamp down tightly. Don't show it, he warned himself. Whatever happens, don't show it or you're dead. He tried to breathe, to fight the horror tearing through him. He tried to keep his hands still. Gilberto Rey was thin and neat, light-skinned, wearing a white shirt and gray silk slacks. The face, the short hair, the twinkling yet vacant eyes—the whole look of the man was unmistakable.

"Hey," Rey exclaimed, "Steve Gallagher and Luz Almeida. Nice to meet you. How do you like Lima?"

Not trusting his voice, Brody shrugged.

"Haven't really seen much yet," Luz replied, glancing at Brody uncertainly. "We slept all afternoon. I don't think Steve's up yet."

They entered the suite and followed Rey to an old-fashioned veranda and a wrought-iron table surrounded by captain's chairs.

They took a seat, and Rey poured some drinks—vodka for Luz, Scotch for Brody, both on the rocks—before returning to the phone call their arrival had interrupted.

Brody took a sip of his drink, rose, and sauntered over to the railing. He knew he was badly on edge. The hotel pool glimmered beneath him, the pinks and greens of the cabana awnings aglow in muted lantern light. His eyes began to follow the sandy paths that ran through the trees and around the bushes of trumpet flowers to the grill, and he tried to regain his composure, hoping his shock wasn't too obvious.

Luz came over and slipped her arm around his waist. "What's the matter?" she whispered.

"I'll tell you later."

"You okay?"

"Okay enough. Nothing to worry about." He leaned on the railing and stared at the paths around the pool. "Some place, huh?"

"Mm. Very pretty."

"Just like you."

She laughed. "Well, whatever it is, chill out—you're going to spook the guy."

He nodded and took a deep breath of the scented night air.

They returned to their seats when Rey had completed his conversation. "Sorry if I'm a little edgy," Brody told him. "Neither of us has ever done this kind of thing before."

"No sweat," Rey said appraisingly. "It's good to be a little edgy. That way you don't get reckless."

"Nice place you have here," Brody said, casting an eye about.

"Isn't it? So much nicer than those new American joints. So what if the towels are a bit ratty?"

Luz flashed a lustrous smile. ''Do you stay here often?''

''I lease it. It's my own little world, all to itself.''

''So I see.''

''Yeah. You get a chance, you'll see the rest of it. And it's low profile, actually. Hey, you have to be careful in this business. I hate surprises.''

I bet, Brody thought. Well, you're going to get a real big surprise as soon as I can figure out how to lay it on you. ''You did say you're closing the deal by morning?'' he asked.

Rey took a slow sip of Scotch, his cold eyes faintly whimsical over the rim of the glass. ''You *are* a bit edgy. Stop worrying, man. The deal's all set. You'll be back in Paris on Tuesday.''

Brody shrugged. ''I just like to know where I am.''

''Stuff'll be here.'' The twinkling eyes bore down on him. ''You know, there's still time to back out of this, if you don't think you can handle it.''

''I can handle it,'' Brody replied flatly. ''For thirty grand, once it's on, I'll be fine. You want to tell us what it is?''

Rey waved the thought away. ''Tomorrow. There's plenty of time. As for now, relax, man. We finish our drinks, we go for din-din.''

''Best idea I've heard all night,'' Luz replied cheerily.

Rey drove a forest-green Jaguar convertible with cream-colored leather seats and inlaid walnut panels, the sort of car one sometimes sees in Beverly Hills. He drove with one hand on the wheel and the other tapping happily away on the driver's door to the rhythm of the salsa music blasting out of the radio. They quickly covered the distance to Miraflores, where a premium table at an exclusive fish restaurant awaited them.

The food was good, though Brody had lost his appetite, Luz thought. The service was slow, one course leading languorously into the next. Brody seemed pensive, easily slipping into the use of words like ''business'' and ''merchandise.''

"But you see," Rey was saying to Luz, "for me, now, all that air travel's a real gas." The waiter had just finished brushing the tablecloth and was serving black coffee and cognac in oversize snifters. "For me, it's a dream come true."

"How's that?" asked Brody.

"I grew up poor as dirt," Rey explained. "When I was a kid, I used to take the third-class bus to the airport, with a cardboard suitcase in my hand, and just wander around the place, pretending I was going to fly away to Rome or London."

"Like a sort of game," Luz observed.

"Yeah, right. But with me, it wasn't a game. It was *training*—being there so close I could practically taste it, smell the fuel burn-off, even. The works."

Brody nodded thoughtfully.

"You dig?" Rey continued. "*I* made it happen. When I was twelve years old, I stuffed old newspaper in my baggage, and I came back with them stuffed with duty-free clothing. We sold that stuff in my mother's stall in the *central* for triple the cost of the whole trip."

He seemed, after twenty years or so, to still relish the memory. "Entrepreneur from the beginning, huh?" Brody asked him.

"You bet."

"So this now is just a refinement. Tell me, where'd you learn to speak English so well—New York?"

Rey nodded enthusiastically and took a long sip of cognac. "Been up there, on and off, for years now. You live there?"

"I have a place in Chelsea. Had it since I left the army. Rent-controlled."

"No kidding."

"Sure keeps the overhead down."

"I bet. Cigar?"

"No, I gave up smoking," Brody replied, unwrapping a piece of pineapple gum, reminding himself that his supply was running low, and where in hell was he going to find sugar-free tropical flavors in Peru? It made sitting at the table with the man easier. Looking at Luz made it easier still.

"You really work as a stew?" Rey asked her.

She nodded.

"Bet you never thought you'd land here."

She laughed. "Sure as hell not. Do you think we'll have a chance to see any of it?"

"Well, maybe. Tomorrow morning, we work. After that, the two of you can do what you want, check out the city. Hey," he said, snapping his fingers, and pulled a wad of bills from a thick roll in his pocket. "Here, expense money." He handed the bills to her. "It's the least Alex and I can do for the two of you, right?"

"Very thoughtful of you," Brody answered.

"Not at all." Rey leaned forward and added, "I'm telling you, we take care of our people. You hang out with us, you play the game right, and you'll have so much money in your pocket you won't know what to do with it. It's like water, man. It's like *air*."

"*Yeah*," Luz murmured.

Brody turned to her and smiled. "How do you like it, huh?"

"I love it. I *love* it."

Brody leaned back and studied Rey. "You know," he finally said to break the easy silence, "I could swear I've seen you before."

"Where?" Rey replied.

"I don't know. New York? In Barney's, maybe?"

Rey laughed. "Could be."

"Probably. But you get around, I gather, and I sure as hell get around . . . I don't know, it's just something about you looks familiar," Brody concluded.

"We could have run across each other lots of places," Rey suggested. "You travel a lot, don't you?"

"Do I. You name it. Say, could it have been—do you spend any time in Portugal? I was there last month."

Rey shook his head.

"What the fuck," Brody replied. "But you wait. Give me a little time, and I'll bet you I remember it."

Rey shrugged and took another sip of cognac.

They parted in the hallway and made plans for the following morning. Rey leaned toward them and murmured, "Ta ta. Don't do anything I wouldn't do." He was weaving slightly as they watched him stroll off. When they were alone, Brody removed the sliver of tape on the door and they entered their room.

"He's one of the men who killed my sister," he said as soon as the door shut behind them. "I saw him coming out of the house that day."

Luz's eyes widened in shock. "What are you going to do? You can't let on."

"I know."

"So?"

"So," Brody said grumpily, and drew her to him, breathing in the wonderful scent of her hair. "I've been trying to control myself for the last four hours. I wanted to move on the sonofabitch right there, and fuck the consequences. I haven't been able to think."

She ran her hands over his back. He felt taut as a drum. Then she could hear him breathing deeply.

"All I know is, he's meat. I'll find a way. But first, he's going to tell me why it happened."

When they got up the next morning, they ordered breakfast from room service and ate it at a table before the window. Afterward, Brody went down to the newspaper stand in the lobby and grudgingly purchased a few packs of Juicy Fruit gum. Luz was taking a bath when he returned to the room. "Anything happen?" he called out.

"No."

He entered the bathroom and started to take a shave. "How are you doing?" she asked.

"Pretty well." He turned to her for a moment and ran his eyes over her body. "You?"

She smiled back at him. "So long as you're okay, I'm fine."

"Good." He turned back to the mirror and started drawing the razor down his left cheek.

"It's so corny."

"What's that?"

"I like watching you shave."

"Really? Most boring thing in the world."

"It just feels . . . comfortable, like I know you."

He started in on the other cheek. "Maybe you do. I feel the same way. A little lost down in the lobby before, like I ought to be here. It's strange. I mean, I'm so used to being on my own—"

The phone started to ring, and he went for it, taking the thin hotel towel with him.

"Yes?"

"Hi," he heard Rey say. "It's me. Care to join the party?"

"You bet," Brody replied. "Give us fifteen minutes—she's taking a bath."

"You got it."

Brody came back into the bathroom just as Luz was standing up in the tub and reaching for a towel.

"Our little sweetheart?"

He nodded. "It's going to start moving pretty soon now. You ready?"

"As ready as I can be." She wrapped the towel around her head and left. He quickly ran the razor over his chin and upper lip, rinsed his face, combed his hair. He found her drying her hair, a pair of bikinis hugging her luscious ass. He couldn't resist giving her an appreciative pinch.

"Beast," she murmured. Then, "Hey, finish what you were saying before."

"About what?"

"You know."

"Oh. Well, just that I've been on my own for so long, you're a real surprise. Being with you like this—I don't mean sleeping alone. . . . "

She smiled tenderly at him over her shoulder. "I'm

glad I'm not the only one who feels that way. Hand me
that skirt, will you?''

Ten minutes later, he was ringing the buzzer of Rey's
upstairs suite. A few moments went by, the door opened
a crack, and a short, dark-skinned man with wide cheek-
bones and a hawklike nose peered out at them. "Gilberto?'' Brody said.

"Eh, Jaqui!'' the Indian called out. *"Venga."*

Rey appeared behind him, and the door opened the
rest of the way. The Indian was carrying a Mac-10 at his
side. "Hi,'' Brody said to Rey. Then, nodding at the
automatic, "Heavy artillery, huh?''

"Better safe than sorry. Come in, come in.''

"What'd he call you? Jackie?''

"Nickname,'' Rey explained. "It's an old story.''

They followed him in. Luz gasped when they saw the
ropy pile of cocaine sitting on a table in the middle of
the living room, looking just like taffy hot off the candy
machine in Atlantic City before it's stretched and
chopped and wrapped.

The Indian returned to his seat at the far side of the
room and leaned his weapon against the leg of the table.
Another guard was lounging against the wall, arms
crossed over a substantial chest, a military .45 hanging
listlessly in his hand. *"Dios mío,"* Luz finally murmured, transfixed by the coke. "How much is there?''

"Three kilos,'' Rey told her. "Pure.''

Three kilos, Brody was thinking—enough to put the
man away for twenty years.

Luz nodded, staring. "How much does that *go* for?''

Rey shrugged. "Here, a hundred and a half. Way down
the other end of the line, so much a gram, so many
grams to the ounce—hey, we don't even bother to figure.
Who *knows* what that's actually worth?''

"Ay! No me dices."

He grinned. *"Pero sí, chica."*

Brody nodded admiringly before adding, "So what's
the deal, Jackie? Graf sent us here to pick this up and
deliver it to him. He said you'd tell us everything else.''

Rey was already nodding. "Come into the bedroom."

They followed him down the hall. Brody was startled to see a fan-shaped display of knives covering nearly five feet of the wall facing the old Spanish bed. There must have been fifty of them up there.

"Sit down," Rey said, offering them the armchairs beside the bed; he himself sat on the edge of the mattress. "Okay, look, first of all, you're going to take it back to Paris."

"What do you mean, 'first of all'?" Brody muttered. "We take it back and somebody meets us there, no?"

Rey shook his head. "It's not that simple. We got to sell the stuff in the States."

There was a dead silence. Luz heaved a sigh. "Oh, great. You want us to smuggle it past U.S. Customs? This was supposed to be safe!"

Rey smiled agreeably. "Listen to me. I'm telling you it's *foolproof.* And worth thirty grand to you. But hey, you can still back out."

Brody thought for a moment. "If it's so foolproof," he asked, "why don't we just fly it to the States from here? Why go all the way to Paris? It's sixteen fucking hours in the wrong direction."

"Exactly."

Luz's face slowly broke into an enlightened grin. "Of course! Why would anybody do it if they didn't have to? God, that's brilliant. That's genius!"

"Right?" Rey nodded in excitement, his feral eyes full of pleasure. "It's the whole damn thing, okay? You don't think we're going to send you into the U.S. of A. from South America, do you? Any place in South America. Hey, Uncle Sam'll be checking out your grandmother on that kind of flight, *hombre.* This here is where the drugs come from."

"What about when we get to Orly?" Brody asked, warming to the discussion. "Won't they be looking too if we're coming from Lima?"

Rey shook his head. "It's not like the States, man.

There isn't enough of a market. It's all society stuff, and it's tight, very private.''

He paused significantly. "Anyway, nobody at Orly's going to be expecting a shipment of coke from Peru."

"Right."

Luz took a deep breath, and Brody looked at her and nodded. "Sounds pretty sharp so far," she said.

Rey held up his hands and continued. "Okay, you fly to Paris. You're Americans, combining a little pleasure with some business down here, took you a few days to wrap up—hey, you're cool, no big deal."

He paused. "I guarantee they won't spot the fake passport, any more than they did here. I can't tell you how, but I guarantee it," he insisted with great mystery. "So, you get through Customs, and you take the evening flight to Los Angeles."

"Los *Angeles*?" Luz exclaimed.

"Hey, this is great, man!" Brody said.

"Well, look," Rey replied. "I ain't going to kid you—U.S. Customs, that's the tough part."

Raising a hand to forestall comment, he got up and started to pace. "But let's look at it. You been in the air another eleven hours, but you lost time flying west, so it's eight at night or so. Agents are busy, airport's just packed with tourists coming home at the end of the summer."

He put up a finger. "But nothing about your trip's going to ring any bells. You show the agent your own passports, and what does he see? You been in Europe, mixing business with a little pleasure—same story exactly—and you had to fly to L.A. before returning to New York. It's all there on the exit and entry stamps."

"So far as he knows," Brody replied, "we flew New York to Paris to L.A. We were never here at all!"

"That's it," Rey declared, pleased. "You were never here at all."

Brody let the idea sink in. "But those Customs agents have opened my bags plenty of times anyway, for all kinds of reasons. What do you want me to do, tuck three keys of coke up my assshole?''

Rey laughed. "No way, José. What do you think, we're looking to get caught? Come on."

"That's some collection of knives," Brody said with a gesture as they were getting up.

"Like 'em?" Rey asked.

"Beautiful."

"I got a thing for blades. Go ahead, take a look."

Brody removed a U.S. combat knife and took a few swipes with it.

"Bring back memories?" Rey asked.

"A few," Brody answered, putting it back. There were a few dirks hanging above it and a number of beautifully forged hunting knives.

Rey reached out for a streamlined stiletto with an ivory grip that occupied a position at the base of the display. "Here's my favorite," he said. He flicked it, and the blade disappeared soundlessly. Smiling, his eyes blank, he handed the knife to Brody.

"Nice balance," Brody observed, and released the spring. The surgical blade shot out instantly. "*Really* nice. A little short, maybe.

"Not for some things," Rey said with a snicker. "Take it with me whenever I can. Fits any place—you dig?"

"Yeah, I dig," Brody whispered, staring down at the knife. Like right between your ribs. He was inside striking range. A step and a lunge would do it. Two seconds. His fingers tightened around the grip as he pictured his hand twist to the left and up at the end of the stroke, and the look of shock on Rey's face, and the shriek that would end in a spray of blood. He tensed for the thrust and lifted his eyes.

"Come on, Steve," Luz said with a barely concealed edge to her voice, "let me see it, too." She took it from him, and the moment passed.

Chapter

12

Rey told them to take a seat at the table where the shipment lay waiting. As they did, he glanced at the standing guard. The Indian shrugged.

Brody's face expressed relief and a sober enthusiasm that masked an even greater glee. Finally, he was thinking, deep beneath all the other thinking, as consciously as he had since he had first entered the suite—bingo! Criminal possession. Evidence. Just ride it out, Brody. Yes, sir. No fucking heroics, Brody. No, *sir*. He smiled gratefully at the pile of cocaine.

Rey opened a cupboard and removed a tray containing neat rows of empty Marlboro 100s boxes, their carefully preserved cellophane wrappers, and a few ordinary teaspoons. He set the tray on the table and, slipping onto a seat opposite them, reached into a drawer for a few stacks of plastic pouches and a small, battery-operated soldering tool.

"And now," he said with a grin to the coke, "we make you disappear, you pretty thing." He glanced up as he broke a chunk off the pile and began mashing it with the bottom of a spoon.

"You get into that Customs line," he explained, "nobody's going to notice *nothing*. Got to be that way, so even if they start to poke around a little, they don't put it together."

Brody rubbed his nose.

Rey studied the coke. He had left a few peanut-sized chunks in with the powder. "For the dealers. They like to see pieces that show the crystal."

He switched on the soldering tool, rested it against an ashtray, and, opening one of the plastic pouches, began to scoop up the merchandise and deftly spoon it in. "Please," he said with a trace of irony to Luz and Brody. "Give me a hand."

They both mashed up a few chunks that Brody broke off the pile. Afterward, Rey scooped up the coke and added it to the pouch. When the pouch was completely filled, he sealed it shut and rubbed the seal between his fingers. " 'Course," he said, "you don't want to free-base it by accident. But the iron never gets that hot." He slid the pouch into an empty Marlboro box.

"Now, that's seal number one," he said. It fit perfectly.

He took a cellophane wrapper from the supply on the tray. "And here's number two," he went on, easing the box into the cellophane. When he had fit it back in place, he pulled a tube of industrial glue out of the table drawer and resealed the upper edges of the cellophane.

He cooled the seal and handed the pack to Brody. "Of course, they go back in the cartons, and we seal *them* in the international wrappers. That's number three."

He pointed his teaspoon at Luz for emphasis before breaking off another chunk. "Three seals. Even if they used dogs, they wouldn't make you."

He looked at Brody. "Say they open your bags, they want to go fishing. They find zero, man. *Nada.* Who's going to fucking open a carton of *cigarettes* just on speculation? You're respectable people, and *everybody* takes

184

home duty-free cigarettes, even if they don't smoke. Shit, they could even do a body search, they're going to miss it.''

"What happens,'' Brody drawled, "if they don't?''

"I don't know. It never happened.''

"Never?''

"Not once.''

"You're kidding.''

"No. It's like taking candy from a baby. We move a lot of product like this, and they ain't looking for it. That's the best part. It's the big move they hear about— guy tries to land a fucking boatload, you know somebody's going to cop him somewhere along the line. Not this, man. We got it figured.''

"It's pretty funny,'' Brody said to Luz, "me giving up smoking.''

It took five hours to assemble the four cartons—the Marlboros for Brody, Virginia Slims (recently a hot item in South America—nice touch, Rey said, didn't she think?) for Luz. After a while, it began to feel like building model airplanes—not boring, but no remarkable thrill, either.

The conversation in the room dwindled. Rey looked across at them every few minutes to see how they were doing and seemed pleased by the neat and disciplined approach Luz had adopted. Teeth securely clamped to the tip of her tongue.

Just nervous enough, Brody thought. He stretched his arms, yawned, and rubbed his eyes. "Wow, what is it, the climate?''

"You got it,'' Rey replied, and chuckled. "No sun and lots of snow.''

They returned to their work. The guards remained at their posts. Walls of meat, even more impassive than Brody had first been aware. He whistled a show tune.

The Indian on the chair looked up at the slowly revolving ceiling fan and down again. He'd done that a few times and occasionally glanced out the window beside him, down past the filigree of wood carving that framed it, to the manicured turf that led away from the side of the club.

The second guard moved around now and then, peeked through one or two of the other windows in the room before returning to roost against a wall. Brody did not have to wonder whether the safety catch was on on the big bad .45.

Each of them had also been watching Luz—impassively, yes, but Brody was not thrilled about the prospect of the guards.

Rey was very cool, on the other hand, very much a dealer, and the coke made him cooler still, precise, methodical. What kind of habit, Brody wondered, does a dealer in kilos have?

When they had finished preparing two complete cartons, Rey suggested a break for lunch. They helped him carry everything in from the kitchen—not much more than an efficiency, Rey declared, but better than nothing. "Hey, we ain't calling room service today."

"You know, it's interesting," Brody observed when they had taken their seats at the table under the veranda awning, with their dishes of warm *papas rellenas*, bread, salad heavy on the onions, and good cold beer. The light was less harsh than it had seemed the day before. It could almost have been painted by Vermeer, the way it fell on Luz's face as she ate.

"What's interesting?" Rey asked, busily pouring beer.

"It's like there's nothing to *talk* about."

Rey laughed and wagged his head. "You said it. Would you have believed it if I told you?"

"Nope," said Luz.

Brody shook his head, swallowing. "Not in a million years," he agreed. "Does it ever get to you?"

Rey smiled slowly and took another sip of beer. "It's a gas, man. Every part of it."

"I could still swear I recognize you from someplace," Brody declared, putting down his glass.

Rey grinned. "Don't worry, you'll think of it." He

pointed to his watch. "Time to get back to the slave mine."

They worked quietly for another hour and a half, under the watchful eyes of the two Indians, neither of whom moved much. The one on the chair seemed to grow more interested in Luz as she crossed and uncrossed her legs while she worked. The other kept up his sluggish patrol of the windows.

Brody dropped back to his seat in relief and returned to crushing cocaine into a fine powder with, here and there, a nice little peanut.

"Looks like we're nearly done," he observed with a merchant's cordiality when he had finished scooping his pouch full and Rey had sealed it. "How about another beer?" he asked, rising from his seat.

"Sure," Rey replied. "Don't bother, he can get it." He told the standing guard to bring three beers.

The Mayan slid the .45 into his belt and loped off.

"So what's next?" Brody asked as he stretched the kinks out of his back. "We just hang out until the plane leaves?"

"Just about. But it looks like you won't have much of a chance to see the city. We had you set for tomorrow, but we're moving you up. You leave tonight."

"Oh?" Luz seemed disappointed. "I thought we'd get a chance to look around town."

Rey shrugged. "Hey, this is the business. I gotta move product, you know?"

"Sure," replied Brody.

"And I'll be coming with you—just in case you run into any problems."

"Glad to hear it," Brody said, relieved. He had been idly figuring how long it would take him to nail the seated Indian, grab the Mac-10, and eliminate the second one he could hear returning from the kitchen with the bottles of beer. Three seconds at the outside. He had already decided that he was not going to let Rey loose, and he was grateful not to have to do it with Luz as exposed as she was. At moments like that, you never knew.

"Yes, I'm serious," he was saying to Luz minutes later as they were packing to leave. "I came that close."

She shuddered. "How?"

He unsnapped his briefcase. "I figured to kick the first one in the nose. I weigh enough, the way he was sitting."

She stopped what she was doing and looked at him. "And the other one?"

Brody shrugged. "He was sleepwalking. Coming back with three beers in his hands—he wouldn't have reacted fast enough. The Mac-10 was leaning against the table, right there."

He paused, looking for the right words. "You understand, don't you? They were armed, with three keys of evidence sitting there on the table. I could have nailed him for twenty years. You figure what twenty years is like in a South American jail."

"And let Graf off the hook?" she asked in amazement. "No. That's crazy."

Brody's eyes flickered. "Hook? What hook? We haven't got *máximo jefe* on any hook." He passed a hand across his face and squeezed his lips into a pout.

"Luz, you didn't see her. Corky Reddon told me she was on her back when it happened, with her legs spread. That little bastard up there shot her where the baby was. The fucking blood was still fresh. And the *way* he did it. The way he killed *Jorge*—"

"Maybe now you still have a chance to find out why," she replied decisively. "I don't know." She shook her head and stepped closer.

He sat down on the edge of the bed, and she sat beside him. He said in a whisper, "I stared at the ceiling of that hotel room for seventy-two straight hours, except for calling the funeral parlor and talking to the cops. I could barely walk."

She started to rub his shoulder. "It wasn't the . . . physical facts," he went on with some effort. "I mean, I've never worked in a stockyard, but I've smelled enough blood, and compared to mortar wounds . . . But *why*? I kept thinking.'' He winced. ''She was my only close kin. And here's—''

''Darling, look,'' Luz said after a long moment of studying his broad face. ''This is a lousy time to start acting like a client. You took a pass on Roper Gance in Key West—why?''

''Ah, Gance,'' he said with an impatient wave of the hand. ''Man was fucking doing a favor. Doing a *favor*,'' he repeated with a smirk. ''I got one slow look at Roper Gance on that big boat of his, with the guard on the deck chair cradling an M-11 right out where anybody could see it.''

''So what are you saying?''

''The man is trapped in. For him, it's just one big circle. I doubt he thought about it at all—two easy set-ups, two hits, and somebody owes him a favor. The less he knows about it, the better.''

''Yeah? Well, *somebody* is Alexis *Graf*,'' she reminded him. After a pause she added, ''Would you have killed Rey, too?''

Brody stood up and rested his palms on his hips. ''He'd have tried something.''

''Oh?'' she demanded. ''And if he was too smart to try?''

He scowled. ''Okay, okay, I'd have had to cart him all the way to Paris with my fist up his ass. I get the drift.''

She grabbed his hand and pressed her cheek against it. ''You really do operate that way, huh?'' she said after a pause.

He seemed surprised. ''Sure. I bend the rules, I don't break them. It would have been murder.''

''Well, then,'' she replied, ''thank God he's coming with us.''

Brody turned to his briefcase, removed his Beretta, released the clip, and examined it. Luz reached for her blouses and was tucking them into her bag when he laid his arm around her shoulder and drew her close.

"Thanks," he said. "I guess I've been getting rattled all through this case."

She turned to stroke his face. "You'll do."

"We really don't have Graf on any hook, you know."

"No, but we're sitting on the coke. Boy, that's all we would have needed, explaining to Graf that his man in Lima—*Ay, qué pobrecito Jaqui, qué lástima*—that he suddenly met with an accident. You'd have never got close to that sweet old fellow again."

Brody grunted, replaced the clip, set the safety, and put the gun back in his briefcase. "Meanwhile," he asked, "how friendly do you think I should get with our boy Gil?"

"Better you than me." She chuckled and kissed him before she returned to her packing. "There's no point speculating, anyway," she said, folding her skirt with a flight attendant's practiced hand.

Suddenly he let out a low hiss.

"What is it?" she asked, looking up at him. He was lost in thought, his eyes narrowed. He held up his hand.

"I don't know," he said finally. "Something about Key West. Not about Graf. It wasn't Katie."

He snapped his fingers. "That's it. Jorge. My brother-in-law."

"Jorge?"

"Yes, goddamn it, Jorge. We still don't know how Katie got to be a courier. Well, maybe she was forced to." He glanced at his watch. Nearly six o'clock. "I've got to call Marty. There's a public phone about two blocks east of here. Rey drove by it last night."

Luz thought a second. "What if they're watching you from up there? Wouldn't you be? What else have they got to do, those two animals?"

"It's still worth the chance. There's a blind spot under the clubhouse eave. You can't see it from the third floor."

She looked at him, impressed. "I'll finish packing," she said.

He grabbed his jacket. "Lock the door," he ordered.

* * *

190

Brody strolled down to the lobby and spent a while selecting a cigar at the news kiosk, a light panatela. Finally he strolled out past the carved wooden doorframes that led to the pool.

He lit the cigar and puffed on it contentedly, taking a seat at one of the wrought-iron tables, whose umbrellas were already closed for the night, and watched the gray-blue sky warm to a muted olive with the sunset.

After a while he stood up, stretched, and continued his stroll. He took in the prospect from the other end of the pool, nodding to a few other early evening holdouts, paused to examine a venerable stand of trumpet flowers, and seemed momentarily undecided about where to go next before he slipped onto the terrace and disappeared beneath the generous awning that swept around the side of the hotel.

He came out under the north eave and hurried to the wooded boundary ahead of him. From there he figured he was safe, but he kept to whatever cover he could find anyway, senses keen.

The phone booth was free, sheltered by trees a few yards from a corner bus stop. He waited, scanned the cover. Nothing. He took another puff of his cigar and walked over.

He gave the operator Marty's number and a priority code number. Who said modern technology's a drag? he asked himself as he rolled the cigar between his lips. Just picture getting the right change now. In a few moments she said, "Your call is going through now, sir."

"Thank you," he said. Marty picked up the phone on the fourth ring.

"How's it going?" Brody asked.

"Great," Marty replied. "You ought to be here."

"Ah, listen—I'm still in Lima. I'll be leaving for Paris tonight."

"Oh? Keeping the clients happy?"

"You bet. I'm working with a thirty-K memory package. We'll just have to reconfigure it. But I'm supposed to fly to L.A. right afterward. Maybe you can call Henry and let him know—maybe he can meet me.''

"Sure. He still losing his hair?''

Brody chuckled. "Hey, don't let *him* hear you say that. And listen—I have another prospect, a guy named Gilberto Rey. That's with an 'e' and a 'y.' He's involved in a few businesses down here. He's the one that got called into Key West. Check him out, will you?''

"Sure. Anything else?''

"Yes. You remember that Reddon character? Ask him if he ever pulled a rap sheet on Jorge.''

Marty couldn't resist asking, "Why? Are they trading them in for green stamps?''

Brody laughed. "Seriously, Marty.''

"Okay, you got it. What about *número uno*?''

"He's supposed to meet us himself in L.A., though I still don't know why.''

"I do. There are rumors the man is shaky. I just found out today.''

Brody pressed his ear closer to the phone. "Are you kidding me? He's loaded.''

"Nope. Maybe he looks loaded, but he's short of cash. Not like your Houston supplier at all. And speaking of that one, guess what? He took a trip to Toronto last spring. The two of them had a meeting there.''

"Marty, you're a jewel. When last year?''

"In May.''

"May what?''

"Does it matter?''

"It might, if it was around the twelfth.''

"I'll try to find out. Enjoy.''

The line went dead. Brody replaced the receiver and headed back to the hotel in the dusk, retracing his steps once he reached the overhang.

His cigar was down to a stub by the time he had finished taking the long way through the ornamental shrubbery that curled around the pool area. He saw Rey skipping down the steps from the hotel and waved to him.

"Where you been?" Rey asked.

Brody waved his cigar. "Pain in the ass to smoke one around a woman."

"I thought you gave them up."

"These? No. I gave up cigarettes. Once in a while, to take the edge off."

Rey nodded. "Got some 'ludes if you want."

Brody grinned. "This is fine. I want to be clear in the head."

Rey seemed skeptical. "Ready to go?"

"Just about. When do you want us?"

"Meet me in the lobby in half an hour."

"Fine. Beautiful night, isn't it? Too bad we couldn't stay."

"You'll be back."

How much you want to bet? Brody said to himself. Not me, and not you, either.

"Finished packing?" he asked Luz when he reentered the room.

She laughed. She was on her hands and knees, looking under the bed. "Are you kidding? I can pack in nine minutes flat. How did it go?"

"Fine. Rey was looking for me when I got back."

"I thought so. He stopped here first."

"What did you tell him?"

She rose from the floor and began dressing. "I was in the bathroom when he knocked. I said I didn't even know you'd gone out. God, what's that smell?"

"My cigar."

"You smoked a cigar? Oh, you needed an excuse to get out of here."

When he told her what Marty had said, she dropped onto an armchair. "How did he find out that Graf's short of cash?"

It was Brody's turn to laugh. "I told you, Marty can find out anything."

"That's why Graf's going to meet us himself. He needs the money. I knew it wasn't just me."

Brody shrugged.

She started fastening the strap of her sling-back shoe. "When are we leaving?"

"He wants us downstairs in half an hour."

Her eyebrows rose. "Half an hour?" she smiled up at him and unfastened the strap.

Brody was tipping the bellhop in the lobby when Rey emerged from the hotel office, gabbing expansively with the manager, a dour and exceedingly reserved gentleman with brushed hair and the general appearance of an aging polo player.

Introductions were made; the manager regretted he had not personally had the pleasure of meeting Señor Rey's American friends. Brody assured him the feeling was mutual.

It was all very pleasant. Yes, Brody was perversely tempted to say, it's a pleasure using your place to package cocaine, we must do it again soon, yes, yes. He half suspected this was exactly what Rey was thinking—throwing his weight around in a place in which, a generation before, he would have been lucky to mop floors.

Musn't be catty, though: that would be suicidal. The manager excused himself. Rey ordered margaritas while they stood around waiting for their taxi to appear. Very elegant. The drinks came with remarkable speed. When he had finished his, Brody set the empty glass on a table, folded his hands in front of his linen jacket, and nodded politely at a story Rey was telling about conquistadores.

"Oh, yes," Rey added when the car arrived and the bellhops were out carrying their bags, "here's the cigarettes you wanted."

"Thanks," Brody replied. He negligently shoved the Marlboro cartons into his carrying bag while Rey handed Luz the Virginia Slims and she did the same. He reminded himself to think of them as cartons of cigarettes, that's all, a few cartons he was bringing home for a friend. He and Luz got in the back of the cab, and Rey slid into the front.

Luz kept up a conversation with Rey, in rapid Spanish, on the way to the airport. Brody shut his eyes and yawned, grateful for the chance to sink into himself. He had seen little enough of Lima in two days and couldn't say he wanted to see more—now then, anyhow. He was writing scenarios. Most of them were silly and involved ways he had not yet thought of to kill Gilberto Rey.

They had a long flight to look forward to, and another one after that almost as long. He thought it would probably be a good idea to divide the possibilities of killing the man into separate categories, "no weapons" being the first, "explosive device" the last. He opened his eyes a crack and added lateral strangulation to his no-weapons list.

Nobody checked their hand luggage at the airport. Brody stowed his briefcase in the compartment above his first-class seat, next to Luz and across from Rey, who smiled often but seemed lost in thought and said little.

That was fine with Brody. He was already breathing the way they had taught him to breathe, the way the big cats breathe to rest before a run. He didn't think he had much time left to rest.

Dinner wasn't bad, first class on an expensive flight: good-size shrimp, Argentinian beef, a small salad, and two more margaritas. Brody knew from hard experience that there would barely be enough food for him to see, let alone eat, on the in-flight tray the steward set before him. Six bites, even if he were as extremely polite as Mother had taught him to be.

Rey went to the john after they had finished their coffee. He came back and slid gracefully onto his seat across from Brody, who nodded.

"Not bad, hey?" Gilberto murmured.

"Better than working the flight, you better believe," replied Luz with a wink.

"Hey, you stick with me, maybe you never have to serve a meal again."

Brody grunted approvingly.

Luz continued, "And you never get tired of traveling, huh?"

"Never. *Never,*" the thin man replied with a giggle.

Thank God for bathrooms, Brody thought. I wonder if he always snorts up during a flight. I wonder if he always snorts up, period. "Say," he asked, "do you two mind if I grab a nap?"

"Whatever you like, man," Gil replied. "My plane is your plane."

Brody closed his eyes to the silver bell of Luz's high, effortless laughter, opened them to watch her lovely mouth as she chatted the man up in incomprehensibly rapid Spanish, and closed them again when the conversation trailed off. After that, Rey stared out the window and Luz began to read. Brody planted a kiss on her shoulder and fell asleep.

Chapter

13

When Brody woke up eight hours later, Luz and Rey were both asleep. He was tempted to look for the knife, but he thought better of it. There were other stirrings on the plane, the light still dim, the attendants readying breakfast. Dawn was beginning an accelerated rush across the horizon; the flight was half-over.

Luz shifted her body and settled back to sleep. Brody slipped out of his seat, headed for the lavatory, and washed up. Time to start in on the little bastard, he was thinking. Time to start scaring him. When he returned to his seat, Rey was just waking up.

"I got it," Brody said, pleased with himself. "Florida, that's where I saw you. Key West. Couple of weeks ago, right?"

For a few moments, Rey said nothing. "Oh. Hey, yeah, I was there a few weeks back. Right."

"Where were you staying, the Pier House? That's where I was."

197

Brody knew he had stung the man. Luz blinked and came awake, still curled in her seat.

"No," Rey replied cautiously. "The Marriott."

"Sure," Brody concluded with satisfaction. "That must be it. I must've seen you in the lobby or something. I knew I'd figure it out!" he declared to Luz. She nodded, yawned, and looked out the window.

A smile that was more a grimace passed over the thin man's face, and Brody could practically hear him calculating as he patted his leg. Good, you little fuck. There's more where that came from.

Breakfast came half an hour later—a bacon omelet, fresh orange juice, good rolls, and plenty of coffee. Luz fell to it with eagerness and had nothing to say.

Rey, toying with his food, kept glancing at Brody out of the corner of his eye, but no further mention was made of Key West. It seemed as if the little detail of memory, once recovered from memory, no longer held the slightest interest.

When they were sipping the last of their coffee, Rey made up his mind. "So what were *you* doing in Key West?" he asked Brody casually, but there was no concealing the threat in his voice.

Brody looked up from his plate and replied agreeably, "Consultation. For the head office. They needed . . . you know," he concluded, "I'm not really supposed to discuss it with anybody."

Rey leaned forward over his tray. "Just between us, man."

"They needed a better credit system," Brody said, catching a whiff of cologne. "Just between us."

"Oh?"

"Would you believe it?" Brody stretched his shoulders in the discreet manner of a man warming to a favorite subject. "Tough time keeping track of the bucks—and they're completely legit. They *needed* help."

Rey's lips broke into a grin. Brody studied the man's slim face, lit by the nearly horizontal sun. "What about you?'' he asked, leaning closer. ''What were you going there?''

Rey instantly grew taut. ''The fuck business is it of yours?'' he growled.

Brody raised his shoulders and let them drop. ''Well, I could say, 'Jeez, what's the big secret?' '' he murmured, ''and leave it at that. But I figure I'd better level with you,'' he added in an even lower whisper. ''Alex told me you were having some trouble with one of the couriers. He said two people got killed—and guess what? The courier was living in Key West.''

Brody kept his eyes on Rey. The flight attendants had come to remove the breakfast carts. They did, amid a dead and impatient silence.

When they had left, Brody leaned over again and whispered, ''Now you tell me to mind my own business, Gil, okay, I will. But you're a killer, man. I can tell. I saw the way those guys with the automatics treated you.''

Rey was growing more excitable by the moment. ''Maybe you talk too much,'' he snarled.

''And maybe the cops are after you right now.''

Rey's eyes glinted ferociously. Brody could hear the jet engines humming.

''Look, Gil,'' Luz said quietly, with just the barest hint of fear in her voice, ''*este*—you know, we have a right to look out for ourselves, too.''

''Better believe it,'' Brody agreed testily. ''Hell, if I hadn't recognized you, I would never have asked. As it is—for Chrissake, we're in this now. We have to know what we're up against.''

Rey wiped his lips with the linen napkin on his tray and said, ''I do what I do, *comprende*? That's all the two of you got to know about. And we flying into Paris, not Key West.''

''I'm just not looking for trouble,'' Brody told him, breathing hard.

''I don't leave traces, man.'' An ugly smile spread across Rey's face, the warning in it unspoken.

Luz nodded. "I didn't think you did," she said, appeasing, and Rey thought he had the upper hand again.

"Besides," he said, his lustrous eyes meeting Brody's, "I give them all my blessings."

"Blessings?"

Rey kissed his fingernails and flicked them across his chest. "From up in the mountains, man. From how my people butcher the meat. You just look after your end, and keep your mouth shut."

Brody didn't say another word.

Five hours later, they landed in Paris. It was cloudy, and a light rain had begun to fall. Customs was jammed, they discovered when they got off the plane, flight bags slung over their shoulders, Brody carrying his briefcase as well. They walked the long distance to baggage claims. Evening weekend traffic in the summer, Brody considered. I wonder if this smuggling business is seasonal?

They waited around as the baggage conveyors started up. Rey took a slow glance around the room and murmured to Brody, "Okay, you ready?"

Brody nodded.

"You too?" Rey asked Luz. "This is the easy one, right?"

"Right."

"Okay. When your bags come up, you get on one of the lines. Don't wait for me. I'll see you outside."

"Where?" she asked.

"Outside, in the main lobby. Wait for me near the Hertz counter." He drifted off to the other side of the claims area.

Luggage started moving around the conveyor. After a few minutes Luz spotted their two weekenders, and Brody grabbed one, waited for the second to come around, and grabbed it, too. She found a cart and wheeled it over. He heaved the luggage on and picked up his briefcase, and they joined one of the lines.

"I hope you don't mind if I go first," he said dryly.

"No, not at all," she replied. "You can do it every time."

Some time passed. Brody glanced around to see if he could spot Rey, knowing that he wouldn't. He took a look at his watch and reset it when he saw Luz checking hers against the clock on the far wall. Twenty-three and a half hours, with the time zones.

The line grew shorter. They looked around, made small talk. He slipped his weapons ID out of his briefcase and into his passport. And then it was his turn.

He handed their papers to the man with the kepi, turned his broad frame to the side, and, as soon as the agent saw the ID, said in amiable, precise French, "We're being watched. Before you give the signal, examine the baggage. Please."

The agent pursed his lips and asked them to unzip their luggage. He gave it a systematic search, smiling all the while, then scrutinized the passports again and picked up a phone.

Brody glanced around nervously, and Luz folded her hands in front of her. Two more agents arrived, made some more noises, and asked Brody and Luz to accompany them to one of the side rooms.

She was surprised and turned to ask Brody why. He shrugged.

The agents escorted them through one of the nondescript doorways. It caused a low murmur to spread in their immediate vicinity. "Just take it easy," Brody said to Luz. "I'm sure it's nothing."

Inspector Massaing was blowing smoke rings in the air when one of the agents pointed to another doorway and they went through it. *"Enfin,"* he said.

"Enfin yourself. There's about two keys of coke in these cartons of cigarettes. I'm taking them with me to L.A."

"Oh? Really?"

"Now don't be difficult, Henri. I'll give you Marlot's killer, and I'll give you the knife he cut him up with, and I'll give you another kilo—right here, now."

Massaing sat up.

Brody nodded. "He's the one who murdered my sister, too."

The inspector leaned forward on his elbows and took a puff of his cheroot. "And then you leave? Why can't you take ordinary cigarettes?"

"The coke is Alexis Graf's, Henri, and he's meeting us in L.A. to take delivery. We just found that out, though we've suspected it."

Massaing motioned to an aide, an older man who was scanning one of the computers across the room, and told him to find out if Alexis Graf was still in French jurisdiction.

"I'll bet your ass he isn't."

"*Merveille.*"

"Is it true he's financially shaky?"

"Why, you want to invest in his firm? If he's out of my grasp already, forget him. At the moment, you are asking the French Republic to aid and abet in—"

"I can nail the fucker, Henri."

Massaing's jaws clenched in disgust. Then he shrugged, picked up a phone, and, turning his back to them, asked to speak to someone at headquarters. "What about Marlot's killer?" he asked, staring back at Brody.

"His name is Rey, Gilberto Rey. Slim, short hair, insect eyes. He flew in with us. He's still out there, I'm sure. Pick him up and put him on hold—but tell him it's a routine check. Don't spook him."

The inspector called one of his men over and sent him out. "Ah, *oui*," he said into the phone, and began an animated conversation in a grave and patient undertone. He talked for quite a while.

When he finished and hung up the phone, Massaing took a meditative puff on his black cigar, turned to them, and said, "All right. We give you what you want. Now— why do I not have to 'spook' him?"

"I'd swear he's got that knife in one of his pockets."

Over his cigar, Massaing glanced at Luz. The inspector came back in and reported that Rey was waiting on one of the slow-moving lines.

Massaing grunted and told him to do what Brody asked. "And search the baggage for a knife, a—"

"It's an ivory-handled stiletto about twelve centimeters long," Brody explained. "Not very heavy."

"And the suspect?"

"Just put a guard on him."

"One thing I will not tolerate, though," Massaing warned Luz when the inspector had left, "Is a seepage, let us call it, *ma chère*. A seepage. At this moment, I can close the Marlot case. I will have the killer in my custody. And we will locate his accomplices in Paris, believe me."

He turned to Brody, "As to Graf . . . you say you can 'nail' him. What if you can't, and the whole case against him blows apart?"

"What whole case?" Luz replied snidely. "Anything you have right now, you got from us."

"All right," the inspector snorted. "I do what I can."

The aide looked up from his console screen and said that Alexis Graf had left for London on the five P.M. flight.

Brody wasn't surprised. "Okay. He'll move from there. Can you keep Rey on ice for us?"

"Until when?"

"Tomorrow night."

"This is when you meet Graf?"

"If we don't, it won't matter."

Massaing threw the end of his cheroot into an ashtray. "*D'accord.* Twenty-four hours. Let's go."

He led them down a hallway and into another part of the building. They met the inspector on his way back. "No weapon in the baggage," he told them.

"Then he's got it on him," Brody said.

"If he has it at all," Massaing drawled, and checked his service revolver.

A uniformed cop was standing beside one of the interrogation rooms. Massaing stopped and nodded. *"Après vous,"* he said to Luz.

He opened the door, and she walked into the room. Another uniform was standing to one side, and Rey, cool as could be, was sitting across from him on a wooden bench.

Cool for sure; but, Brody could tell, unnerved to see all three of them walk in.

Massaing opened the passport he had in his hand. "Your name is Gilberto Rey?"

The thin man nodded and looked at Brody, who shrugged. "Anything else," Rey told the inspector, "talk to my lawyer."

"Why, because you know I found the cocaine? I don't care about the cocaine. Can you account for your movements on the night of August twenty-sixth?"

Rey's mouth opened in shock. "The—what?" he blurted. "The twenty-sixth? You mean—"

"I mean last Tuesday." Massaing smiled indifferently. "I know you were here," he added, nodding in Brody's direction.

Rey screamed, "You bastard!" and Brody heard the blade flick open as Rey darted toward him.

It was like flying into a moving train. Brody drove his foot hard into Rey's forearm, kicking the knife sideways before following through with both fists, sledgehammering Rey's exposed face until he fell over backward. Brody grabbed his neck and started to squeeze.

"Katie Castillo was my sister, you little fuck," he hissed. "How does it feel, huh?"

Rey was tearing uselessly at the stranglehold.

"Why'd he tell you to do it?"

The glittering eyes lolled to the side, vivid against his choking face. "*Why*, goddammit?"

"Enough!" Massaing barked.

"Why?"

"I said *enough*!"

A little more, Brody knew, and the man would be dead. He let go of Rey's neck and punched him again in the face. He threw all his weight into it. "You're going to fry, you fuck, you hear me?" he snarled, leaning over. A cry of heartache deep in his gut escaped in a long sigh that was almost like a wounded animal's, and he rose slowly to his feet. Luz came closer and reached for his hand.

Massaing took out a handkerchief and lifted the knife from the floor. To Rey, whose eye was beginning to swell shut, he said, "I am placing you under arrest for the murder of Alain Marlot. Your victim had a rare blood type. You didn't know that, did you?" Rey closed his eyes.

Ten minutes later, Massaing was handing the flight bags back to Brody. Luz had gone to what passed for a powder room in a restricted Customs area. "So. You have twenty-four hours, *mon ami*. Is not much time. Good luck."

"You haven't located Jacqueline Ebert yet, have you?"

"Pah."

"Once it hits the papers, she'll show up. And thanks, Henri. I mean, in there—"

"You had the right. But not to kill him, Steven."

"I know."

"Share a brandy with me?"

Brody nodded, and the inspector poured two cognacs from a bottle in the desk. He seemed tired beneath the odd version of suburban dapper that he always maintained. "This one anyway is finished," he remarked. "You can be sure of that."

"What do we do now?" Luz asked Brody when they had checked their luggage and emerged, flight bags and all, into the main lobby of the terminal.

"I don't know. We have at least an hour to kill before I call Miss Leila." He looked at his watch. "Can I buy you a coffee? They must still be open."

They passed a kiosk on the way, and he stopped to buy a *Herald Tribune*.

When they were seated in the airport cafe with two

café crèmes and a plate of cookies, he gave in to the fatigue that had begun to dog him. He would sleep on the plane, he told himself, and started glancing through the paper as Luz immersed herself in her book.

Sipping the hot, rich coffee, he turned another page and nearly dropped his cup. "Oh, shit!"

She looked up. "What's wrong?" His lips had contracted to a thin line. He slammed his palm on the table and handed her the paper, pointing to a headline that read FLORIDA POLICE LIEUTENANT SHOT.

"No," she said. "Oh, my God, no. Critically wounded by unknown assailants. . . . Steve?"

Brody had run for a phone. Luz grabbed the flight bags and hurried after him.

When she caught up, he was giving an overseas operator his priority number and telling her to hurry, his fingers drumming nervously on the side of the booth. At last, the call went through. It rang three, four times.

"Well?"

"He's not answering." Five, six, seven.

"Jesus, Steve—it's Labor Day."

He let it ring. Eight. Nine. He was about to hang up when Marty picked up the phone.

"Thank God," Brody exclaimed. "Where were you?"

"I was just going out for the fireworks. Why?"

"Did you get through to Reddon?"

"No. He wasn't in the office. I'll—"

"Damn it. He's been shot, Marty. He's critical. I just read a UPI dispatch in the *Trib*. Look, we just nailed Gilberto Rey for murder, and we have to fly to L.A. to meet the big man. I don't want to spoil your fun, but you'd better get your ass down there right away. Whoever shot Reddon may try to finish the job." He gave Marty Luz's address. "Just tell whoever's there you're a friend of hers. We'll join you as soon as we can."

"I'll be waiting." The line went dead.

Brody looked at his watch again. "Okay," he said to Luz. "It's nearly eleven. Time enough to wait. We've been here three hours."

He dialed Alexis Graf's number in Enghien. When Leila Moore picked up the phone, he said in a nervous rush, "Thank God it's you."

"Who is this?"

"It's Steve. Steve Gallagher. Listen, we don't know what to do. It's been three hours, and Gil hasn't left Customs. The fuck is going *on*?"

She lowered her voice. "Where are you calling from?"

"The main terminal, where he told us to meet him. Is Graf around?"

"No."

"Well, what do we do if he doesn't, you know . . . show up?"

"Did they question either of you at all?"

"No. It went just like he said it would."

"Then you're clear. Look, nothing has changed. There's nothing to tie him to you."

"How the hell do you know?" Brody shouted. "He could be singing through his ears by now."

"He won't talk. He won't say a word."

"Jesus Christ, lady, you think I was born yesterday? I'm plenty worried about this."

There was a long pause. "All right," she finally said. "Drive down here. But come alone. I don't think I could stand having your little friend along. I'll make a few calls in the meantime."

He hung up and told Luz. She touched his cheek and kissed him. "Be careful," she said.

"You too. Check into the Claridge, and don't leave the room until I get back. This may take some time."

"Don't be so sure. Maybe she wants to tell you something she'd rather I didn't hear."

He drove quickly through the suburban sprawl that thinned into farmland. When he reached the château in Enghien, the place seemed almost deserted. He rang twice before a maid let him in and gestured toward the staircase.

There was an open set of double doors across from

the second-floor landing. He heard Leila's voice and entered a silk-paneled salon with a high ceiling and swagged curtains. She was wearing a quilted housecoat and talking on the telephone.

He waited for her to finish. When she had, she turned to him and said, "He's been arrested for murder. They won't let anybody speak to him."

"Oh, great, great. What if he fingers me?"

"He won't finger you or anybody else."

"Leila, he knows I'm taking the stuff to L.A."

"No, you aren't."

Brody paused, surprised. "What are you talking about?"

"You and the girl are going to Miami instead. Alex is already there."

"He's not on the coast?"

She started flicking the cuticles of her long fingernails. "He never was. He changed his plans day before yesterday. He'll meet you in Key West. There are tickets waiting for you at the Pan-Am desk for the twelve-thirty flight. Check into the Pier House when you land. He'll be in touch."

She opened the French doors at the side of the room and walked out. She seemed uncomfortable, he thought as he followed her onto a balcony that overlooked the gardens behind the château. "Anyway," she remarked, facing him, "you know Gil won't finger you."

"Why do you say that?"

She shrugged. "Your name isn't Gallagher, either, I bet."

"Ah," he said after a long moment. "No, it isn't. It's Brody. I'm a private investigator."

"Yeah, and you're the one who busted him, aren't you? And now you're after Alex."

Brody sighed, not taking his eyes off her. "You blow the whistle on me yet?"

She uttered a distracted laugh, slumped onto one of the chairs, and offered him a smile full of pain. "No, man, it's not like that. I can't do this anymore. It's coming apart, the whole scene.''

''What, all this?'' he asked, looking around in disbelief.

''He rents this little hideaway, he doesn't own it. Big fancy life, you know? But you can't pay cash for everything, and the man has made mistakes. He's been acting crazy for weeks. And then Marlot and the American girl—I figure maybe it's time to get out of here.''

''What did those two do to Graf, Leila?''

She buried her face in her hands. ''Marlot wanted more than Alex was paying him. He had something on him—something about a drop in Toronto a while ago. He said he'd go to the cops.''

''And the girl?''

''I don't know. She got caught up in it somehow.''

''She was my sister.''

The woman looked at him and bit her lip. ''Oh, Christ.''

''Anything at all you can tell me?''

''Shit. You think the man discussed it with me? He didn't even trust Gil, had to switch the drop without telling him first. Maybe she was in it with the truck driver. Maybe she just knew too much. All I know is, something big is coming down. He's short on cash, and he went to Miami to square it.''

Her eyes dropped to the herringbone brick of the terrace floor. ''You going to bust me, too?'' she asked.

''For what, coming along for the ride?'' he replied, and took a seat beside her. ''You want to play rough in bed, that's your business. But don't try living that way. You're too honest for it.'' He slapped his hands on his knees. ''Let me give you a piece of advice. Disappear. Wait till I'm gone and then get the hell out of here. Use cash. Don't let anybody find you.''

She nodded. He lifted her chin, planted a shamelessly soft kiss on her lips, and left her sitting there. He drove to Paris.

"Enjoy yourself?" Luz asked wryly when he entered the room she had taken at the Claridge.

"Tough girl," he replied. "Trying to be, anyway. She hit the limit when she found out they're holding Rey for murder. And she had us figured out, too. She asked me. I told her."

"She won't tell Graf?"

"Nah. And we aren't going to L.A. after all. We're going to Key West at twelve-thirty."

"No kidding. Home sweet home."

He sat on the bed, and she threw her arms around him. "You're trembling," he said.

"I'm scared. It'll be the finish, won't it."

"Maybe."

"I mean, for us," she said, stroking the back of his neck.

"Hey," he murmured, "that's no way for a junior partner to talk." He kissed her neck and started nibbling downward. She sighed and gave herself up to him, raising her breasts to his touch.

"I love you, Steve."

He rested himself on an elbow, stroking her smooth hip, and watched the lamplight play on her face and the dark splendor of her hair. They seemed chiseled indelibly against the oceanic movement of his life, the swift current of faces and action; he could barely remember the fading sun behind him as he sat eating *ropa vieja* at the little sidewalk cafe in Key West, three continents away. Yet he could instantly recall each glance she had given him. "I love you, too," he said.

Chapter

14

Luz and Brody landed in Miami at four o'clock in the afternoon. Caught up in the stream of passengers making their way to the baggage area, they said little; there was little left to say. He had told her what he thought might happen once they got through Customs, based on his experience. It wasn't much. Most likely they'd be followed to the hotel—maybe, he half expected, by Chucky Rio.

More and more, Brody felt it was a stroke of fortune that Graf had suddenly changed plans, though he wished he could predict the man's next move.

When they presented their passports and declaration forms at Customs, he showed the agent bills for the evening dress, the shoes, the silver beret pin, and the set of embroidered sheets they had selected at the Marche aux Puces. The agent paused in his gum chewing and nodded. Then Brody showed him his firearms ID.

There was no fuss over any of it—they were using their real passports and looked comfortably chic in an understated way that conveyed the clear impression they were well traveled. The agent thought no further of the weapon, as was his job; he had already given the signal.

And that was that. The agent had a poke at Brody's flight bag that revealed little out of the ordinary, only the three packs of sugar-free tropical fruit gum that constituted Brody's dwindling hoard. The agent glanced at him. Brody shrugged. "I gave up cigarettes. These here are for a friend."

The agent nodded. "Can't tell some people, can you. Never touched the stuff myself."

Hardly a glance at the cartons of cigarettes; Brody was grateful enough, though peculiarly disappointed, when the agent finished stamping the forms and added, "Welcome home."

Hardly a glance. They checked Brody's Beretta in one of the side rooms, ran the registry number through, and came up with Massaing's advice that Brody would be arriving.

"Pretty neat," he murmured to Luz as they left the Customs area and entered the main terminal to check their bags onto the Key West flight.

She shook her head in amazement. "It was over before it even started. All that talk, all that traveling . . ."

He patted his flight bag. "Yes. It's an awfully good scam. Smooth as butter. I'm glad we're going to put the whole damn thing away for keeps."

After their bags were checked in, they strolled around the terminal as they waited for their flight. "I still think you could have explained it," she observed.

He nodded. "Sure, but it would have taken too long. They would have had to talk to Massaing first—once I convince them to—and in the meantime, what? We wait, they do a little more poking around, and I wind up saying, 'By the way, sir, this is, well, two kilograms of cocaine.' " His voice was very low. "I can just see it. We'd have checked into the Pier House tomorrow afternoon sometime. No good."

Luz frowned. "When do you think Graf will call?"

"He'll give us an hour or two, maybe. He's hungry, though. Once the meet is set, we start to move."

They made their way up the stairs in time for the five o'clock flight to Key West. Business people were standing around in the boarding area, along with a young Florida couple and their children.

A few minutes later Val, Luz's male roommate, came up the stairs in his steward's uniform and uttered a jovial greeting when he saw them. "You're working the flight?" she said after he embraced her. "What a great way to come home."

Val was pleased. "See you on the plane," he said, and dashed off.

After they were airborne, it was all he could do to grab a seat across the aisle from them and start gossiping.

"Hmm," he said, casting a practiced eye over them. "Just a trace of fatigue around the eyes. Obviously staying up late enough, but not *too* late."

"Well," she began.

"Can't fool me," he rejoined with a little leer. "But, seriously, you're both looking great, I must say."

"Yeah," Luz said. "Well, we did have a lot of rest on the plane."

"Where'd you come from?"

"Paris!"

"Ohh. You always wanted to get there. Was it everything you *dreamed* it would be?"

She signed and squeezed Brody's arm. "It was better. It was perfect, Val. We took long walks, and stayed at a hotel right on the Champs-Elysées just down from the Arc de Triomphe? Flowers in the halls and everything. And the shops!"

"Didn't I tell you it would be like that when you finally got there?"

"And the food—*ay*, I must have gained five pounds. Oh, and we even bought a few antiques. One deco."

"I'm green with envy."

"Everything at the house okay?"

"Just the way you left it—I think. I haven't been there since yesterday, and I'm flying right back tonight—your shift, just in case you forgot."

"Don't be catty," Luz replied. "I'd do the same for you."

"Doesn't mean I can't tease you. I'm just so thrilled to see the two of you looking so laid back."

"Hah! We're blitzed, that's all."

"It's nearly midnight Paris time," Brody added.

"Oh, to be in the jet set," Val wailed. "And you still have a few days of your vacation time coming, don't you?" he asked Luz. She nodded.

They left him on the tarmac at Key West. It was a clear night, and a breeze was blowing steadily. "See you tomorrow," he said, shaking hands with Brody and blowing Luz a little kiss. Brody glanced around as they entered the building. Chucky Rio wasn't there.

They collected their luggage and took a cab to the Pier House. The town seemed quieter, on the day after Labor Day, than he remembered it. There were already fewer tourists making their way up and down Duval, taking pictures of the church and Sloppy Joe's.

He glanced past the driver at the sun sinking lower in the sky, the clouds taking on greater and greater character, the palms starting to fall into silhouette. He turned in his seat and took a peek out the rear window, but there were too many cars behind them to see if they were being followed.

The cab turned right at the foot of Duval and, a minute later, deposited them at the entrance to the hotel. Brody checked in under the name of Gallagher and asked for a second-floor room facing the water.

After they had showered and changed, Luz joined him on the sun porch. "Hungry?" he asked as she sank onto the lounge chair beside his. He reached for her hand.

"A sandwich, maybe. Dinner was pretty filling."

He ordered beer and coffee with the sandwiches. When the food arrived twenty minutes later, they were still watching the horizon. Brody was yawning, breathing again like a cat.

"You really are impressive, you know," he said to Luz as he watched her finish a turkey sandwich.

"My appetite?" she asked, looking up at him, her face a reddish gold in the deepening light.

"No," he said, and reached out to touch her cheek. "Your nerve. You don't seem the slightest bit scared."

"Are *you*?"

"Sure I am. This is the end of the line."

"Well, you don't look it, either. I guess I'm learning it comes with the territory. Are you telling me it's time to start worrying?" she added in a small voice.

"Uh-huh."

She shrugged. "It's okay, Steve. I don't care about that anymore."

"Maybe you'd better. I can't predict what's going to happen from here on in. It'll be Graf's setup, and you can bet he doesn't plan on us walking away from it."

He took her hands in his and kissed them. "I couldn't have pulled this off so far without you. I came pretty close to blowing the whole nine yards back there in Lima, and you've been like a rock. But maybe it's time for you—what I'm trying to say is, I'll understand if you don't want to take the chance."

She smiled. "Forget it. I've been taking the chance since we left here, and I'm not backing out now. It isn't heroics, Steve. It's just, we're a hundred percent or we're nothing. How about some coffee?"

He nodded, and she poured two cups. "Listen," he said after a long silence, "if this thing works out, do you think you can bear me a while longer?"

She gazed at him over the rim of her cup. "How long a while?"

"Let's take it decade by decade."

She smiled. "Anything you say."

The phone rang. It was Graf. "Hello again. Are you ready to make the delivery?"

"Yeah. You hear about what happened?"

"A shame. But we are still here, aren't we. A man will meet you at the snack bar in front of Malory Square at nine o'clock. You know where that is?"

"I'll be there. We're just having a bite now."

"I want both of you to be there."

"Oh. Fine."

Brody hung up, looked at Luz, and said, "Well, you were right. He wants to see us both. I've got a little under two hours. Stay right here and wait for me—and don't forget to put on the damn short skirt."

"*And* reapply my makeup," she replied with a wink.

He enclosed her in his arms and kissed her long and hard. Then he removed the Beretta from the briefcase beside his lounge chair, clipped it to the waistband of his dark slacks where it would be hidden by the navy shirt, and eased himself over the side of the sun porch.

He made his way down to the ground in the cover of a clump of palms that rose from the edge of the water. He waited there for a minute or two, then moved silently around to the left, preferring to avoid the beach area, which he had decided was too exposed and too close to the main entrance.

He found a service alley and edged down it. Pressing himself against the wall, he glanced around the corner. Chucky Rio was leaning against the fender of a car in the shadows at the end of the parking area, watching the entrance. His neck was enclosed in an orthopedic brace, and he was smoking a cigarette. Another man was with him, sitting in the car. There were no other people around.

He returned the way he had come and made a long detour along the water's edge before cautiously crossing MacArthur and making his way to Luz's apartment. The streets were quiet, and he could feel his adrenaline begin to rise, his muscles begin to hum.

Finally, he slipped across the pathway to the apartment and rang the bell.

Rosalee opened the door. She was wearing a halter top and a pair of dungarees. Brody slipped in, and she shut the door behind him. Marty was just coming out of Rosalee's bedroom, barefoot, tucking his unbuttoned shirt into his slacks. It was hard to tell whether he had been taking off his clothes or putting them on.

"What took you so long?" Marty asked.

"I had to wait until Graf called," Brody replied. "The drop is set for nine o'clock."

"Huh." Marty finished tucking in his shirt and began to hunt for his glasses. "Rosalee," he sighed when he had them perched on the bridge of his nose. "Not that I forgot what you looked like, but oh, are you lovely."

She smiled back at him.

"Well?" Brody asked with a trace of impatience.

Marty found his briefcase and pulled out a 10-K notepad the size of a credit card. "Okay. Reddon was out. He won't regain consciousness until maybe tomorrow morning. And the hospital's tight as a drum—State, Special Narcotics, you name it. The lieutenant is very well thought of."

Brody rubbed his chin. "He'd *better* fucking make it, that smart-assed old cracker. They could bust us for possession if he doesn't."

Marty smiled and shook his head.

Brody's eyes lit up. "You didn't. You found the stash?"

"Well," Marty said, punching keys on the pad, "after all the fuss about your brother-in-law's rap sheet, I snooped around."

"Where is it?"

"Safe, in a nice little branch bank in Key Largo. Talk to me."

"Is Roper Gance in town?"

"Since yesterday," said Rosalee. "I heard the boat was coming back from Houston."

"When did Graf get here?"

"He flew in from London last night with two other men—a Frenchman and an L.A. hoodlum." Marty's fingers were already flying over the keypad.

"My, my," said Brody. "Didn't expect such a welcoming committee."

"Neither did I," Marty replied. "You want descriptions?"

"No, I'm sure I'll recognize them. All right. We meet a man in Malory Square."

"Could be he takes the coke from you right there."

Brody shook his head. "The Austrian wants to see Luz."

"Does he want to see you, too?"

Brody shrugged. "You're right. I'll keep it in mind. Probably just being cautious, though. My guess is, whoever we meet takes us someplace."

"And you make the drop," said Marty, "and then you're meat. They don't know how much Rey told you. They won't take a chance."

Brody pressed his lips together. "Probably not, but we're going. We have to. We try playing games now, they'll disappear. Where do you figure they'll take us?"

Marty paused. "The boat, no?"

"Could be a car, too, or one of the hotels, or a house. Just let it play. But the minute anything out of the ordinary happens, blow the whistle and start wading in. What did you bring with you?"

"Only what I had up there—Smith and Wesson."

Brody pursed his lips. "You shouldn't have to use it."

It was Marty's turn to shrug. "Anyway, if it *is* a car, I'll follow you. I'm driving a dark-blue LTD. *Amor y pesetas.*"

"*Amor y pesetas.*" Brody cuffed him on the cheek and turned to leave. Rosalee was standing there, waiting for a kiss. He gave her one and said with a smile, "Sorry to have interrupted."

"Still have plenty of time," She giggled. Marty cleared his throat and, removing his glasses, waved goodbye.

Brody was back at the clump of foliage on the sand beneath his room by eight-fifteen. He rubbed his hands on his slacks and, grasping the inner tree trunk, began his silent ascent. He reached out to hoist himself over the railing.

Luz looked up, startled, from her book.

"Sorry I took you by surprise," he whispered.

"You might have sent your card," she replied. "How'd it go?"

He told her. "How much time have we still got?"

"Forty-five minutes."

"I'd better get ready." Under her kimono, she was wearing sheer black stockings. The short skirt was laid out on the bed, black heels on the rug beneath it. She had waited to finish her eyes.

"Your friend Chucky Rio's downstairs," he called out.

"Oh?"

"Keeping an eye on us." Brody changed into his linen suit and a pair of loafers and took a seat on a chair beside the bed to watch her put on the finishing touches. She slipped into the skirt one leg at a time and slid it up, pulled a loose blouse over it, and raised her collar. "Mmm!" he said.

"Yeah, that's about right," she agreed, studying herself in the full-length mirror beside the bathroom door. She found her perfume on top of the chest and dabbed some on. By then it was a quarter to. She threw her makeup pouch into her handbag and slung it over her shoulder. "We forget anything?"

Brody, who was leaning over for the flight bag in which he had deposited all four cartons of cigarettes, reached into his pocket for a piece of cantaloupe gum and unwrapped it. "I don't think so."

They took the elevator down and dropped the key off in the lobby before strolling out through the main entrance and up the pathway to the street, past the parking lot. Brody tried to spot Chucky Rio out of the corner of his eye but couldn't. The stars were out, and the wind was hurrying white clouds across the sky.

Luz took his arm, and he shifted the flight bag higher on his shoulder. He paused under a street lamp to check the time again before crossing the street ahead of the excursion train stop and entering the square.

He glanced at three or four people before he and Luz

made their way to the far end of the square, where the curio building ended in a stand of palms. They passed through the archway to the pier.

Suddenly Chucky stepped from behind a tall banyan and studied the square behind them. "Well, well," he finally said to Luz. "So we meet again, right on time."

"Right on time," replied Brody.

"You and me got a score to settle," Chucky told him, his voice somewhat altered by the neck brace. "But that can wait. You're taking up the man's time. You got the stuff?"

Another man had emerged from the mass of plantings. He was carrying an automatic pistol. To Brody, he looked like the Frenchman Graf had brought along.

"Right here," Brody said, patting the flight bag. "Lead the way."

"You first," Chucky barked, pointing down a path that took them to a big old Buick sedan. Chucky left the Frenchman guarding them and took another look around before telling Luz and Brody to walk on. They followed the shoreline for a few blocks and then turned in and around to a cover where the *Sea Legs* was tied up. The dock was deserted, dark but for the wash of spotlights on the wooden planking and the vessel itself.

"Get on," he said.

Two more men were waiting for Brody when he boarded, one the guard with the M-11 he remembered seeing on the after deck of the yacht, who told him to raise his hands and waited while the other, also a Cuban, frisked him. As they were checking him over, Brody nodded at Graf, who was sitting on a deck chair, a russet smoking jacket over his white shirt.

Brody helped Luz off the ladder, and she said, "Hello, Alex."

"Ravishing," the Austrian replied as he rose from his seat.

He showed them into the saloon and told the Frenchman, who had followed them on board, to keep his eyes open. The dark man with the M-11 came in last, closing the doors behind him. A beefy American was leaning against the bar. There were a few empty glasses on it and a sweet smell of bourbon in the air.

"Sit down," said Graf, leaning on his cane. "A drink?"

"No thanks."

Graf's hooded eyes seemed not to blink. "Your trip went well?"

A side door opened, and Roper Gance appeared. Up close, Brody noticed the man's suntanned face was marred by a fine pattern of age lines and hair-thin capillaries. He slid onto a barstool.

"Not as well as you said it would," Brody replied testily. "Leila told me they arrested Rey for murder. What the fuck happened?"

"That's not all," Luz added. "He told us that he killed that American woman, too, right here in town. What—"

Graf licked his upper lip. "He told you?"

"*Told* us?" she replied, nonplussed. "*Ay, Dios mío*— he was so high on coke on the plane from Lima, I could barely shut him up. What kind of a mess are you people getting us into?"

Graf glanced at Roper Gance, who sat up on the stool and shook his head. "The cops don't have a thing on that," he said flatly.

"Oh?" said Brody. "Well, we're here, anyway. I guess we're stuck with it. Who's your friend?" he asked Graf.

"Mr. Gance."

"Nice boat you guys have," Brody remarked. "Gorgeous teak. Okay," he said to the Austrian, "here's the coke. Where's our money?"

"Don't be so impatient." Graf held up a finger and wiggled it at the flight bag.

Brody pulled out one of the cartons and handed it to him. Graf passed it to the American, who removed a penknife from his pocket and gingerly slit open the carton. He pulled out a pack and slit it, too, touching a bit of the powder that escaped to his tongue. He tasted it and nodded.

"Hey," Brody said, "we wouldn't fuck with you."

"What a pity." Graf laughed and signaled the Cuban, who lowered his rifle and pointed it at Brody.

"Hey, man," Brody said, "what are you doing? Where's our money?"

Graf laughed again and said, "Lock him up downstairs. Soon, we will take a little trip. Meanwhile . . ." His eyes fell on Luz.

"Wait a *minute*," she said. "This wasn't—"

"You bastard!" Brody growled, raising his hands as the Cuban motioned with the muzzle of his rifle. "You had this planned all along."

Graf chuckled. "Mr. Gallagher, you disappoint me." The American who had been leaning against the bar pulled out a revolver and chuckled, too.

"It isn't Gallagher. The name is Brody. I'm Katie Castillo's brother."

A flash of sudden rage passed through the Austrian's eyes. "All the more reason to quiet you."

Roper Gance's jaw stiffened. "He's her brother?" he snarled.

"That's right," Brody went on. "Remember the little favor you did for him?"

"Shut your fucking mouth. She had it coming to her."

"Like me?"

Graf's face hardened into a frightening grimace. *"Now!"*

The Cuban hustled Brody out of the room. As he left, Brody saw Graf turning to the aft stateroom, dragging Luz with him. *"Stop* it," he heard her say. "I'm coming, all right?"

Hands raised above his head, he walked as he was told to through a forward passageway and descended a metal staircase to the lower deck. The Cuban motioned him to the left, past the engine room, to a storage cabin with a heavy door.

"Listen," Brody said, "I—"

222

The Cuban slammed the butt of his rifle into Brody's kidneys, knocking him down, and kicked him viciously in the face. "No talk," he snarled, unlocking the door. "Get up."

Brody managed to rise on one knee and reach for the wall. He could feel blood trickling in his ear where the man's heel had met it. The room was spinning, and he didn't know if his calves would bear his weight. He took a ragged breath, willing himself into a hard, focused knot, knowing he wouldn't have another chance. He shook his head to clear the nausea that was starting to overcome him.

"I say get *up*," the Cuban barked again impatiently. *"Now!"* He grabbed Brody's wrist and started dragging him to his feet.

He didn't expect Brody to suddenly pull him down, or the knee to the groin that sent a jolt of pain through him as he was falling. And then Brody, who had forty pounds on him, landed on top of him, grabbing his throat with one hand and twisting the rifle back against the man's clenching fingers before he could fire it. It fell from his grasp as the Cuban struggled frantically to free himself from Brody's choke hold that had already begun to tighten. But he had no leverage, and Brody smothered him with his size. He kept up the pressure until the violent lurching came to an end and the man stopped twitching.

Brody dragged the body back through the corridor and into the engine room. Wincing in pain as he forced himself upright, he glanced around in the darkness until he spotted a pile of rags in a carton. He grabbed a long one and rolled it up, unscrewed the gas tank on the generator, and stuffed in the rag.

Coarse but effective, he thought, searching in his pockets for the Pier House matches he had brought along just in case. He would have a minute, maybe less.

He picked up the M-11, held it in the crook of his arm, and lit the rag. He waited until the fire took, then hurried aft and found another staircase, which he mounted carefully. It led to the deck. He crept toward the doorway at the back of the saloon, pressed himself against the wall beside it, and marked time in the star-light. Eerie seconds passed. He could hear the water lapping against the hull and the sound of faraway laughter.

Then the boat was racked by a shattering explosion that tore a hole out of the forward end and sent smoke and fire billowing outward. He heard shouts on the other side of the ship, the pounding of feet on the deck. He heaved the door aside and came in low.

The beefy American, his body hidden, the heavy, long-nosed Smith & Wesson braced in both hands on the top of the bar, swung around and began to fire. Brody lunged to the left and fired back. The man ducked behind the bar and shouted something through the smoke before coming up again. In that instant, Brody squeezed off a few more rounds that splintered the bartop and caught the man in the neck and head. He shrieked, eyes frozen open, and Brody started emptying the rest of his magazine across the saloon, aiming through billowing smoke at the glass doorway that the Frenchman and the second Cuban were rushing through.

Brody saw the short one go down, and he ducked behind a table as a barrage of slugs ripped into the teak paneling above him. He crept around the table and squeezed off another burst of fire from a kneeling position.

Then his firing mechanism jammed. Muttering an obscenity, Brody threw himself prone to the floor and started crawling through the smoke toward the Smith & Wesson the American had been using. He heard a terrible creaking noise, and the yacht heaved, rolling him over. When he landed on his stomach again, he saw the Frenchman step through the doorway with a hard smile on his face. Brody didn't have a chance: the revolver was still eight feet away.

The Frenchman was bringing his weapon down when the door of the aft stateroom flew open. Out came Alexis Graf, the belt of his smoking jacket untied, fly open, followed by Luz, who was holding the back of the jacket in one hand and had Brody's Beretta in the other. Without a pause, she pointed it at the Frenchman and shot him twice in the chest. He staggered and fell, firing blindly until Brody laid his hand on the .44 and finished him off.

Luz was breathing hard, her face white as a sheet, when Brody looked up. She had the muzzle of the Beretta pressed against the soft recess at the back of Graf's neck.

"You swine," Brody growled, staring at the Austrian. "What was Katie going to do to you?"

"Talk!" Luz ordered. "Talk or I'll kill you, so help me."

Graf shivered, and a bead of sweat began to form above his lip. Smoke was still pouring from the forward section, and Brody could feel the floor tilting.

"She was going to spill the beans about Toronto, wasn't she? You took Gance's cut, and you blamed it on her."

Graf's lips clenched in a sneer. "Very clever."

Luz suddenly leaped behind the doorway, and Brody hit the floor. Blood streaming from a wound in his forehead, his torn shirt glistening with blood, Roper Gance had stumbled out of the smoke and flame of the forward stateroom. He had a chrome-plated revolver in his hand.

"You scum!" he shouted at the Austrian. He took a few more shaky steps and raised the gun. "Greedy scum bastard!" He fired four times, the force of the slugs driving Graf back against the wall. Brody came up with the .44, but Gance was already falling, disappearing into the smoke. When Brody got to him he was dead, the wound caused by the explosion turning the carpet dark.

Brody coughed and came back. Graf's legs had crumpled, and he had slumped to the floor, head jerking, blood pumping from his neck. He tried to speak but couldn't. Brody watched the life go out of his hooded eyes.

For a moment there was no other sound but the fire crackling and the ship's groan as it tilted farther.

"I knew he wouldn't check your bag," he said.

She slumped against him. "I've never been so frightened in my life," she said.

He looked down at her and saw that the color was returning to her face. He smiled. "Oh, I don't know. I think you could do this for a living. Let's get the hell out of here."

They came out on deck. Chucky Rio was spread-eagle on the dock, along with a few other crew members, and Marty was keeping an eye on them with his Smith & Wesson. He looked up. "We're fine," Brody said. In the distance, he could hear the wail of police sirens growing nearer. The flames were spreading through the forward bulkheads, the smoke rising higher and higher. "I hope they get here before it sinks."

"If not, they'll just get wet," Marty replied.

"Okay," said Brody. "The two of you handle it now?"

"You bet," Luz answered.

"Then I'm gone."

"The LTD's right over there," Marty told him, waving his revolver at a spot through the trees.

Brody was sipping a glass of orange juice when he heard a key turn in the lock. He set down the glass and slipped into the darkness without making a sound.

A man entered and was halfway across the living room before he saw the muzzle of Brody's gun pointed at a spot just above his eyebrows.

"Don't even think about it," Brody snapped, and the man's hand froze in midair. He had started to reach for his gun, but Brody's muzzle was still aimed at his forehead.

"Nothing would please me more," Brody said in the deadly calm that followed. "Take it out with your pinky."

"What are you—"

"Do it! And do it slowly."

The tension continued until the man's service revolver fell to the rattan rug with a clunk.

"Good. Sit down—over there," Brody snapped, flicking his automatic at the big armchair across from the T.V.

The man did as he was told. Stooping to unload the revolver with his free hand and shaking the shells out onto the floor, Brody never took his eyes off him. "Now," Brody asked when he had him face to face again and had reached over to turn on a lamp. "You want to start, or should I?"

Detective Baar, teeth clenched, said nothing.

"Okay," Brody said. "Have it your way. You tried to kill your boss the other day. Why?"

Baar laughed at him.

"Found something, didn't he?" Brody continued. "Sniffing around you like an old hound, I bet."

"Try to prove it," Baar said, and laughed again.

"I don't have to."

Baar's eyes fell on the automatic. "You wouldn't," he said, cautious and alert.

"Oh?" Brody replied. "That the way you were trained to think?" He waited, working his hand on the grip, his face devoid of expression, tired, the blood caked on his ear and neck where the Cuban had kicked him. It would have been easy, and Baar knew it. His lips began to tremble.

Brody picked up his glass and took another sip of juice. "Well, you're right and you're wrong. I know you have another weapon around someplace, maybe even down the small of your back there—I guess I forgot to check. You try to use it on me before we're through talking, I'll be glad to kill you. That'd be a sportsman's way out. But you won't take it."

Brody drained the glass, set it down, and took a few steps closer. "But I'm not here because of Reddon. I'm here because of *them*. My sister, man. My flesh and blood. And you're going to tell me all about them."

He got a sneer in response. He extended the gun and wrapped his left hand under it, and Baar shrank back involuntarily. "Hey, no—no, *wait!*"

Brody lashed the barrel of the gun across his face. "What was it first put you on to Jorge Castillo?" he asked through clenched teeth.

Baar's eyes narrowed. "What? What do you know about that?"

"We found the stash, cocksucker."

The man's mouth fell open.

"That's right," Brody went on. "The safe deposit box you opened in Key Largo, after Katie's first trip."

Baar slumped back against the seat. "It took me a long time to figure how she got into it in the first place," Brody went on. "I was in Lima when it finally hit me. She wouldn't have taken a chance like that by herself. She stuck to him like glue through all the shit they went through up north, all the promises and disappointments, even when he lied to her, lied to himself—nine years of it. But he finally had his act together, and she wouldn't have done anything to risk it. And she certainly wouldn't have gotten pregnant if she'd still been worried about him, either. That much I know."

Brody lowered the Beretta. "But they didn't figure on you. Gance had you in his pocket from the beginning, and he was always looking to recruit runners. She was perfect for the part—that you saw right away. But how to get her to agree to it?"

Brody rubbed a hand across his weary face and down his lower back to the sore spot above his kidneys. "Then you heard the rumor about Castillo trying to deal drugs and getting squeezed out, the same rumor Tiny Johnson heard. Didn't mean much to anybody, happens down here all the time. But it meant plenty to you, because you had the badge. It was just the kind of leverage you needed over her. So you called New York and found out he had two previous convictions for possession. So what if the state's case was a little shaky the second time and his lawyer pleaded him wrong—he went up anyway. Once more, good-bye for life. He knew it, and so did she.''

Brody suddenly cocked the Beretta and brought it back up. "So you framed him, easy enough for a guy in your position to do. Planted some coke in his car, maybe, or around the house, but real careful about avoiding entrapment, I bet, and then you threatened to bust him. Am I right so far?''

Baar nodded in resignation.

"Then you had them both where you wanted them,'' Brody continued in a voice that had become flat, almost indifferent. "What choice did she have? You hooked her up with Gance, just doing the man a favor. And she did her job well—three runs, and no fuck-ups. But what Gance didn't know, she was handing those fifteen-grand payoffs to you. Had to, or you would have turned Castillo in.

"But then something happened. You didn't know what, of course—they didn't warn you it was coming down. You were just their friendly crooked cop,'' he concluded witheringly.

There was nothing Baar could say.

"When Graf set her up,'' Brody continued, "she must have come to you. But you didn't do a thing for her. And you didn't tell them about me, either, after the murder. Scared to, I bet. Scared they'd somehow discover that you had the stash. You kept quiet after I broke Chucky Rio's jaw—even when I starting coming up with Gance's name. You figured it would all just blow away. And you were nearly right.''

He stretched his shoulders. "Of course, you didn't know I found Gance's business card in one of her passports, with a New York phone number on it. I guess I forgot to mention that to you and the lieutenant. So you kept quiet. Too bad. If you hadn't, I'd be a corpse by now. You have anything to say to me?''

"Why should I?''

Brody shrugged and turned to the wall phone. He was punching the police emergency number when he felt rather than heard Baar turning on his seat. He started firing the Beretta as Baar's hand came up with the revolver he had hidden in the chair. Three slugs slammed through Baar's forehead and into the back of the chair. He slid sideways, blood trailing across the fabric. He was dead before his body hit the floor.

Brody slowly rubbed his face, turned back to the phone, and dialed again.

On a blustery November day in New York, Brody was pulling up the collar of his overcoat as he followed Luz out of the Abercrombie's at South Street Seaport. He held open the door for Detective Lieutenant Reddon, who had come to the big city for the first time and was enjoying his stay immensely.

"Can't hardly believe it," the lieutenant said, shaking his head. "Alligator valise for fifteen grand. Fifteen *grand*. If I hadn't taken you up on your offer to visit, son, I'd never have known."

Brody laughed. "Bring in a key of coke, you can make an even exchange for that valise."

Reddon nodded. "Been a great week you've shown me," he said, absently rubbing his chest.

"Still giving you pain?"

"A little sluggish yet. Be fine in another month."

Luz wrapped herself in Brody's arm and shivered. "I'm sure not used to this weather," she murmured, sheltering herself against him. "Where can we get a cup of hot coffee?"

"I know just the place," Brody replied.

They started walking north, the crisp light rapidly fading behind the Wall Street skyscrapers. "You planning to stay up this way, Miss Almeida?" Reddon asked.

"Maybe," she answered, squeezing Brody's arm.

"Catch your death of cold."

"I doubt it," she said.

"Me too," Brody agreed as they walked.